TIXƎ STRATEGIES

EXIT STRATEGIES

PAUL CRESEY

Freehand Books acknowledges the financial support for its publishing program provided by the Canada Council for the Arts and the Alberta Media Fund, and by the Government of Canada through the Canada Book Fund.

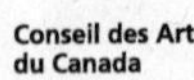

Canadä

Freehand Books
515–815 1st Street SW Calgary, Alberta T2P 1N3
www.freehand-books.com

Book orders: UTP Distribution
5201 Dufferin Street Toronto, Ontario M3H 5T8
Telephone: 1-800-565-9523 Fax: 1-800-221-9985
utpbooks@utpress.utoronto.ca utpdistribution.com

Library and Archives Canada Cataloguing in Publication
Title: Exit strategies / Paul Cresey.
Names: Cresey, Paul, author.
Description: Short stories.
Identifiers: Canadiana (print) 20230152279 | Canadiana (ebook) 20230152317 | ISBN 9781990601316 (softcover) | ISBN 9781990601330 (PDF) | ISBN 9781990601323 (EPUB)
Classification: LCC PS8605.R4655 E95 2023 | DDC C813/.6—DC23

Edited by Naomi K. Lewis
Book design by Natalie Olsen
Author photo by Tristan Davies
Printed on FSC® recycled paper and bound in Canada by Imprimerie Gauvin

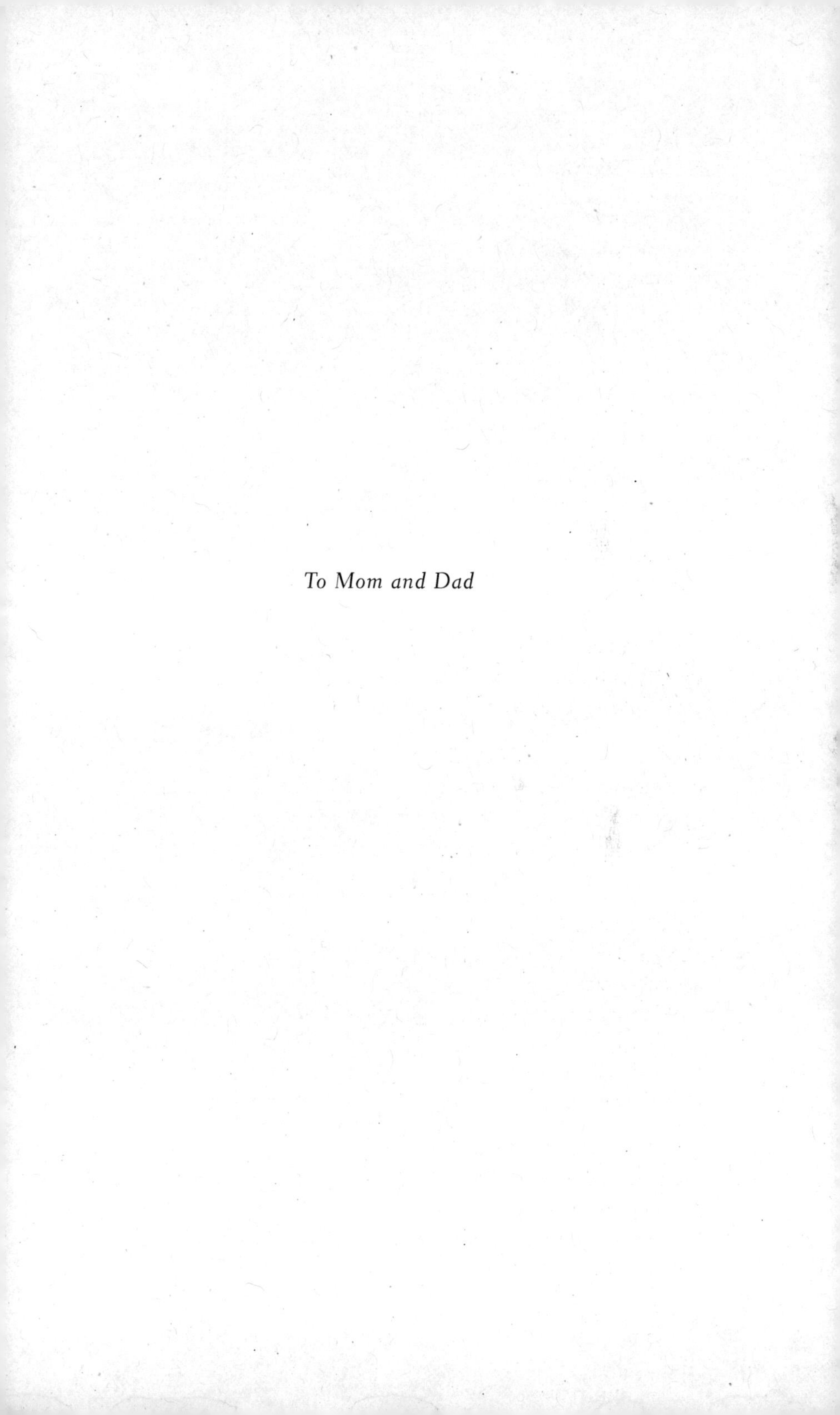

To Mom and Dad

#1 *The Love Story of Vladimir Fiser and Marika Ferber*

ON OCTOBER 13, 2013, Vladimir Fiser and Marika Ferber jumped to their deaths from the eighteenth floor of their apartment building in Toronto, Ontario, in an apparent double suicide pact. Friends and neighbours reported that Ferber, a retired ballet instructor and former ballerina, had long suffered from chronic back and leg pain, and it was for this reason police believe the married couple jumped. (Suicide notes exist but, for obvious reasons, have never been made public.) Why they chose to end their lives in such a sensational manner when more private methods remained available to them – Fiser drove, Ferber took pain medication – is certainly the more compelling question than why they chose to end their lives at all. That Ferber was wheelchair bound at the time, and physically incapable of climbing the balcony railing without Fiser's help, favours a motive beyond mere convenience. Both were also Holocaust survivors, and the similarity of their suicides to the suicide of Primo Levi, who threw himself from a third-storey apartment landing, cannot be overlooked. Perhaps there is something that happens to a person psychologically after having experienced such unimaginable violence, which can later induce them toward a violent end. Or perhaps it was survivor's guilt, and jumping an act of solidarity with those friends and family lost to the Nazi scourge. But this is unfair speculation, people are never so simple as that, and surely a summary of their lives up until that point is required before any answer can be surmised.

VLADIMIR FISER WAS BORN IN 1924 in the city of Osijek, in what would become modern day Croatia. At the time Croatia existed as part of the Kingdom of Serbs, Croats, and Slovenes, one of many such conglomerate countries formed during the dissolution of the Austro-Hungarian Empire at the end of the First World War. Five years later, in 1929, King Alexander I would proclaim a royal dictatorship over the newly named Kingdom of Yugoslavia. That same year Marika Ferber was born, also in Osijek. There, Fiser and Ferber would first meet, growing up together amid the city's tightknit Jewish community.

Before the Nazis invaded in 1941, there were approximately three thousand Jews living in Osijek. By the end of the war, fewer than six hundred would remain. Only ten of those ultimately deported to concentration camps would return alive. Among those who perished in the first year of the invasion was Vladimir Fiser's father.

Not much is known publicly about Marika Ferber's experience during the Holocaust. She might have gone to the camp at Djakovo, but that is unlikely, for almost all of the twelve hundred women and children sent there ended up perishing in either one of Auschwitz or Jasenovac. She might also have fled, as Fiser had, to Italian-occupied Yugoslavia. Or she might have been one of the few Jews hidden in Osijek until the war ended.

More is known about Fiser's path through Nazi-occupied Europe, though details are still limited. After his father's death, Fiser fled to Italian-occupied Yugoslavia, where he remained until 1943, when he was smuggled into neutral Switzerland, apparently aided by the controversial police officer Giovanni Palatucci. Upon returning to Croatia at the end of the war, Fiser received a degree in economics. Shortly thereafter, Fiser and Ferber settled independently in Israel and reconnected as platonic friends.

For most of their adult lives, Fiser and Ferber were married to other partners. Ferber conceived two children with her husband; Fiser remained childless his entire life. It was only after their spouses died of cancer one day apart (a remarkable and tragic coincidence of which great love stories like theirs seem preternaturally rife) that Fiser and Ferber ended up marrying one another and moving to Toronto – and many years later jumping seventeen floors[1] to their deaths.

I ARRIVE AT PEARSON INTERNATIONAL AIRPORT around noon and take the 52 bus to Kipling Avenue, then the 45 to Widdicombe Hill Boulevard. From there I walk the remaining distance to the apartment building where Fiser and Ferber took their own lives. The semi-circular north-facing front of the building is a layer cake of brick and concrete. At one time this might have passed for a luxury high-rise, but in the twenty-first century, the uniform, sparsely windowed exterior calls to mind the Khrushchyovka of Soviet-era Russia. I cannot imagine anyone would ever be tempted to call it beautiful. The front courtyard, however, is well maintained, and the floral arrangements and tall trees are a welcome distraction from the oppressive architecture.

1 As with most apartment buildings in the West, floor thirteen is skipped. Thus the eighteenth floor is really the seventeenth floor, and so on.

Earlier in the week I made an appointment to view the apartment with Mr. Wenutu, the current tenant. Being aware of the morbid history, he was, at first, reluctant. But I explained to him that I was a journalist, that I was writing an article about "exit strategies" and merely hoped to include Fiser and Ferber's story in it, with perhaps even a mention of his name. I believe it was this final appeal to his vanity that led him to consent.

I dial the apartment number and am buzzed in. In the elevator I time how long it takes to travel seventeen floors and discover it takes almost three times as long as a fall from the same height: ten seconds as opposed to three and a half.

Stepping out onto the eighteenth-floor landing, I look left and see a short, stubble-faced man lingering in his doorway.

"Mr. Wenutu?"

"Please," he says, "call me Wayne."

We shake hands in the hallway, then I follow him inside. The apartment smell is a blend of Lysol, vacuum cleaner, and burnt coffee. He leads me on a path through the apartment that purposefully avoids the balcony, saving it for the end of the tour. Everything in the apartment appears in its proper place. Even the messy parts have an order to them that evince a morning of obsessive cleaning.

"And this is the balcony," he says.

The stone balcony runs the entire length of the living room wall, about fifteen feet. I am surprised to see there is nothing on it. No furniture, no barbeque. Not even a plant.

When I ask him about this, Wayne answers, "I never had a problem with heights before. But for some reason, standing out there, I get this weird feeling like I'm going to fall. I guess you'd call it vertigo." He pauses. "That's what you're here for, isn't it? To look over the edge?"

"I was hoping it might help me answer the question of why they jumped."

"There's no one knows why but them and God." He bends over, picks a crumb off the ground, and squirrels it in his hand. "To think if it had been three years later, they could've had the doctors do it. But what would be the story then?"

It is believed Fiser and Ferber jumped sometime between seven-thirty and eight in the morning. According to weather reports from that day, the skies were cloudy over Toronto. Today the skies are clear. I open the sliding door and, stepping over a lip tall enough to stop a wheelchair, walk out onto the balcony. I put my hands on the solid cement railing and peer over the edge.

I imagine myself as Vladimir Fiser. I have survived dictatorships, wars, persecution, exile, the death of most of my family, the death of my first wife. Yet even as I have suffered there is someone who has been with me since the beginning, who has suffered as I suffered. *Marika.* I remember how she danced. I remember her poise, her perfect control. But for this gift of dance, the gods demand recompense, and Marika is made to pay dearly for those years. Her body, once an attuned instrument of time and space, disharmonizes. She is confined to a wheelchair. And when the pain becomes too much, Marika begs me for an end to her suffering, which is also my suffering, and which I know will require an end to us both. I carry her onto the balcony. My own weak heart strains from the effort, but as this will be my last effort in life, I am able to see it through. I set her down on the stone railing, then climb onto it myself. Once more I take her into my arms.

And for three and a half seconds, we dance.

#2 *Reward*

SHORTLY AFTER MIDNIGHT Sam Pederson of Sam's Corner Store and Video admitted his fifth customer of the day. He had been about to step outside for a cigarette when he spotted the boy crossing the neighbouring Glanford Middle School soccer field. Usually the reflection of the inside of the store prevented Sam from seeing anything beyond the front lot, but that evening the moon was bright – two days away from full – and the boy was stumbling. Drunk, probably. They always were this late at night. Before they brought in the new hours, Sam had met only the occasional drinker. Now it seemed half the customers who came in were either drunk or high.

Eventually, the boy arrived at the chain-link fence before the road. Sam watched him struggle to carry himself over it. He knew right then that the boy wasn't from the neighbourhood, because if he had been, he would've known about the square hole not ten feet south of him, which even the parents crawled through sometimes.

Also, he was injured. Sam wasn't sure it was blood until the boy entered the store.

"You're bleeding," Sam said.

"You sell cigarettes?" the boy asked.

"I can get you a Band-Aid. There's some gauze next to the Tylenol."

Sam leaned over the counter to peek at the wound above the boy's right knee. The boy hovered a shaking hand over it. Sam smelled for booze but got only the tinny odour of blood. He glimpsed the boy's pale green eyes. Pale as a husky's blue.

"Canadian Classics," the boy said, "if you got them."

"I'll need to see some ID."

Sam didn't think the boy was old enough to buy cigarettes, but then he had been wrong before. Just last week a girl buying cigarettes, whom he had pegged for a student at the high school, turned out to be the same age as his oldest daughter, twenty-one.

The boy removed his wallet from his back jeans pocket. He handed his driver's license to Sam. Sam read the birthdate. *July 20, 1997.* Fooled again. Out of curiosity he read the boy's name. *Lang, Donald Frederick.*

Sam handed the license back. "Canadian Classics, you said?" He opened the drawer underneath the register. "King size or regular?"

"Regular." The boy looked about the store. He snickered when he saw the aisle for DVD rentals. "You still rent videos?"

"The odd one," Sam said.

"I can't remember the last time I rented a video."

"Not many people can." He rang up the cigarettes. "That'll be fifteen forty-five."

The boy handed him a twenty.

"Sure you don't want some Band-Aids? I'll sell them to you at cost."

The boy shook his head.

"All right," said Sam.

He handed over the cigarettes and change.

Outside, the boy lit a cigarette in the glow of the store windows and then continued north along the road.

BEFORE NETFLIX, Sam and his wife, Samantha, earned enough money from video rentals alone to keep the store running. But this was a post-Netflix world, and with rental sales all but ruined, the Pedersons were forced to diversify. Junk food had always been lucrative for them, so they stocked more of it. Chocolate bars, Maynards, slushies, ten-cent candies, Doritos, Lay's, Pepsi, Coke – Sam's offered as much selection as your average 7-Eleven. Thanks to health consciousness, however, children were spending less on sweets than they ever had. Samantha suggested they expand to include healthy options like vegetables and fruit, but most of it rotted on the shelves. They considered selling alcohol, but the licensing proved too costly for them. If it hadn't been for their two daughters, both in college, both relying on their parents' support for tuition and lodging, Sam and Samantha might've just retired, sold the business, and moved upstairs permanently. Instead, they branched into pet supplies – Samantha's idea – and Sam agreed to put the DVDs up for sale. (Of course, what movies hadn't sold, they continued to rent.) At the same time the Pedersons changed to their new hours. Before, they had opened at seven and closed at seven. Now they opened at six in the morning and closed at two in the morning, with Samantha taking the morning shift from six to six and Sam the evening shift from two to two. It was hard at first, not seeing each other more than four hours in a day. Samantha, too, struggled with falling asleep alone. For Sam sleeping in was the problem.

Nevertheless, given the choice between their own comfort and their daughters' continuing education, the responsible Pedersons put their daughters first. Besides, in three years both their children would be graduated. And then they could do whatever they wanted with the store.

The same night he served the boy, Sam was unable to sleep before Samantha awoke for her shift, so he helped her open up. He turned on the lights and started the coffee. Meanwhile, Samantha made fresh breakfast sandwiches upstairs. This was another of Samantha's ideas: a sandwich and a coffee for five dollars. The Pedersons placed a folding sign by the road to attract customers on their commute to work. After he had started the coffee, Sam carried the sign across the lot to the easement, stood it up under the streetlamp, and lit a cigarette.

That was when he saw the blood. It looked like motor oil in the dawn light. There wasn't much of it, a couple of spots on the grass. Sam ambled back to the store and found more on the pavement. When he mopped the floor last night, he had only noticed a small spot by the counter. Back inside the store, he checked again to be sure. Nothing. He considered dragging the hose out front and spraying off the lot, but the cigarette had tired him, and he went to bed.

Sam slept until eleven. Knowing that the middle school would soon let out for lunch, he decided against trying for an extra hour. After a quick shower and a shave, he went downstairs to help Samantha through the rush.

At twelve-fifteen the bells rang at Glanford Middle School. Hardly a minute passed before the students came pouring through the square hole in the fence and running across the road to the store. Samantha stayed behind the counter to ring in their purchases, while Sam roamed the storefront like a supervising teacher.

He ordered the children into lines and answered questions about prices. Some of the younger children asked him to count their change to see if they had enough for what they wanted to buy. All the while Sam watched out for thieves, particularly by the ten-cent candy bins, where stealing was easiest to get away with. One boy he recognized had a peculiar habit of chewing the ends off Twizzlers. Also present was the infamous Gobstopper girl. Though neither of them had caught her in the act, Sam and Samantha would find an empty Gobstopper package on the shelves after the girl's every appearance. How she smuggled them out was a mystery: she carried no purse, sported no jacket, and always wore pants without pockets. They guessed she hid them in her cheeks like a chipmunk.

Sam heard his wife call to him from behind the counter. "Could you help this little boy put up a poster?" she asked. "It's for his lost puppy."

Sam approached the boy at the counter. The boy wore grey sweatpants and a Scooby-Doo shirt, and chewed his nails while he talked.

"What's your name?" Sam asked.

"Mark," he said, chewing.

"So I hear you lost your puppy? What's his name?"

"Bella. She's a girl."

Mark handed the poster to Sam. It was crumpled on the side where Mark had been holding it and stained with saliva from his fingertips. The picture of Bella showed her crouching, ready to pounce at the camera. She was a Yorkshire Terrier with brown and white fur. Along with a short description and a phone number, a reward of fifty dollars was offered for her safe return.

Sam led Mark to the window where the Pedersons hung posters from around the neighbourhood. But they were out of space;

an older one would have to come down. Sunlight enabled Sam to read the posters backwards from inside. There were advertisements for dog walking and landscaping, two for lost cats, one for a lost budgie, another for a lost dog, and a missing person poster for Emma Fillipoff, which had been there since both his daughters were in high school. Six years and a twenty-five thousand dollar reward, and still no one had come forward. He decided to swap Mark's with the poster for the lost budgie.

"Would you like to tape it up?" Sam asked.

Mark nodded.

He handed Mark the tape and resumed his surveillance. The Twizzler boy was still there, hovering dangerously close to the licorice, but the Gobstopper girl had already gone. He looked across the road and saw her playing on the other side of the fence.

Later, Sam found the empty pack of Gobstoppers where he always found it, hidden behind the display box. He showed it to Samantha, and they had to laugh.

AT SIX-THIRTY Samantha came downstairs to see Sam. She usually visited him twice an evening, once at seven, to bring him dinner, and again at nine, before she went to bed. But never three times.

"What's wrong?" Sam asked.

"There was a murder," she said. "On the news."

"Who? Where?"

"A mother and her daughter. Over on Carey Road."

"That close?" Sam said. "Do they know who did it?"

Samantha shook her head. "They know nothing." She peered out the front windows in the direction of Carey Road. Then she turned to Sam and said, "I think we should close early for a while. Go back to our old hours. At least until they catch who did it."

"Don't be ridiculous," he said.

Samantha turned the bolt on the front door. "Just for a week. Until they know more." She reached for the switch under the neon sign and turned it off as well.

Sam came out from behind the counter. He bumped past his wife to the door and unlocked it. "We're not closing," he said. "We can't afford to."

When he reached for the neon sign, Samantha grabbed his arm in protest. He swatted her hand away. "Anyway, what are you worried about? Nine times out of ten it's the husband that did it, not some psycho killer. You think you would've learned that watching all those *Datelines*."

Samantha stuck a finger in his chest. Sam knew she was mad then. Every time they fought it began this same way, with a prodding finger, as if she were pushing a button to start it.

"I'm talking about a mother and daughter stabbed to death in their home, and you want to leave our front door open all night?" She jabbed her finger harder into him. "No, I won't have it. I have as much say whether we stay open or not, and I'm telling you, we're closing."

Sam remembered the boy from the night before. He had come from somewhere across the field. He was bleeding. A cold feeling rushed over him. He grabbed Samantha by the shoulders.

"Last night there was a boy," he said.

"What boy?"

Sam closed his eyes so that he could better picture him in his mind. What was his name again? Lang. Yes, that was it. Donald Frederick Lang. Green husky eyes. Matted brown hair. About five-foot-eight, five-foot-nine. Medium-wash jeans. Round blood stain. Black rain jacket. Sam recalled the position of the boy's injury.

Right leg just above the knee. The blood stain itself was only an inch or two across. Could he have gotten it from a knife? Perhaps he jabbed himself running away.

Perhaps the blood wasn't even his.

"What boy?" Samantha asked again.

"Around midnight a boy came in and bought cigarettes," he said. "His leg was bleeding. I thought he was drunk."

She gasped. "That's about the time they say it happened!"

"I asked him for his ID," he said. "Donald Frederick Lang. That was his name. I thought there was something odd about him, so I remembered his name."

"I'm calling the police."

Samantha turned to go upstairs, but Sam seized her by the arm. "Wait," he said. "Wait a minute." He didn't fully understand just yet why he wanted her to wait, only that he wanted it.

"What else would we do?" she asked. "Sam, what else would we do?"

He squeezed her arm tighter. "I'm thinking."

"What's there to think about?"

"You said they don't know anything yet, right? That's what they said on the news?"

With her free hand Samantha massaged the back of her neck. "What are you on about, Sam?"

"Because sometimes there's a reward," he said. "When they don't know anything, when they don't have any leads, sometimes they offer a reward."

After the briefest silence, Samantha said, "Shame on you."

Sam released her arm. If Samantha wanted to call the police, then fine, he would let her go. But she stayed. She was red faced and shaking, and there were even tears in her eyes, but she stayed.

Sam walked over to the posters. He found the one for Emma Fillipoff and peeled it off the window. He showed the poster to Sam.

"Do you remember when this happened?"

"I remember," Samantha snapped. Sam could tell, however, that she wasn't as impassioned as she wanted to make him think.

"Twenty-five thousand dollars," he said. "That's tuition for both our girls for the next two years. That's us going back to the old hours. No more going to sleep alone and no more sleeping during the day. That's us spending the whole of every day together. Waking up together. Eating breakfast and dinner together."

"It's not right," she said. "We'll be arrested."

"I have every intention of reporting it. But what would be the harm in waiting a week or two to see if they offer a reward?"

"He could kill again." Samantha clawed at Sam's breast. "What if he kills again?"

He reminded her of the boy's wound. "He's not going to kill anyone anytime soon," he said. "Not while he's still . . ."

Just then Sam remembered the blood. He was relieved that he had been too tired earlier to wash the lot. Those spots were evidence now. Physical evidence. Even if the police didn't believe his story, Sam would give them the blood, which they could compare to the blood the boy was almost certain to have left at the scene. He made a mental note to go outside later with a rag. Something to wipe it up with and set aside for when the day came.

"I don't feel well," Samantha said. "I need to sleep."

"Sleep is good," said Sam. "We'll sleep and then talk about it tomorrow. You're right. We should close early. I don't think he'll come back, but you never know."

AFTER SAMANTHA HAD FALLEN ASLEEP, Sam went back downstairs and outside to wipe up the blood. He sponged what he could off the pavement with a rag and then brought the hose around front and sprayed everything clean. The more he thought about the reward, the more convinced he was the idea would work. But he had to be careful, meticulous. That meant no evidence except what he kept for his own purpose. Nothing that the police might find and test themselves. Only after the reward was posted would he go to them. He would tell them he hadn't thought about the boy until weeks later when he saw the murders on the news. He didn't watch TV very often. Too busy running the store.

That morning Samantha said nothing about the reward. In fact, she hardly spoke a word to Sam the whole twelve hours they were open. Sam interpreted her silence as passive protest. She meant to punish him for making her agree to something she knew was wrong, but which she couldn't bring herself to right by going over his head.

At six o'clock Samantha went upstairs to watch the news. She returned twenty minutes later with nothing to report. The murderer was still on the loose, and there was no reward. Sam remained hopeful. A high-profile case like this one wouldn't be allowed to go unsolved for long. Soon the public pressure would become too great, the police would get desperate, and the Pedersons would collect their reward.

A week passed. It was long enough that Sam went many hours a day without thinking about the reward. Long enough, too, that even Samantha seemed to have forgotten about it. Working together for the first time after almost a year working apart, the Pedersons had remembered a simple and easy happiness.

They decided never to return to the new hours.

This was not to suggest Sam and Samantha had forgotten their priorities: they intended to keep paying for their daughters' education. But when Sam compared the difference in profits between this week and the last, he found the numbers were not so disparate as they originally thought, barely three hundred dollars, which was almost negligible considering the increase to their overall well-being.

One evening Sam was tending the counter when he heard Samantha call for him from upstairs in a panicked voice. Fortunately, there were no customers, so he locked the door, turned off the neon sign, and ran upstairs. By the time he found her in the living room, Chief Manak had already begun his announcement:

"*—was found dead in his home yesterday. No foul play is suspected. We believe there is sufficient evidence tying Mr. Lang to the murders. As of this moment, we have no further suspects in this case. We will now open the floor to any—*"

Sam took the remote from his wife's trembling hands and muted the TV. "There was nothing we could've done," he said. "Anyway, it's over now." He sat down beside Samantha on the couch.

"He killed himself," she said. "If we had called . . ."

"It wouldn't have made any difference."

The Pedersons never said a word about the boy again.

The next day, they brought back the new hours.

#3 *The Crooked Salvor*

THE RANCH HAND located the missing cow behind a small bluff. At the sight of him, she lowed weakly. Her voice was strangled, like the wind had been knocked out of her. She tried to stand, but her legs remained buckled underneath her.

She lowed again.

"Shhh," the ranch hand said. "Shhh."

He looked toward the feedlot and slaughterhouses, and beyond them to the Canyon Crossing arch at the entrance to the driveway. There, a white Volvo was just turning in. He rang Phil.

"You find her?" Phil asked.

"I did."

"And?"

"Same as the others."

The ranch hand unslung the rifle from around his shoulder. He took a few steps back from the cow in case of any spray. He aimed at a spot beside her left shoulder blade.

WHEN ANDERS SVENSSON heard the gunshot, he slammed on the brakes, grabbed his Ruger from the glove compartment, and crawled out the passenger door. He checked to see how many bullets were left in the cylinder. Two. But where were the other three? Oh, yes, now he remembered. Last month he had gone on a date with the sugar shacker from Kamsack, Jocelyn, whom he met on the maple syrup job. Somehow it came up that she had never fired a gun, so after dinner he took her to a deserted part of the Assiniboine to shoot some rounds. She fired the gun three times and never called him back.

Anders felt for his cellphone; he had left it in the car. Fortunately, he was wearing his Bluetooth headset. "Call Phil Holler," he whispered. While the phone rang, Anders watched for the shooter through the driver side windows.

"Canyon Crossing, Phil here."

"Call your man off," Anders said.

"Who is this?"

"Anders Svensson."

"Who?"

"The salvor."

"Right. Now what's this about a man?"

"Not *a* man: *your* man. He shot at me."

Phil laughed. "Oh, that? That was just Travis." Anders heard floorboards creaking. "Is that you there in the white – Dodge is it?"

"Volvo." Anders hid the Ruger behind his back. He stood and waved in the direction of the ranch house.

"Miss Dunn's already here," Phil said. "Parking's around back."

"Miss Dunn," Anders repeated. "Of course."

Angela Dunn was the representative from the Canadian Farm Insurance Corporation who had hired him for the job. The night before, Anders had learned everything he could about her from her LinkedIn and Facebook, and by combing through all 267,000 Google search results of her name. From LinkedIn he learned that she held a Master of Financial Insurance from the University of Toronto. From Facebook he learned she was slender and tall, with black bobbed hair. Her relationship status was Separated. Google provided him other extraneous details: she owned the record for high jump at St. Patrick High School in Thunder Bay, she volunteered for the Salvation Army as a career consultant, she had uploaded a series of YouTube tutorials explaining insurance jargon like liquidity and tort.

Anders resumed the drive. With its excessive pediments and windows, the ranch house ahead reminded him of a quaint prairie inn. He imagined many rooms inside. Perfect for an evening tryst with Angela. Behind it, however, there loomed the slaughterhouses, towering grey buildings like chemical plants, and these made the house seem only a poorly conceived front for something sinister in back.

Anders parked behind a blue Ford King Ranch with the vanity plate HOLLER1. He checked his appearance in the visor mirror. He noticed a small shady patch under the right side of his chin where he had missed shaving. He rubbed at it, hoping it might be a gun oil stain from the Ruger. It was not.

Phil met Anders outside. "Howdy." He tipped his black Stetson hat and offered a hand to shake. "Mr. Holler," said Anders, accepting. The rancher's fingers were the texture of petrified pepperoni sticks and his palm like the rind of a ham. Anders glanced around the Herculean man for Angela. "I'm assuming Miss Dunn is –"

"Inside." Phil gestured to the slaughterhouses behind him. "Want a tour?"

Anders politely declined. "I should like to see Miss Dunn."

"Right," he said. "This way."

Anders followed Phil across a cobblestone patio. They passed through a BBQ setup that looked like the kitchen of The Keg. Enclosed grills, open grills, spit roasters, griddles – Phil seemed to own the gear to cook any animal on the planet. "Kalamazoo," he remarked. "Top of the line stuff. Any other year and I'd be out here with the steaks. But you know."

The back door led directly into a spacious kitchen, the centrepiece of which was a white marble island about the size of Anders's Volvo, give or take a foot. Angela was seated on the opposite side of it, insurance papers scattered in front of her. She hadn't noticed them come in.

Phil cleared his throat.

"Oh, sorry," Angela said. "I didn't –"

Abruptly, she rose from her chair and crossed the kitchen to Anders and Phil. She wore a black skirt suit and a red dress shirt with the top two buttons undone, enough to show the contours of her collarbone. Anders realized with some consternation that she was two inches taller than him. Not that he didn't like tall women, just that he had never met a tall woman who liked him back.

"You must be Mr. Svensson."

"Son of Sven," he said. "And you must be Miss Dunn."

"Angela, please," she said. Then, "Daughter of angels."

Almost as soon as she said it, Angela began to laugh. Anders answered her laughter with a self-satisfied grin. In all the times he had used the quip, it never failed to break the ice.

"Well," she continued, composing herself, "shall we start?"

"Anybody want coffee?" Phil asked. "Never mind. I'm putting it on."

Anders followed Angela to her seat. He stood beside her while they talked, propping himself up with a hand on her chairback. She tugged on the ends of her skirt until it came down over her knees.

"I assume you've read the briefing?" she asked.

Anders nodded. "How many cows do we know are infected?"

"Three," Phil said. "Travis found another this morning."

"Are any more showing symptoms?"

"None as far as we know."

Angela interjected, "How many isn't important. We still have to liquidate the entire stock. That means 232 head, insured at $140 per hundredweight, at an average weight of twelve hundred pounds –"

"Just under 400K," said Anders.

"Yes, exactly."

"What percentage are you hoping to recuperate?"

"Sixty-five."

"On 139 tons of tainted meat?" He scoffed. "I can get you thirty, maybe forty percent."

"Fifty," she countered.

Phil set two coffee cups on the table. "I know you take it black," he said to Angela. Then to Anders, "What about you?"

"Black is fine," he answered. Phil poured the coffee. Anders returned his attention to Angela. "Like I said, I can get you thirty, thirty-five percent. That includes shipping and cold storage. Of course, I can only ship fifty tons at once, so there may be additional loss incurred by the farm."

"But I still get my 400K, right?" said Phil.

"That doesn't change." Angela glanced over her shoulder at Anders. "I was told you could get fifty percent. That's what you got the Coombs in 2003."

"Iraq was a godsend," Anders said. "Besides, all my contacts in the Middle East are either dead or in exile."

"Then where is the meat going?"

"Libya, to the government in Tobruk."

Angela cocked an eyebrow. "Are they aware it's tainted?"

"They are aware."

Yes, they were aware. Aware that only 229 cases of variant Creutzfeldt-Jakob had ever been reported in humans. Aware that if they removed specified risk materials – head, organs, spinal cord – the odds of transmission were statistically zero. Aware that they were getting enough beef to feed their army for a month, at half the price. Compared to other jobs he had done, this one had been a relatively easy sell.

"And Libya agreed to thirty-five percent?" Angela asked.

"No," said Anders, "they agreed to fifty percent. But factoring in the cost of shipping and cold storage, and my percentage – that leaves thirty."

She sighed. "All right. Thirty percent."

Angela picked up her coffee and sipped it. Anders tried his coffee too, but it was lukewarm. He let the drink slip back out of his mouth and into the mug.

"What do you think?" Phil asked. "It's Kopi Luwak. Best in the world."

Angela pushed her mug away from her. "I'm all coffee-ed out."

"Kopi Luwak?" Now that Anders knew what it was, he tasted the tepid coffee purposefully. "You know," he said, "I once arranged for a sale of civet cats from a foreclosed exotic animal farm on Vancouver Island to a bean man in Sulawesi." He swirled the drink around his mouth and swallowed. "I got a bag of shit in the mail for a thank you note."

Phil laughed boisterously. Even Angela permitted herself a chuckle. Anders hid behind his mug so as not to let his pleasure show. He watched Angela satisfy an itch on her shoulder. He imagined her hand sliding further sideways, removing her top as from a coat hanger.

Angela checked her watch. "Well," she said, "I suppose I should be going." She gathered the paperwork in front of her into four piles, then stacked them haphazardly on top of each other. "We can meet back here tomorrow at, say, eleven? I'll prepare the contracts tonight, so that they'll be ready for us to sign in the morning."

"You're not staying here?" Anders asked.

"The Palliser, actually."

He did his best to feign surprise. "Really? You don't say. That's – what a coincidence. I'm staying at the Palliser as well."

"But I thought –" Phil started to say before Anders cut him off.

"I thought it best not to inconvenience you."

"Right," Phil said. He gave Anders a knowing nod. "Right, right."

"In that case," said Angela, "do you mind if I follow you?"

"Not at all," Anders said. "We could even carpool, if you'd like."

"I'd feel more comfortable taking my own car."

"Of course."

HEADING NORTH OUT OF CANYON CROSSING, Anders plugged the Fairmont Palliser into his GPS. He read the route time in the top right corner of the screen. One hour and thirteen minutes until his destination. He wished he'd been more adamant that they carpool.

What to do with all this time? Anders tried the radio, but all he could pick up were two country music stations. He checked his rear-view mirror to make sure Angela was still behind him. He was certain that she would agree to a drink with him when he asked; no woman had ever rejected him straight off. Only after the drinks were served did there seem to arise any complications. Perhaps he should take this time to strategize. He considered Angela in terms of a buyer–seller relationship. How would he sell himself to her? Easy. At forty-one years old he had a net worth of just under 2.3 million, including properties in Vancouver and Edmonton, and a lake house in the Okanagan. He was single and childless, never married, never divorced. Lean for his age, he still showed four out of six abs in the right lighting. Not to mention that he worked in the exotic, some might argue *dangerous*, field of black-market salvages and sales. Even the word "salvor" bore connotations of the romantic, like the title of some Spanish folk hero.

At Calgary's city limits Anders sped through a yellow light and lost Angela. Sometime earlier he had realized it would be best if he got to the hotel ahead of her. That way he could book a room, get his bags in, ruffle the bed to make it look as if he had checked in the day before, and return to the lobby in time to catch her arriving. He would apologize for losing her, then offer to make it up to her with a drink.

The Fairmont Palliser reminded Anders of the head of a giant fork. Paired with the spoon-like neighbouring Calgary Tower they appeared together like the world's largest salad servers. Out front, he tossed his keys to the valet and whistled a porter for his bags. In case Angela had somehow caught up to him, Anders surveyed the downtown traffic for any black Honda Civics. He spied a lot of Fords. No Civics, though.

He turned to the porter. "Do you have a razor and some shaving cream?"

The porter nodded. "Would you like that now, sir? Or when you are checked in?"

"I had better get it now."

The porter left to get him a razor and shaving cream. Anders continued to the front desk. He entered a line with three other men. Two of them were either cowboys or merely dressed up like them, and the other looked to be here on business. Anders checked his watch. Three forty-six. He estimated he had ten minutes before Angela arrived. He took out his money clip and removed a fifty-dollar bill from it. He tapped the businessman on the shoulder and showed him the bill. "Fifty bucks to budge," he said. The businessman stepped aside. He tried a similar method with the cowboys; they too stepped aside. By then the porter had returned with the razor and shaving cream, and Anders, knowing the porter had seen him give the other men fifty dollars, begrudgingly tipped the same.

A minute later Anders was waved forward by a front desk agent named Harriett. If things went sour with Angela, perhaps he could talk Harriett into joining him for a drink after her shift. She was just his type, slim and small-chested, tall but not taller than him.

"Good afternoon," she said. "Are we checking in or checking out?"

"Checking in."

"Could I get your first and last name?"

"Anders," he said. "Svensson. Son of Sven."

"All right, Mr. Svensson, son of Sven." Harriet's eyes darted across her computer screen. "I don't seem to have your reservation on file. Did you make a reservation? I might have misspelled your name. That's S-V –"

"I didn't make a reservation."

Harriett winced. "I'm sorry, Mr. Svensson, but we're all sold out. If you would like, I can call another hotel to –"

Anders set his money clip on the counter. "There must be something you can do."

"I apologize, Mr. Svensson," she said, blushing. "But it's Stampede weekend."

He pulled a one hundred dollar bill from the clip. "Listen, Harriett, I can give this to you, or I can give this to your manager. I don't care if it's a supply closet, I just want a bed and a place to put my bags." He palmed the bill and extended his hand for her to shake. "It's up to you."

"Like I said, it's Stampede weekend."

Anders groaned. "Your manager, then."

He checked his watch again. Three fifty-seven. Angela would be here any minute – if he hadn't already missed her while tied up at the desk. He hoped that wasn't the case, because if it was, then he would need to get her room number. And to do that he would have to ask Harriett for it. Honest Harriett, Harriett the honourable. Daughter of hairdressers. Anders chuckled to himself. If she had been quick like Angela, she might've replied with something like that.

Just then he spotted Angela gliding through the lobby. "Angel!" he called. Her head jerked out of reflex, but stopped short of glancing in his direction. She sped up. Probably she thought him some creep. Anders called her name again, correctly this time, and Angela whipped around. She held her hands open in front of her as if about to receive a benediction. Anders mimicked the gesture.

"What happened to you?" he asked.

"I could ask you the same thing," she said. "Was that you shouting about angels?"

"A slip of the tongue."

"Freudian?"

"Judeo-Christian."

She laughed. Now was his chance to ask her out for a drink. How could she say no to him after a joke like that? But before Anders could say anything, Angela pointed behind him and said, "I think someone wants to talk to you."

Anders had almost forgotten.

Harriett.

The manager.

Anders spun around on his heels. "Yes." He read the woman's nametag. "Joy, I was wanting to thank you for the wonderful, uh, dessert you had sent to my room last night. It went perfectly with my Shiraz."

"My pleasure," Joy answered. She exchanged a bewildered look with Harriet beside her. Anders scrambled after the hundred dollar bill floating in his pocket.

"I apologize, sir," Joy continued, "but Harriett seemed to –"

Anders grabbed Joy's hand and pressed the hundred dollar bill into her palm. He removed another from his bill clip and gave it to Harriett. "I wanted to say I appreciate it." He spoke the words slowly, with emphasis, also dipping his chin and widening his eyes, so that there could be no mistaking he was paying them to leave. "Thank you, sir." "My pleasure, sir." With that, Joy and Harriett left.

"That was bizarre," Angela said.

"I've never been very good at giving tips," Anders said. Then, "So how about that drink?"

"What drink?"

"Oh right, I was about to ask if you would like to join me in the lounge for a drink."

Angela cocked an eyebrow. "Is that you asking?"

"I suppose so."

"All right," she said. "Let's say nine o'clock?"

OF ALL THE JOBS he had ever done, Anders was most proud of the sale of eight thousand pounds of salvaged yellowcake to the Democratic People's Republic of Korea.

"When they closed the Cluff Lake Mine in 2002," he told Angela, "I was hired to sell the leftover yellowcake. Almost that same day, I was in talks with Khatami's government, but ultimately we couldn't agree on shipping. Then a week passed without a single decent offer. I tried Vajpayee in India. Nothing. Jamali in Pakistan. Nothing. Of course, these are countries with uranium deposits so substantial that eight thousand pounds was like offering a handful of sand to a beach; it just wasn't worth their trouble." Anders paused to sip his Sauvignon Blanc. "Then I thought, what about North Korea? They are probably in the market for the stuff. So I went on their government website and sent an email to what I honestly suspected was a dummy contact explaining my proposal. The next day, however, I received a reply from Choe Thae-bok."

"Who is . . . ?" Angela asked.

"At the time one of Kim Jong-il's closest advisors. Chairman of the Supreme People's Assembly. Anyway, he offered to pay me in full, as well as an additional hundred thousand dollars upon arrival. How could I refuse? I arranged for the transport of the yellowcake to Vancouver, and they took care of the rest."

A food runner appeared with the appetizers. Anders had ordered Korean Gochujang wings, Angela, a plate of assorted olives and artisanal bread. "After all that talk of meat," she had said, "I don't think I could stomach anything else." But for Anders all their talk of meat had had the opposite effect. In fact, during the long drive to Calgary, whenever he wasn't thinking about Angela, he had been thinking about meat. Specifically chicken. Before

Anders decided to follow Angela here, Phil had promised him a fresh-slaughtered rotisserie chicken for dinner. "I know just the one," he had said. "Looks just like you. Same yellow hair. She's got your little belly, too."

Anders picked up his first wing. He imagined biting into his doppelgänger. Ba-gock!

"But aren't you afraid of anybody finding out?" Angela asked. She fished through her olives for a kalamata. "What if, for example, CSIS found out? Or the CIA?"

"Or what if the package never made it to North Korea?" Anders shrugged. "Hypotheticals. The reality is, no one ever did find out."

"And if they had?"

Anders devoured another wing. "Then you'd find me one night in my library with a single gunshot wound to the head. Possibly hanged from the landing of my grand staircase."

Angela laughed. "*I'd* find you? What makes you think *I* would find you?"

"Or drowned in my swimming pool," he continued. "Or floating face down beside my lake house dock."

"Lake house, huh?" She plucked an olive pit off her tongue and dropped it on her plate. "Are you seriously bragging about all the places somebody might stage your suicide?"

"Do you own many properties?" Anders asked.

"I have a house in Scarborough."

"Married?"

"Separated."

"Kids?"

Angela shook her head.

"Me neither," he said. "But I want to have a son one day. Somebody to carry on the Anders name. An 'Andersson,' so to speak."

"Kid talk on the first date," Angela said. "That hasn't happened in a while." She took a large swallow of wine. Anders refilled her glass from the decanter.

"Do you want kids?" he asked.

"Maybe let's quit it with the kid stuff," she said. "Why don't you tell me another story? Like about the time you sold sarin gas to Assad or something equally awful."

Anders contemplated his half-eaten appetizer of chicken wings, then looked to the discarded bones on the plate beside him. The sight of the bones, some cracked in half, others still wearing flesh, made him suddenly self-conscious. For being a carnivore. For eating with his hands like some primitive. A beast. He pushed the plate away.

Angela apologized. "Sorry, that was rude."

"Apology accepted," Anders said. "Although, in one sense, you're right, I've done jobs I'm not proud of." (He was thinking specifically of Asbestos, Quebec, and the Jeffrey mine. When they closed the mine for decontamination in 2012, he had been hired to sell what was left of the asbestos reserves. And he did. Nearly nine thousand tons of it to Bangladesh. He had made forty thousand dollars off the deal, which he used, in part, to buy the Volvo.) "But I would never sell anything I thought was going to be used purposefully to kill."

"What about the yellowcake?"

"Useless unless you can enrich it."

"Didn't they?"

"It's what they would want you to believe."

Anders divided what remained of the Sauvignon Blanc into his and her glasses. He waved down the waiter and ordered another bottle.

"I hope you plan on drinking that yourself," Angela said.

"I can ask for nuts if you're feeling tipsy."

She yawned. "Just tired."

"Should we go to bed, then?" he asked. "I can cancel the bottle." He searched the dining room for the waiter and, spotting him at the bar, signalled for the cheque.

"You better not have meant what I think you did," Angela said.

Anders affected confusion. "What did you think I meant?"

"Never mind."

Angela reached around her chair back, where she had hung her handbag. She set the handbag in her lap and dug through it. Anders waited until she pulled out her wallet before making it clear that he was paying.

"That's all right," said Angela. "I don't mind."

"I insist," Anders said.

"It's really no trouble."

"Get me next time."

She guffawed. "Doubtful."

The waiter arrived with the wine and the cheque. Anders surveyed the dining room for a table to send the unopened bottle. He spied three women sitting in a booth nearby and instructed the waiter to send it to them.

"Shall I say it's from you?" asked the waiter.

Anders glimpsed Angela in his periphery. "I prefer to remain anonymous," he said. Besides, if Angela rejected him, he could always come back later and announce himself as the purchaser.

The waiter left to deliver the bottle to the table of women. Anders searched Angela's expression for any trace of acknowledgment for his generosity, but she remained unimpressed.

"Anyway, it's just money," Anders said. Simultaneously, he and

Angela reached for the cheque. She succeeded in wrestling it away from him. She set her credit card in the plastic slot and held it out for the waiter to take.

"It's just money," she said.

When the waiter returned with her credit card, Anders offered to walk Angela to her room. "It's the least I can do after you bought me dinner," he said.

"You can walk me to my room. But I'm not going to sleep with you."

Anders and Angela strode silently through the lobby to the elevators. They took the elevators to the seventh floor, also in silence. Anders followed behind Angela to the door of her room, 715, at which point she finally spoke.

"This is me," she said.

Anders moved to kiss her.

Angela slapped his face. The sharp sound made her gasp. "I'm sorry!"

Anders felt his cheek. Hot like he had been leaning over a fire. He opened his mouth. *Click*. He closed it. *Click*. Apparently his jaw was yet to heal from his tussle with Jocelyn. He swore he could taste maple syrup.

"Are you all right?" she asked.

"I'm fine," he said. He rubbed his left mandible. *Click*.

"Look," sighed Angela, "I'm not saying that I didn't enjoy myself tonight. You strike me as a gentleman. A nice guy. And you're not bad-looking. You're even – yes, I would say you're even attractive. But I could never be with somebody who does what you do. You understand that, don't you?"

Of course Anders understood. He was forty-one years old, never married. Childless. He had nothing but time to arrive at such understandings. But what did these women expect? That he wasn't going to try?

Anders showed Angela the left side of his face. "Is it bad?"

"It's a little red," she said. Then, "You should go."

So Anders left. He took the elevators down to the lobby and returned to the restaurant. There, he introduced himself to the table of three women. He told them he had been the man who had bought them their bottle of wine.

"Really?" one said. "I was told a woman bought it for us."

Another remarked on his face. "You can actually see the fingers!"

Anders abandoned the table to the roar of their laughter. He went to see Harriett at the front desk. Perhaps he could still get a room. Perhaps somebody hadn't shown up for their reservation or had cancelled last minute. This time around he didn't have to pay his way to the front of the line. He asked if any rooms had become available. They were still all booked up.

Harriett's eyes lingered on the slap. "Did you want some ice for that?"

Out front, Anders asked the valet for directions to the carpark. He walked around back to the carpark, found his Volvo, took the emergency blanket from the trunk, and made a bed for himself in the passenger seat. For a time he tried to sleep, but without luck. He heard the echo of footsteps nearby. He took the Ruger from his glove compartment and held it tight against his chest. All that talk of North Korea and the CIA had made him paranoid. If there had ever been an opportunity for assassination, it was now. He worried that every moment of his life had been leading him to this spot, to what would surely be an ignominious end, a murder framed as suicide. More than dying, he worried that Angela would think he killed himself because of her.

A knock at the window.

Anders pulled the trigger. A reflex. The Ruger fired into the car roof. A woman screamed. Because his ears were ringing from the gunshot, the sound was warbled, almost alien. Anders peeked out the back window. He watched the woman get inside a black Honda Civic. *Angela.* The car tore backwards out of its spot and crashed into a parked Mercedes-Benz. Then Angela, in her damaged Civic, sped away.

ALL THE WAY TO CANYON CROSSING, the gunshot hole whistled overhead like a mischievous child. Anders tried plugging it with gum, a pen, even a wadded Kleenex, but none of them held for very long. Eventually, he decided to drown it out with one of the abundant country music stations. He lasted exactly two songs. Between the whistle and their twang, Anders would take the whistle every time.

At the ranch Anders was disappointed to learn from Phil that Angela had dropped off the papers for him to sign and left.

"Did she mention why she wouldn't wait for me?" Anders asked.

Phil shrugged. "Said she was in a hurry."

Anders signed the papers. He and Phil shook hands.

"It was a pleasure doing business with you," Anders said.

"Got something for you before you go." Phil went to the fridge, opened the freezer bottom, and took out a plastic bag with something in it the size of a human head. Phil handed the bag to Anders. Anders peeked inside. A chicken. Only a chicken. He wondered how, in his current condition, he was going to survive the drive back to Vancouver.

"Truth is," Phil said, "I don't let anyone leave without trying my meat. That there is free range organic. One of our best birds. Did I tell you she looked just like you? I might've mentioned it to you yesterday."

"You did," Anders said.

"She's a good bird." Phil chuckled. "Plenty of meat on that bird."

Anders thanked Phil for the chicken and exited the ranch house by way of the patio.

ANDERS ARRIVED HOME IN VANCOUVER just after ten o'clock at night. Not a minute had passed during the drive when he didn't think he was going to fall asleep behind the wheel; but now that he was home, he found himself, impossibly, awake. He checked his messages. None. He made himself a bowl of cereal and watched TV. (He might've cooked the chicken, but he had thrown it out the window on the Coquihalla after it began to stink.) Afterward, he dusted off his thirty-pound weights and did a few bicep curls. In the middle of his second to last set, he heard his cellphone vibrating on the coffee table. He knew the caller only by his initials: JP.

"How'd you fare with the cows?"

"Better than expected," Anders said. "If you could believe it, they actually agreed to thirty percent."

JP laughed. "Dumb fucks." Anders heard papers rustling on the other end. "I've got another job for you. This one's in Churchill, so pack your parka."

"What's the merchandise?"

"Polar bears," he said. "Furs. A friend of mine discovered six crates of them while digging up the land for a hotel she's opening up there. She says they're dated from the seventies and have kept pretty well on account of the cold. For obvious reasons she doesn't want to go through legal channels."

"What's her name?" asked Anders. He went to his computer and turned it on.

"Donna Bagley," JP said. "I told her she could expect you by Monday."

While JP shared with him the relevant information, Anders started a pot of Kopi Luwak coffee. Since having it lukewarm at the ranch house, he had been craving a hot cup. He returned to his computer. He opened his internet browser and typed Donna Bagley into Google search. 411,000 results. Even more than Angela. He was in for a long night.

#4 *Not the Summit but the Plummet*

TENZING AND I AWAKE at eleven for the summit push. We don't realize until we are dressed and standing outside our tents at Camp IV that the team from Rapid Ascents has left already. They are perhaps one or two hours ahead of us by now; it is impossible to know how long because neither Tenzing nor I heard them leave. In all likelihood this means we will meet them coming down the Hillary Step, where bottlenecks are apt to form. Having slept fitfully for the three hours Tenzing allotted us, I am frustrated by the coincidence of my deepest moment of sleep arriving at the moment of their departure and have to suck a breath of oxygen from my portable Mountain High to interrupt my anger before it barrels out of control. At twenty-six thousand feet, I experience oxygen for what it truly is: the fire of life, substantial, burning, and for whose wielding we, as Prometheus's spawn, are slowly pecked away. But I am alluding to the wrong myth. I am, in fact, a contemporary Icarus – though, if told correctly, the myth would not see his wax wings melted by the sun, but instead frozen in the thin air of high altitude.

In the same way it is "not the summit but the plummet" that makes the difference in any climb. I put quotes around the aphorism because it is rightly Tenzing's, not mine. Tenzing is full of little sayings like this one, which are particularly useful in occasions of extreme stress, when the mind slackens into fancy. It is much easier to remember "not the summit but the plummet" than it is to remember "the descent is four times more dangerous than the ascent" or "it is a well-known fact many more people die on the way down than on the way up."

In our fifty-five-litre backpacks, we carry two oxygen bottles each. These will provide ten to twelve hours of continuous oxygen, and sustain us to the peak and part of the way back. To complete our descent, we will need to stop on the South Summit and pick up a third bottle, placed there ahead of time when Tenzing and the Sherpas from Rapid Ascents fixed the ropes.

Before we leave, Tenzing reminds me, "Not the summit but the plummet, okay, boss?"

I give him a thumb's up because it is easier than talking. I hate it when Tenzing calls me boss, but he uses the tag unconsciously, like a waitress uses honey, and though I have told him a dozen times to please call me John, he seems incapable of shaking the habit.

As we ascend The Balcony, a strong westerly wind crowds the darkness of night with flakes of ice and snow. With my left hand I trail the rope like an arthritic senior using the railing up a steep set of stairs, taking each step with judicious care, fighting against the screaming of my bones and the pins and needles in my feet and the stiffness of my muscles. An oxygen revolution foments inside me at a cell level. My fingers, too, are beginning to numb, though I am so familiar with this feeling by now that I don't have to commit conscious thought to maintaining a grip on the rope; my fingers simply work in the unfeeling reality like one of those mechanical hands reacting to signals from the brain. I am only scared when transferring between anchor points. But Tenzing is never far behind. Attached to me at the waist, he scrutinizes my every movement for error, knowing any mistake of mine will have potentially deadly consequences for us both.

Not the summit but the plummet. Plummet is not exactly synonymous with descent. Icarus plummeted; we descend. There is a spot along today's route where plummeting is a genuine concern, and that is the Cornice Traverse. When several hours into our journey we stop at the South Summit to exchange oxygen bottles, I experience an anxiety of the prophetic kind, knowing the Traverse comes next. Words have power in repetition, and there seems even extra power in words that rhyme. "The peak is only the halfway point" would be an inarguably weaker expression of the same idea. "The descent not the ascent" is too easily jumbled in the mind.

Fortunately, the weather clears precisely as forecasted by Rapid Ascents, and soon we can even see their party up ahead, their headlamps like Christmas lights stringing toward the peak. They have successfully surmounted the Hillary step. To the east, weak blue light descries the Himalayan peaks. It is almost morning.

On the Cornice Traverse, I hesitate to glimpse down the eleven-thousand-foot Kangshung Face. It appears a never-ending chute into the void of space. At this point my exhaustion seems total. But there is much farther to go, and my mind whips my body into suffering submission. My strength of spirit both inspires and perplexes me. I have never known such power over self before. No wonder the Tibetan people view the mountain as holy, the seat of the gods.

Death attends my every footstep. And to die is to ascend.

We have not seen any bodies, but they are easily mistaken for exposed boulders in the snow.

We arrive at the Hillary Step in full daylight. Five team members from Rapid Ascents await us at the bottom of the narrow passage. There is one person currently descending and three more atop waiting to descend. Fixed ropes have greatly reduced the difficulty for less experienced climbers; but even so, without Tenzing's close encouragement, and nearing my energy's expiration, I am nervous whether I will be able to summon the individual effort required to deliver me up the sheer rock face. If this is the most challenging part of the summit, it is only because I must tackle it alone.

Five times Tenzing and I unclip from the rope to pass the other climbers. Each time we do this, the odds of a fatal error rise exponentially. One mistake, one misstep, and we risk embarking on the longest and last toboggan ride of our lives. With the arrival of their sixth member, the leader of Rapid Ascents radios for the others atop the step to wait while Tenzing and I take our turn. I go first. Almost immediately my crampons slip, and I am forced to retest them against the ice.

"You got it, boss," Tenzing says. "Don't wait for me at the top. Keep going. I'll play catch up."

Left foot up, right pick up, right foot up, left pick up – using this careful alternating method, I ascend. When fear strikes me halfway to the top, I remind myself that eight other climbers have already succeeded today, and it is unreasonable to think my fate will be any different from theirs. And, afterward, only a short jaunt to the peak. A leisurely stroll compared to other sections of the mountain.

Half an hour later I make it to the top of the step. I am congratulated by the two waiting climbers with pats on the back and rear end.

"How is the peak?" I ask.

They tell me it is beautiful, indescribable.

I continue alone. For the first time I experience what is called "summit fever," an adrenaline high that comes upon the realization of certain victory. My steps quicken; I am crazed with joy. People with the condition can sometimes find it impossible to turn around, even in the face of certain death. Summit fever is the siren call of the mountain, the god's final trick of seduction. But what is the trick? To obscure this truth in ecstasy: not the summit but the plummet.

I am halfway to the peak when the wind picks up. Though it has been blowing steadily the entire way, I feel the difference like a small change in acceleration; it is there one moment and gone the next. I look to the south and notice a haze settling over the Western Cwm. To the north the sky is azure blue, but to the south it appears a lighter cerulean. A pale mist spreads over the Lhotse face, and in it I discern the delineations of clouds, inchoate, frail, like I could clap my hands in their direction and scatter them. Still, they frighten me. If Tenzing were here, I might point them out and ask his opinion. But he has just made it atop the Hillary Step and will be another fifteen minutes in reaching me. And I cannot stop now. Not when I am so close to the peak.

My mind fractures. One half descends the mountain ahead of me, to secure my way back. The other half rushes me forward to my accomplishment.

Tenzing catches up steps from the peak. "What's the hurry, boss?"

I point toward the Lhotse face.

"Nothing to worry," he says.

I spy the flapping prayer flags, green and yellow and red. Tears come to my eyes as I reach over them to lay my hand on the peak.

Though I have seen pictures of it before, I am still disappointed there is no exposed point of rock. It appears merely a hump of snow, of the sort one might find dumped beside a shovelled driveway. All around it are scattered the trinkets and tokens of hundreds of climbers before me, who, in hoping to leave their special mark, have instead perverted the highest point on Earth with tiny vanities. To light a candle in a church, to set flowers on a grave, to clip a lock to a bridge – those are supplications. An empty Coke bottle, a teddy bear, a keychain from the Space Needle – that is litter.

"Say cheese!" Tenzing snaps a photo.

Once the picture is taken, I start back the way we came.

"Where are you going?" he asks.

"Not the summit," I say. "But the plummet."

He shakes me gently. "Relax. Enjoy. You deserve it."

But I cannot enjoy it. I have three hours of oxygen left. A new oxygen bottle awaits me at the South Summit. If I leave now, I will have an hour to spare in case of disaster. It is nowhere near long enough.

"Why have you come all this way, huh? To turn around?"

I don't have an answer for him other than I shouldn't have come. I shouldn't have come. A loud cracking noise makes me flinch. Tenzing laughs. We watch a piece of glacier ice tumble down the mountainside and vanish in a splash of snow.

TENZING AND I MAKE IT SAFELY DOWN to Base Camp the following day, after an overnight at Camp Three. While packing up my tent, I am approached by another climber about to embark up the mountain. She is curious to know what it was like to reach the top. I am not lying when I tell her that I never got there.

"Was it bad weather?" she asks.

"No," I say, "the skies were clear."

"Then what happened?"

I tell her the moment you start planning a way back is the moment you stop going up. I tell her if you worry about the plummet, you'll never reach the summit.

"Worry about the plummet, never reach the summit." She thanks me for the advice and heads off to join the rest of her team.

#5 *Hard Time*

IF THERE WERE A PRETTIER GIRL in all Topeka, I had never seen her. She had the build of a farm girl. Tits fattened with unpasteurized milk. Legs that could squat a horse. I liked my girls big. Tall, too. I could handle pretty much any woman God in his infinite lunacy could throw at me. He had endowed me for it. She looked taller than me sitting down. I bet we weighed about the same. One hundred and sixty pounds of sex. I was a scrawny boy. In prison you're either a Meerkat or a Gorilla. Brains or brawn.

"– so Aunt Clara asked if Marcy wouldn't collect the mail for her. She's staying with your uncle Peter on a job in Wichita. And of course Marcy will do it."

Was she still going on?

"Momma," I said.

"What, Robert?"

"Could you pray for me?"

She smiled. "Sure, dear."

"Make it a long one."

Mom reached her hands across the visitor table. She liked holding hands when she prayed for anyone. A real lightning rod for Jesus. She scrunched her eyes.

"Dear Lord –"

"Don't embarrass me, Momma."

She continued the prayer in silence.

Back to the girl. She dressed with that fake conservatism that drives pious men to pigs. No cleavage, no knees, no shoulders. But her pink dress was cut with enough room in the chest to smuggle watermelons. And it funnelled down to her waist tight as a corset. Standing up there would be no mistaking her dimensions. God, I hadn't seen a girl like her since I was seventeen! Geoff's sister Catherine. With a capital C for –.

"Christ," I groaned. Mom squeezed my hands.

And that's when I caught her do it.

The New Guy had been whispering sweet nothings in her ear for over an hour now. Calling her sweetheart and darling and lass. Plagiarizing John Wayne or Elvis or whoever it was those inbred feather-pluckers learned their English from. But this time, right in the middle of it, she turned her head to look at me. Her eyes flashed at mine, then back at his. Then at mine again. And again. Though even when she was looking at him, I could tell she was hoping to look at me. Something about her irises. Like they were being stretched or pulled, straining to look straight and sideways at once.

"Amen," Mom said.

I closed my eyes. "Amen."

When I opened them, I saw Mom was crying. She cried like an old man. Silent, trembling.

"Visitation is over," a CO bellowed. "Let's go."

Everybody stood. There was no touching allowed, but Mom had stepped into my line of sight. I had no choice.

"I love you, Momma!" I cried, and pulled her in for a hug.

She *was* taller than me! – the New Guy's girl, that is. I had been right about her dress, too. It fit over her hips like a pink pillowcase. Every line measurable to my wanton eyes. She watched me embrace my sobbing mother. Touched at the scene of my tenderness. She raised her left hand to her chest.

Was that a fucking ring?

The COs wrenched Mom and me apart. I pretended my knees had given out, so they were forced to drag me from the room. It was more fun that way.

THE PROBLEM WITH PRISON was that you had too many hours in a day to think. I practised hard at thinking about nothing. But even then sometimes a thought would creep in. Or a picture. It took time to rid yourself of shit like that. Years for some.

Freddy Gilles lost his head with one visitation. His second cousin. She showed up on her eighteenth birthday looking like a Halloween hooker. She took one glance at Freddy's ugliness, turned around, and never came back. Anyway, Freddy was caught masturbating so often afterward that they handcuffed him to the bedposts every night before light's out. His feet, too, when he figured them out. Until one night he yanked so hard trying to free himself the top bunk came straight down on him. Broke his dick like the shinbone it was. Before him I didn't believe you could do it.

That night after visitation I found myself fighting Freddy's virus. I tried to make it sound like I was restless. Breaking the rhythm.

Rolling from side to side. But when you're top bunk, and with the way those exhausted springs squeak, there was no mistaking it.

My cellmate kicked me from underneath. "Fuck off."

"I'll make you a deal," I said.

"No deal."

"If I go tonight, you can go tomorrow."

"No." He kicked me again.

I needed to talk to Officer Friend. Friend was a CO who did favours. All he wanted in return was protection if we ever rioted. His brother had been one of the hostages at the riot in New Mexico. Friend knew the stories.

I saw him at lunch the next day.

"I need to move cells," I said.

Friend shoved me. "Step back, inmate!"

"I want the New Guy."

He smacked my food tray out of my hand.

"Clean it up, inmate!"

He squashed my potatoes under his boot for good measure. Friend was an excellent actor. Not a single CO, Deputy, or Warden who had come through Lansing suspected him of anything but hatred for us.

Four hours later I was locked in a cell with the New Guy.

Seeing him up close for the first time, I wondered if his girl wasn't stark blind. He looked like a meth addict's attempt at building the Frankenstein monster. Eyes staring off at ten-and-two. Spotty facial hair. Jaw crooked as Freddy's cock. What could she possibly see in him? I peeked at his hog when he took a piss; it wasn't that. Probably a country marriage. Square trade for cattle.

"Senior guy gets choice of bunk," I said.

"All right, partner."

"Keep your partners to yourself, partner." I flopped onto the bottom bunk. "Call the wrong guy that in here, and you'll be the partner. How long you been in?"

"I reckon three weeks," he said.

"Jesus Christ! Quit it with the John Wayne already!"

The New Guy climbed onto the top bunk. Some time passed. I whistled the theme song from *The Searchers* to bait him.

"How long you been here?" the New Guy asked eventually.

I whistled the tune again. "Twelve years and two months."

"What for?" he asked.

I crept up the side of his bunk and met him eye-to-eye. Or his version of that.

"Murder One."

The New Guy wormed backwards to the wall. I spread my arms out on his bed.

"How'd you do him?" he asked.

"Well, it was three guys. But they only got me for one."

"How'd they get you?"

"Two of them I chopped up and tossed in Ol' Blue. The third I buried. Couldn't stomach him being eaten by catfish. That's how they got me."

"Why'd you do it?"

"Because it was fun," I said. "What other reason is there? Anyway, what'd you do?"

"Stole a car," he said.

"They really threw the book at you, huh."

"At gunpoint."

"There you go."

"It was a plastic gun."

"Ha! How long you get?"

"Two years on account of it was only plastic."

The COs began running their batons across the bars in preparation for lights out. I got into my bunk just as one arrived at our cell.

"Lights out!" he yelled.

"But I ain't done reading my Bible verses yet!" I returned.

Soon after the lights went out.

"You got a girl, New Guy?" I asked.

"It's George," he said. "I got a fiancée."

I bit my fist to keep from roaring Hallelujah. I knew farm girls. Engaged or not, they doled it out every day of the week and twice on Sunday. Marriage was different. Something about the myth of the farmer's wife kept them honest and faithful and keen.

"What's her name?" I asked.

"Delilah."

"Delilah," I said. I spoke her name again, "Delilah."

"You got a girl?" George asked.

"What's she like, Delilah?"

"She's a sweet girl," he said. "Too sweet for me."

"I mean what's she *look* like?"

"She's tall."

I reached down my pants. "Uh-huh."

George continued to describe her in his simpleton way. Using words you might find scribbled in a preschooler's notebook. But I got my picture. I asked him to describe what she was like in bed. He went into all the exaggerated detail a young guy would.

It hadn't happened that easy in years.

"— **SO AUNT CLARA SENT THE FIFTY DOLLARS**. It's not every day you hear from a Nigerian prince. She hasn't heard anything yet, but they're hopeful. They could use the money. What with your uncle having diabetes."

"That's a scam, Momma."

"Huh?"

"They're thieves! Robbers! Con artists!"

"Oh my."

I beat my head against the table until a CO ordered me to stop. Oftentimes I wondered where in my family's genetic swamp the mutation happened that resulted in me. I would guess I was adopted, except for my gums. The family heirloom. We Crawleys showed them off like brand new sneakers. Like those ugly pink swatches were the pride of humanity.

I resumed watching Delilah. Three months had passed since George and I became cellmates. In that time I had learned everything I could about her. And I mean everything. From the freckle patch under her elbow to the cut of her pubes. Everything. If I were any sort of artist, I would've painted her. A nudie to keep under my pillow.

Delilah visited George every second week. I suffered in the off week, especially visiting with Mom alone. I made her pray for me every chance I got. But even she tired of that. She wanted to gossip. About my sister Marcy. About Aunt Clara and Uncle Peter and all their pathetic sons and daughters and grandchildren. The worst was when she tried to get me to talk. Whenever she did I told her about the most recent shanking. Real grisly stuff. That usually shut her up.

George threw his arms in the air. "Yeehaw!" He spun an invisible lasso around his head.

"Settle down, inmate!" a CO shouted.

I rolled my eyes at Delilah. She blushed and looked away. Poor George was so busy roping his ghost calf, he had no idea his fiancée was embarrassed and making eyes with me across the room.

"Shush, Georgie," Delilah said. "I don't want you to get in trouble."

"That's just about the best news I ever heard," he said.

"It won't be long now."

"We'll be together soon, Lilah."

What was this?

"Marcy said she might visit you," Mom interrupted. "I think she's ready to forgive you for Pa."

One chance. I'd give her just the one.

"I need quiet now, Momma. Can't you pray or something?"

She frowned. "Did you hear what I said? Marcy –"

"I don't give a right fuck about Marcy! So what, she wants to forgive me for Pa? Nobody needs forgiveness that sends the devil back to Hell. I'm a saviour, Momma. A saint. Tell that bitch I'll kill her if she comes around here spouting her forgiveness."

"Robert!" Mom collapsed into her upturned palms and sobbed.

"I'M GETTING OUT." George beamed. "Delilah hired an appeal lawyer. He got me down to six months and parole."

"How'd he do that?" I asked.

"On account of no one got hurt, and the victim got her car back. I was a first-time officer, too."

"Offender."

"That's right."

"So how long you have left?"

"I reckon two months."

I seethed. "I thought I told you to quit it with that cowboy shit."

"No point," he said, "now I'm a free man."

"Friend."

George leaned over the bunk. "What was that?"

"Get your screwy-eyed dog face out of my sight!" I kicked the underside of his mattress. "Can't you see I'm thinking here?"

I hocked at the toilet. My spit hit the bowl and descended like a spider to the floor. When the lights went out, I tried to clear my mind with a quick wank. But I couldn't get Delilah's picture right. She appeared out of sorts. A blur. Like I hadn't seen her in years. In the same way it had happened to Catherine, it was happening to Delilah. I wouldn't stand for it.

After a while I just gave up.

OFFICER FRIEND STRUCK ME in the stomach with his baton. I lost my food tray again. No one paid us any attention.

"It's happening tomorrow night," I choked out between heaves.

He pulled me up by my hair and escorted me from the cafeteria. He marched me down the hall to solitary. Solitary was where COs took prisoners to beat on in private. Friend took us there to talk. He would still beat on us, of course. But at least there he could warn us of what was coming.

"Right hook," he said.

His fist landed hard against my jaw. I dropped.

"That was a good one," I garbled.

"What's happening tomorrow?" he asked.

"Riot."

Friend stepped back. "Left kick."

I raised my hands in protest. "Wait, wait, wait."

He allowed me to roll into a better position.

"Okay," I said. "Go."

Friend drove his boot into my solar plexus. The wind left me like a spooked hummingbird. He positioned me against the wall. "You're fine," he said. "Just keep breathing."

A minute later I was able to talk again.

"Who told you?" Friend asked.

"George," I said. "Apparently he's leading it."

"Holcombe? I don't buy it."

"I think you broke a rib."

Friend paced inside the cell. He scratched the dry spot underneath his pig nose.

"Believe it or not, it's happening," I said. "Help me make it so that nobody gets hurt."

"What do you need?" he asked.

I told him my plan.

OUTSIDE LANSING I was poor as Aunt Clara's hips. Inside I was rich. But in debts. There wasn't a prisoner I could point to who didn't owe me something. The Bank of Robert Crawley had made clients out of the Brotherhood, the Blacks, the Hispanics, and countless other gangs and non-associates. I was owed everything from issues of *TIME* magazine to cigarettes to a toothbrush shiv. Not to mention favours! It would take me two lifetimes just to count those.

That night I collected on them all. Twelve and a half years' worth of debts. Twelve and a half years of lying, trading, withholding, and baiting. Twelve and half years of getting beat on and spit on and passed around. I traded it all. For her. For Delilah.

I made my rounds during supper. By lights out the entire prison was abuzz with talk of the riot. Word had even reached the COs.

Officer Friend stopped by at midnight, pretending to have caught George and me porking. He handcuffed George outside the cell so he could beat on me in private. And he did for a good while before arriving at the point.

"You were right about the riot," Friend said. "Everyone's talking about it. I just wanted to make sure we're still on."

"Why wouldn't we be?"

"Just making sure." Friend peeled his handkerchief from around his knuckles. My blood had made the fabric stick.

"You going to do him?" I asked.

"Holcombe?" He shrugged. "If you want me to."

I sighed. "Never mind."

After Friend left I couldn't get back to sleep. Neither could George. He had also heard about the riot. He asked me if I had ever been through one. I told him that I had.

"What was it like?" he asked.

"A lot of raping and ass-kicking," I said.

"Of cos?"

"Of everybody."

"You don't mean it!"

I chewed my blanket to keep from laughing.

"Don't you worry," I said. "Stick with me and I'll see to it that you stay tight."

THE NEXT DAY I HAD A TERRIBLE TIME at work. I made license plates. Actually, the machines made them: I just fed the sheeting into the press. Two hours in I fell asleep and banged my head on the godforsaken thing. Right in the spot Friend had got me the night before. That woke me up for about an hour. When that wore off I took to slapping my broken rib. A prison-style espresso shot. Worked like a charm.

Supper was tense. The cos knew that if anything was going to happen, it was going to happen now, with everyone together. I sat beside George. Neither of us ate much. I hated fish and chips day, so it wasn't out of character for me to just poke at it. But George usually licked his food tray shiny. Until he pissed himself I didn't know how scared he really was. No one at the table said anything. Not even me, though I ended up sitting in it.

"Mealtime's over!" a CO shouted.

I barely had time to grab George when the trays began to sail. The Brotherhood and the Blacks pounced on each other. The Hispanics dove into the mob.

"Riot! Riot!" screamed the COs.

Taser barbs flew like streamers. Some asshole fired pepper spray.

"This way!" I cried, pulling George.

In the commotion we were able to escape the cafeteria unnoticed. We ran down the hallway past solitary. I led us toward the exit to the yard. As per my instructions, no prisoner followed us.

George was crying and shaking. He gripped onto my forearm like a frightened child. Periodically he would glance behind us, watching for rapists.

"Where are we going?" he blubbered.

"Through here."

I pushed George into the door leading to the yard. He stumbled ahead of me into dusk.

Officer Friend was waiting for us. Him and five of his peers. They were dressed in full riot gear. Shields and helmets and all. I couldn't have asked for a better showing.

George fainted before they beat him.

I wasn't as lucky.

"—AND SHE SAID, 'Darlene, I tried your potato salad and Fran's is better.' So I picked my potato salad right up off that picnic table and went straight to the reverend. I dropped a big dollop on his plate and—"

I hadn't seen George in visitation for months. After the riot we had gotten a week each in solitary. He was loud for two days. I heard him through the food slot. Cursing me, himself. Whimpering in the night like a lost puppy. Even when they beat him for it, he didn't quit. But then the loneliness gobbled him up. Body and soul. I never heard a peep out of him the rest of the week. And when I got out, we weren't cellmates anymore.

Delilah arrived late. I could tell right away something was off. For one she had dressed in her Sunday best. The sort of loose-fitting skirt suit approved by Jesus. Nylons, too. She also had her hair tied in a bun. But she was still my Delilah. With the prominent tits and sturdy hips. That thick frame built for riding. I had never been so happy to see somebody in my life.

"Momma."

"What, Robert?"

"Could you pray for me again?"

"Sure, dear."

While Mom prayed, I dropped in on George and Delilah.

"What did they say?" George asked.

"That you did it," Delilah said. "That you tried to escape."

"I swear I didn't. I was only trying to hide."

She took a deep breath. Sucked back tears bracing to fall.

"What'd the lawyer say?" he asked. "About me getting out?"

"That you're not," she said.

"That I'm not what?"

"Getting out."

George slammed his fists on the table.

"Settle down, inmate!" screeched a CO.

Delilah fiddled with her left hand. "Georgie."

"No, baby," George pleaded. "Lilah, no."

I couldn't believe it.

"Don't," I whispered. "Don't you do it."

She slid the ring across the table.

"Contraband!" a CO yelled.

The COs swarmed the couple. George quickly put the ring in his mouth. The first one to arrive throat-punched him. The ring twirled through the air like a flipped coin and landed at my feet. I kicked it away from me. Into the closest drain. Plop.

Two COs removed George kicking and wheezing from the room. Officer Friend came to escort Delilah out. He grabbed her arm and jerked her to her feet.

"You can't touch her like that," I said.

"In your seat, inmate!" he ordered.

Delilah looked imploringly at me.

"Don't you touch her like that," I said.

I ran at him. Friend let go of Delilah and turned to face me. I tackled him to the floor. He swung his baton uselessly. I seized his wrist and bashed it against the concrete. The baton rolled under the neighbouring table. I pinned him under me. Friend struggled, but I had him stuck. "Oink, oink, oink." I didn't want to let his arm go to hit him, so I spat in his face instead. I spat until I was dry. Until he begged me to stop.

I looked around for Delilah.

"Delilah?" I called. "Delilah!?"

Friend weaselled one arm free. It was all he needed. He found the baton and cracked it across my mouth. My teeth bent backwards like twenty light switches going off all at once. I collapsed onto my back.

And that was when I found her. On the cold concrete. Delilah must've known I would end up there. She looked the same as the first time I saw her. Pink dress. Curly hair falling on her neck. Like a dream. I touched her soft face. Then I told her what I had never told any woman before. Not even Catherine, when I had the chance.

#6 Houses

EVERY SUNDAY AFTER CHURCH, my family drove the Niagara Parkway from Queenston to Niagara-on-the-Lake, looking at houses along the way. Then my father would buy a Lotto 6/49. My siblings and I picked the numbers. I always picked seven and thirteen, but Mary and Jackson picked different every time. My father might've won if we had played the same numbers every week. Part of his deal with my mother, however, was that we children had to pick the numbers. She considered gambling a sin, and that was the only way she'd tolerate it.

But in the beginning we only looked at houses; the lottery tickets came months later. I can still remember the first time my father bought one. It was fall, when the vines of the Niagara wineries are heavy with grapes. That winter my mother developed bunions. She used to dry her socks on the front windshield defogger when her sweaty feet got inflamed. For the rest of the drive home, the cab smelled like wet dog. No matter how much we children complained about it, it made no difference to her or my father.

"It's either that or you can wring them out yourselves," he said.

My father had a way of making anything we didn't like seem the better option compared to something else. When we complained about having to listen to *Gord's Gold* again, he said, "It's either that or Merle Haggard." When we complained about having leftover pork chops the second night in row, he said, "It's either that or liver and onions."

Anyway, by the time we got to Queenston, my mother's socks were dry and back on her feet. The cab still smelled like wet dog, but at least with the windows open, it was mixed with the wet earth smell of the Niagara River.

"That's a nice one, isn't it?" my father said.

"Which one?" my mother asked.

He snorted. "Well, you missed it now."

Passing a house surrounded by a hedgerow, Mary said, "I wish we had hedges like that."

"Fire hazard," my father said. "And who's going to trim them? You?" Then to us, "Hey boys."

"What?" Jackson and I replied.

"Do you see that yellow house there?" he asked. "See that small balcony?"

"Yeah."

"They call that a widow's walk. Want to know why?"

"Why?"

"Because that's where the wives of sailors would stand and watch for the boats to return. And the widow part is because sometimes they didn't."

My mother sighed. "Wouldn't that be nice?"

"Excuse me?"

She giggled realizing her goof. "I meant the balcony, dear."

The further we went along, the less we talked about what we liked and what we didn't. And when we did say something, it was nothing specific, just I like this house or I don't like that one. I never said much of anything. I didn't share my family's obsession with houses. I was more interested in the river and what was on the other side. *America*. About a quarter of the way to Niagara-on-the-Lake, the houses on my side turned into riverbank, with a view clear across to that greatest of all countries on Earth. So while my family looked one way, I looked the other, and imagined crossing, escaping. I was going to be an actor. That or a rock star. And I didn't think you could be either one in Canada.

On that particular day I was daydreaming about America when my father said, "If you would let me buy a damn lottery ticket every once in a while, then maybe we would."

"I don't like you gambling," my mother said. "Or cursing for that matter."

"It's a toonie, honey. It's not like I'm throwing away a fortune."

"Only a toonie?"

"Yeah, three bucks," he said. "Less than you spend on a latte."

"I still don't like it."

"Just think of all the good we could do if we won."

"That's not an argument for doing something wrong."

A moment later my mother said, "I suppose it'd be better if we won than if somebody else did."

"That's what I'm saying!" my father said.

"And it's not much."

"What's three dollars?"

"All right," my mother conceded. "I'll let you buy it. But we should let the kids pick the numbers. That way it's like a game. Just a game we all play as a family."

My father glanced at us in the rear-view mirror. "Doesn't that sound fun."

Not long after that we passed by a smaller house – small compared to the Georgian or Tudor mansions that were most common – with a short white fence, a yard planted all over with trees, and, out front, a RE/MAX "FOR SALE" sign.

"If we win this Friday," my father announced, "I'll buy that house."

"That one?" my mother said. "There's got to be a better one than *that*."

Next, they launched into the usual reverie of poor folk come into a lot of money. Picking what house they would buy. Arguing how much money they would give away and to whom. My sister negotiated for a pair of Dear Frances boots, my brother a Lego Millennium Falcon.

"What about you, Kyle?" my mother asked.

Right then I had been estimating how long it would take me to paddle across in my aunt June's kayak. "Huh?"

"If we won the lottery and gave you a thousand dollars. What would you buy?"

"A plane ticket to LA," I said. "Or Nashville."

"Ho, ho, ho," my father said. "We've got a celebrity in our midst!"

That set everybody laughing, even my mother, though she rolled her eyes to assure me it was all in good fun. Either way, I wasn't bothered. While I was kicking back in my mansion in Beverly Hills, they would still be buying lottery tickets and spending their imaginary money.

And on Sundays – looking at houses.

We bought the lottery ticket at Gale's Gas Bar on the way back to St. Catharines, where we lived. I can't remember what numbers Jackson and Mary picked. But I do remember that when my father checked it the next week, not one of them had been drawn.

#7 *The Parable of the Wild Man and the Priest*

FOR TEN YEARS Simon Styli lived in the wilderness in perfect solitude, until, one day, he heard a loud rustling noise and spotted a Priest passing below his treetop hovel. Simon recognized the man's profession by his clerical collar, which stuck out conspicuously from his more colourful athletic gear. Simon watched him struggle to penetrate the thick foliage. Without tools for cutting, the Priest was forced to tear a wide hole through the landscape instead of removing only the necessary branches. He stumbled over a tree root and cried out in pain. For a time he lay on the forest floor where he had fallen, taking long sucking breaths and staring up at the canopies of trees. Eventually, he regained his footing and hobbled toward what destination Simon could only guess. He did not make it far. Simon found the Priest hardly twenty feet away, collapsed against a Sitka spruce, panting from exhaustion and praying unintelligibly.

"Psst," Simon said. He nudged the Priest. His touch startled the man's eyes open. The Priest went pale at the sight of Simon, crouched like a wild man in front of him, naked except for a single loincloth tied tightly around his waist.

"Get back! Back! What do you want? Who are you?"

"The answer to your prayers," answered Simon slyly. It felt good not only to speak, but also to jest. His tongue flip-flopped about his mouth in ecstasy.

"Your name. Tell me your name."

"I am Simon Styli."

The Priest's eyes glowed. "Then the legend *is* true. Tell me, is it true what they say, that you have found a way into Heaven? That you know the path of perfect righteousness?"

"I will tell you my secret," Simon said, "but first you must allow me to serve you, to bandage your foot and feed you."

The Priest agreed to Simon's conditions. Using a makeshift harness, Simon hoisted the injured man into his treetop hovel. There, Simon wrapped his swollen foot with lichen bandages and supported it with bark splints. Then he upraised the Priest's leg on a stone.

"Lean back against the trunk and rest," Simon said. "I will be back shortly with dinner."

Simon foraged the forest for food and returned an hour later with fresh blackberries, saskatoon berries, and chanterelle mushrooms. He also stopped by the river to fill his canteen. He might've stayed longer to catch a fish, but he worried about leaving the Priest alone for too long knowing there were cougars about. The Priest ate his meal greedily and swallowed three quarters of the water in a single breath.

"How long have you been without food or water?" asked Simon.

"Two days," the Priest answered. "When I sprained my ankle, I thought for certain I was dead. But then you came along."

Simon smiled. "Have you ever wondered if the purpose of your life was for something so innocent as a single, meaningful encounter? The thought struck me suddenly while I was out in the forest that perhaps my whole reason for being here was to be here for when you needed me."

"But I never would have come if you hadn't first settled here yourself."

"What I mean is," Simon clarified, "do you think God conceived of both our lives for the purpose of this meeting now?"

The Priest beckoned for another gulp of water. Drying his mouth on his shirt sleeve, he replied, "I suppose it depends on whether what they say about you is true, that you have found a way into Heaven, the path of perfect righteousness. And whether you were able then to teach it to me, so that I might take it back with me into the world."

"I am afraid the answer you seek is not one that can be taken back into the world," Simon said. "For to take the path of perfect righteousness, which is a way into Heaven, there is only one requirement: to remove yourself from the world of man entirely." At the revelation of his secret, he had expected a different reaction from the Priest than what he saw, which was a face puckered in disappointment and regret, as if to say, *I came all this way for that?* But Simon knew that he only needed to explain himself a little further for the Priest to open his heart to the profound implications of his very simple epiphany.

Simon continued, "Have you heard it said before that no man can go a single day without breaking one of the Ten Commandments?"

"Perhaps there are some who can go a day."

"But how about a week? A month? Or even a year?"

The Priest thought about it for a moment, then shook his head. "You're right. It is impossible."

"And yet I have done it," Simon said. "For ten years I have lived without breaking a single of God's Ten Commandments."

"Aha! But you have broken one now, by lying." So excited was the Priest by his accusation that his foot leapt from the stone. He yelped in pain as it bounced off the hovel floor.

Simon gently returned the Priest's foot to its upraised place. "Let me ask you this: if a man never marries, can he commit adultery?"

The Priest answered, "It has been said that if a man even *looks* at a woman lustfully he has committed adultery with her in his heart."

"And if there are no women upon which to look?"

The Priest stuttered, searching for a rebuttal. "I suppose not," he conceded.

"A similar thing has been said of hate, that it is the same as murder. But if there are no brothers and sisters around to hate? What then?"

"I follow your logic."

"Then you will understand when I tell you that the path to perfect righteousness and a way into Heaven exists, but only in complete and utter isolation from the world, specifically mankind. Man alone is not the problem: the problem is man in relationship. Man alone cannot lie. Man alone cannot commit adultery. Man alone cannot murder. Neither can man alone steal nor covet his neighbour's goods. Man alone –"

"Yes, yes, I see your point." The Priest sighed. Then shooting up a finger, "But you have forgotten one: honour your mother and your father."

"I am an orphan," replied Simon. "How can I dishonour those I do not know?"

"And for those of us who are not orphans?"

"What better way to honour your father and mother than by living in perfect obedience to the Commandments of God?"

The Priest nodded in agreement, before seeming to remember that this was a debate and countering shrewdly with, "And what about God's command to love one's neighbour as oneself? Isn't it true that the Commandment requires not only that we love, but that we put ourselves in a position *to* love?"

"Have I not shown you love? I fed you and bandaged your foot."

"Yes, but –" For a moment the Priest puzzled over this. Simon waited patiently for him to respond, knowing almost certainly what he would say next. "But should we not seek to maximize our efforts of love, even at the cost of our own righteousness?"

"Ah," answered Simon, "but you have arrived at the ultimate conundrum of our faith. Why did God place man in relationship with one another and then punish him for what arises naturally out of that state? He says it is not good for man to be alone. Yet evil only becomes possible, as I have proven, when men are gathered together two or more!"

All of a sudden the Priest became filled with rage. "Blasphemy!" he screamed. "You speak blasphemy!" He picked up the stone that was supporting his foot and struck Simon across the face. Simon fell backward on the hovel floor. The Priest lifted the rock overhead for a second strike, but Simon did not raise a hand to defend himself. Instead, he asked God to forgive the Priest, even as the Priest brought the stone down and ended Simon's life.

AT THE GATES OF HEAVEN, Simon Styli was met by God. And God said to him, "I have found your name written in the Book of Life. Come, there are many here expecting you."

And Simon said, "It is better for man to be alone."

#8 *The Interstellar Voyage of Granger Taylor*

ON NOVEMBER 29, 1980, Granger Taylor loaded his blue Datsun pickup with dynamite and set out from his family farm at Somenos Lake for, in his words, "a 42 month intersteluar [sic] voyage to explore the vast universe." The note in question, discovered the following morning by his stepfather tacked to the bedroom door, has become a point of much speculation regarding the unknowable truth of Taylor's disappearance – namely, whether it was clandestine suicide or indeed conveyance by aliens. For that reason it justifies inclusion in full.

DEAR MOTHER AND FATHER

I HAVE GONE AWAY TO WALK ABOARD AN ALIEN SPACE SHIP. AS REOCURRING DREAMS ASSURED A 42 MONTH INTERSTELUAR VOYAGE TO EXPLORE THE VAST UNIVERSE, THEN RETURN

I AM LEAVING BEHIND ALL MY POSSESIONS TO YOU AS I WILL NO LONGER WILL [SIC] REQUIRE THE USE OF ANY. PLEASE USE THE INSTRUCTIONS IN MY WILL AS A GUIDE TO HELP

LOVE
GRANGER

On the back of the note was drawn a map with directions from Somenos to Waterloo Mountain, an approximate forty-kilometre journey southwest on roads passing largely through unpopulated wilderness. Naturally, Duncan RCMP assumed Waterloo Mountain to be Taylor's destination and focused their unsuccessful searches in and around that area. Six years later a forestry worker would stumble upon the exploded wreckage of Taylor's Datsun truck on Mount Prevost, some eleven kilometres *north* of Somenos. This does not necessarily mean Taylor composed the map as a purposeful misdirection; alternative explanations include reusing a scrap of paper or last-minute capriciousness or a communication from Taylor's aliens of a change in location. What is perhaps more curious than the apparent misdirection of the map are the specific and seemingly contradictory details in the letter. It is well-documented that suiciders often divest themselves of their possessions, so the final paragraph would seem damning evidence to that end, not to mention the dubious reference to his will. But why state that he was going to return if suicide was always the plan? And why the specificity of forty-two months? Wouldn't it have been simpler to leave the timeline for his journey vague?

And, finally, what if Taylor was telling the truth?

GRANGER TAYLOR GREW UP in a large, blended family of stepbrothers, stepsisters, half-brothers, and half-sisters. From a young age he exhibited a precocious fascination with machines, which proved over time to be one of those rare instances of genius seldom encountered and even less seldom understood. He dropped out of school at the age of fourteen, and a year later restored a car from a discarded frame entirely by himself. Such were his skills that neighbourhood children crowded into his makeshift workshop on his stepfather's farm, the so-called "Sleepy Hollow Museum," just to watch him work. It was during that time he met his best friend, Robert Keller, who will become important later as the last person to see Granger Taylor alive.

In his late teens and early twenties, Taylor became locally famous for two restorations that secured his status as mechanical prodigy for the rest of his days on Earth. The first of these was a Climax locomotive engine, which he found overgrown in a forest nearby. After carting it back to his family farm piece by piece, he rebuilt it to working order, even laying down track for the purpose of giving free rides. The second was a Kitty Hawk airplane. Again, he found the parts scattered about in the nearby woods. These consisted of an intact engine and sections of the fuselage, cockpit, and landing gear. With only photographs to direct him, Taylor reconstructed the plane in its entirety, using scrap metal to fill in the missing gaps. Eventually, he sold the plane for twenty thousand dollars, the equivalent of about one hundred twenty thousand dollars today.

Regardless of these triumphs, the press, and the money, being a large man and shy and living far removed from the city, Taylor suffered from common loneliness. This is not to say that he didn't try to find a partner. He posted single-and-looking ads in the local classifieds, but none of these elicited any meaningful response.

Around this same time, the UFO craze reached a fever pitch with the release of Steven Spielberg's *Close Encounters of the Third Kind*, and like many intelligent men early middle-aged and alone, Taylor was swept up in reveries of other worlds, of other lifeforms, of infinite possibility waiting just beyond the firmament. This obsession culminated in Taylor's construction of a mock flying saucer out of two satellite dishes. Shortly thereafter, he would claim to be in communication with aliens. Perhaps coincidentally, perhaps not, these communications accompanied his first experimentations with LSD.

In June of 1980 Taylor made changes to his will, suggesting he knew about his impending voyage as early as five months before his disappearance. In the will, he crossed out the words "funeral" and "death" and replaced the word "death" with "departure." For months afterward he revealed to friends and family his plan to join aliens on a journey across the stars. They cannot, however, be blamed for dismissing the seriousness of these claims or for not recognizing them as cloaked cries for help. Whatever the case, when Taylor eventually did disappear, it came as a shock to everybody who knew him – everybody except, perhaps, Robert Keller.

On the evening of November 29, 1980, a great storm raged over Duncan and the surrounding counties. Around five o'clock Taylor packed the cab of his truck with dynamite of the grade used for exploding trees[1] and drove from his family's farm to Bob's Grill,

---

1 Certainly this appears strong evidence for suicide, though it could be argued to favour better the explanation of accident. It is a well-known fact that dynamite leaks nitroglycerin when wet, and that leaked nitroglycerin can explode unexpectedly. Nevertheless, the questions of *when* and *why* remain. Because no one can know for certain *when* the truck exploded, no one can know for certain if Taylor was in the vehicle or outside the vehicle, or if it was an accident or not. Human bone fragments were found adjacent to the blast site, but were never DNA tested. They are now lost. As to the question of *why*, it could be argued Taylor brought the dynamite along purposefully to destroy the evidence of his abduction, either lighting it himself or allowing it to explode in the above manner described.

where he had dinner and confessed to the other patrons his departure plans. From there he went to visit his best friend, Robert Keller. Because Keller had previously asked to join Taylor on his voyage, Taylor stopped by to inform Keller of the aliens' decision not to let him come along. Disappointed though he was, Keller wished his best friend goodbye and safe travels.

But for the location of the truck, only Taylor knows what happened after that.

I CATCH A LATE FLIGHT from Toronto that lands me in Victoria, British Columbia, at sunset. In the morning I rent a car and drive the scenic Malahat to Duncan. My plan is to visit the BC Forest Discovery Centre, which houses Granger Taylor's restored locomotive, then continue on to Mount Prevost in search of the blast site. Feeling still slightly jet lagged, I am hypnotized by the green repetitiveness of the tall trees winding through Goldstream Park. My eyes teeter between open and closed – until I crown the mountain and am exposed to a sudden burst of sunlight. That and the simultaneous absorption of caffeine and sugar from my Tim Hortons double-double awaken me for the remainder of the drive.

I park in the lot of the BC Forest Discovery Centre and head inside the administration building to buy a ticket. Ahead of me in line are mostly families, mothers, and their small children, which makes sense since they are the demographic to whom the attraction, with its train rides and cartoon colour scheme, clearly caters. If I were here with my daughter, Nella, I might not feel so out of place.

From outside I hear the familiar chugging of a steam engine. I wonder if it is Taylor's locomotive and become excited at the prospect of seeing it in operation. But it is not his. His does not run anymore; instead, it sits on display in the first room beyond the ticket counter. A series of placards tells the history of Shawnigan Lake Lumber Company No. 2, the train's full and accurate name. Built in 1911 by Climax Locomotive Works, No. 2 was first bought by Shawnigan Lake Lumber Company, before being sold a number of times throughout the 1920s and abandoned in 1930, at the start of the Great Depression. For forty years, then, it had awaited Taylor in the wilderness. Seeing it now before me, I can scarcely imagine the effort he must've spent taking it apart, carrying it home, cleaning it, rebuilding it, painting it. The locomotive is almost the length of a bus and stands at least ten feet tall. Each drive wheel alone must weigh in the realm of three hundred pounds. I run my fingers along its bumpy black surface, the cold metal of the boiler, the grainy wood of the cab. I examine the countless nuts and bolts, the complicated gears and connecting rods. How could he have known what went where except by trial and error?

Before continuing on to Mount Prevost, I stop by Taylor's family farm on Drinkwater Road in Somenos. Because I have not made arrangements with the current owners to view it, I merely peek inside and leave. It appears somewhat dilapidated, the bushes thick, the weeds thriving – nothing like the background in the old pictures I have seen of Granger Taylor and his family.

From Somenos it is a short drive to the mountain. I wind up Mount Prevost Road as far as I can go, before being stopped at a logging barricade, where another car is also parked. I continue the rest of the way on foot. Finding the blast site is exceptionally difficult, but not impossible. Taylor's story has achieved a cult status among UFO believers, and excursions to the area are common. I have come equipped with a map given to me after a request-for-information post on Reddit. Not twenty minutes into my hike, I encounter Richard

Sears, the driver of the other car. He is dressed head-to-toe in hiking gear and carries on his back a large stuffed duffel bag.

"What brings you out here?" he asks.

"I'm writing an article," I say.

"What about?"

"Exit strategies. Granger Taylor."

"Same reason I'm here," he says. Richard hesitates before admitting, "I want to be taken."

"By aliens?" I stifle the urge to laugh. "What makes you want that?"

He gestures as if to the air and leaves the question unanswered.

We continue our trek together.

Eventually, Richard confesses. "Wife left two years ago. Affair, younger man. Kids think I'm crazy, cuckoo. Got laid off. Back's fucked. Figured I'd come out here and give it a shot. Spend a night yelling up at the stars." He cups his hands over his mouth and yells, "Hey! Here! Down here!" He slaps his leg, laughing.

"You're going to spend the night on the mountain?"

Richard pats his backpack. "Got everything I need right here."

He asks me if I would like to camp out with him, and against my sounder instincts, I say yes. (I will use the extra sleeping bag he packed in case of rain.) Soon after, we locate the blast site, not ten feet from where my Reddit map said it would be, and bivouac, perhaps irreverently, in the centre of it.

When night settles we light a fire and arrange ourselves on either side. We lie on our backs and look up at the stars.

"There's one," he says, pointing.

"Meteor?" I ask.

"Satellite."

Minutes pass in silence. Richard seems oddly embarrassed.

I can tell my presence has put a damper on his original plan of pleading with the aliens for deliverance. I encourage him by being the first to shout. "Hello!" My voice echoes in the distant valleys and mountains.

Richard follows immediately with, "Down here!"

"We're here!"

"Over here!"

No one comes to take us away. The next morning Richard tosses me a cold-hardened Clif bar for breakfast, and we hike back to our cars chewing on them. We make plans to meet up at the Dog House in Duncan for brunch, but halfway there I change my mind about stopping. With no way of contacting Richard, I continue on to Victoria hoping he will forgive me, that he won't count me among his long list of deserters: his wife, his kids, and, if Taylor is to be believed, the aliens, too.

#9 *Caravan*

IT WAS PALM SUNDAY when Silvia Valle joined the caravan departing San Pedro Sula for the United States. She had heard the story of Palm Sunday first from her abuela, who, before she died, would sit the children around her at the start of Holy Week and tell of Jesus's arrival in Jerusalem. He, too, had travelled in a caravan and was welcomed at the Golden Gate by crowds of people waving palm branches and shouting, Hosanna! Hosanna! Later these same people would call for His death upon the cross. That the organizers had chosen Palm Sunday for the day of departure did not seem to Silvia coincidence, but providence. For the caravan was certain to meet with great resistance at the border, and so it stood to reason that, if she made it across, on the other side would await her life.

For months Silvia saved every lempira she could from her job at the cafetería. She spent two thousand on a new pair of black Nikes, which would equate to one lempira per mile walked by the time she reached her destination. She also spent five hundred on a backpack in which she carted water, some food, the remainder of her money, and a change of clothes.

In the first hour of walking, Silvia met a man named Geber. He was a dark-complexioned mestizo with wispy hair and spacious teeth. A past injury to his left leg caused him to walk with a limp.

"Why are you leaving Honduras?" he asked.

She answered, "All my family is dead."

"I will open a McDonald's," Geber said with a chuckle. "Eat hamburgers all day." He lifted his T-shirt, slapped his shapeless hairy stomach, and slipped away into the crowd.

She didn't see Geber again until late evening. Because she had heard stories of violent men joining caravans only for as long as it took them to commit their evil deeds, she asked if he would stay with her, and he agreed. In the night she awoke to his hand sliding up her stomach toward her breasts. Geber fondled one, then touched upon the thin chain of her crucifix. He followed it down to the image of Christ, at whose figuration his hand abruptly cowered and withdrew.

Silvia and Geber fell easily into this routine of spending their days apart and their nights together. She tolerated his wandering hands, and in exchange, he provided her a sense of security. Even as the caravan grew, picking up thousands on its path through Guatemala, still they always managed to find each other before nightfall.

One night Silvia felt hot tears on her forehead. Geber was crying and stroking her hair.

"Lo siento," he said. "Lo siento."

"I forgive you," she said.

At the southern border of Mexico, the caravan encountered an unexpected obstacle: the Mexican National Guard. The soldiers were stationed on the bridges and along the shoreline of the Suchiate River. It used to be that migrants were able to wade through the river to the other side uncontested, but apparently not anymore.

For every soldier there were at least a hundred migrants, meaning if the caravan rushed the border, many would make it, and only an unlucky few would not. So that was precisely what they did.

Since the night of his apology, Geber had stopped leaving Silvia in the mornings. Mi alma, he called her. *My soul*. With Silvia on his back, Geber waded through the waist-high water. A little shorter than five feet and weighing less than a hundred pounds, Silvia was grateful for Geber's assistance; even with hundreds of bodies obstructing its flow, the current of the river remained strong. Landing on the other side of the river, they ran hand-in-hand. Everywhere there was fighting and shouting and weeping. Mothers cried out for their children, husbands for wives, brothers for brothers. They saw a man stumble; the soldiers beat him where he lay. Many of those arrested were caught because they became separated from their loved ones and made the mistake of stopping to look for them. As for Geber and Silvia, they stuck to the middle of the crowd like schooling fish, and in that way evaded capture. And when others stopped to rest, they continued to run. They ran until their shoes dried, until they could see the lights of Tapachula in the distance. If Silvia had taken every precaution to avoid damage to her feet, then it had all been in vain: after running for so long in wet shoes, her feet and toes were blistered and swollen inside her socks. Geber asked her to show them to him, but she worried if she took the Nikes off she would never get them back on. Against her pleading, Geber removed his own shoes. A putrid smell like toenail clippings wafted up from his partially degloved foot. When he tried to put his shoes on again, the pain was so intense he needed her to do it for him.

Silvia and Geber rejoined the caravan in Tapachula. There, they mixed with thousands of Mexicans also headed north. While they had moved together in one large mass through Honduras and Guatemala, the caravan splintered into smaller factions for the journey through Mexico. Unfortunately, this made them vulnerable to raids by the very authorities they were hoping to avoid. It seemed every second night Silvia was awoken by sirens and screams. Every time this happened Geber would drag her into the jungle, and they would crouch down and wait there in complete silence, heads swivelling and eyes darting, lest they be snuck up upon in the dark.

Then came the traffickers. They used similar methods as the police, so Silvia could never be certain what fate might befall her if she were captured.

She met a mother with a five-year-old girl who liked to sing while they walked. Geber often joined in the chorus with them, which was how they all became acquainted. A week later there was a raid, and the next morning mother and daughter were gone.

That same night Geber said, "No one will ever touch you."

When she fell asleep, he was holding her so tightly across the chest Silvia worried she might never wake up again.

Word soon spread through the caravan of a program called Estás en tu casa. Those migrants who stopped in Mexico instead of continuing on to the United States were promised education, healthcare, and access to employment. Geber believed it was a ruse.

"The moment they have us," he said, "they will send us back."

Still, the program tempted many away from the caravan. Passing through Mexico City, their number halved from six to three thousand.

In the market, Geber found a truck driver named Rafael, who, for eleven hundred lempira as well as the cost of gas there and back, agreed to take them to Guadalajara. Because Geber was out of money, Silvia paid. She noticed Geber looking as she removed the bills from a secret pocket sewn into her backpack. His eyes shone like she had never seen them before: bright and menacing. Beware of wolves in sheep's clothing, her grandmother used to say. But Silvia knew Geber, and trusted him, and couldn't imagine a scenario in which he might steal from her, she who had been with him since the beginning.

For the remainder of their journey, Silvia and Geber used drivers. They rode in the cabs of trucks, in the back of tractor trailers. Some took them short distances for a lot of money, others long distances for free. The break from walking afforded their feet adequate time to heal. And they would need them healthy and strong, for the hardest part still lay ahead.

In Sonoyta, Geber convinced Silvia to abandon the caravan before Tijuana, their planned point of entry.

"We will find our own way together," he said.

Silvia worried about safety. "Alone we will be easy targets."

"Yes," Geber said. "But the Americans know we are coming."

That was true. Nothing else could explain Mexico's initial blockade and then sudden receptivity. Silvia relented. They spent the next hours buying supplies to survive a trip across the desert. If they wandered in the wrong direction, they might go a week without seeing a person or being detained, so they needed to be smart about it. To start, Silvia bought Geber a backpack. He picked out a pink one too small for him and flaunted it around. Silvia laughed as if she had just remembered how. She wished she could spare a few lempira for a disposable camera, but wanted to save the extra money for when she would really need it. They also bought hats, two blankets for the cold nights, enough food for a week, and two one-gallon glass bottles of water, because in the continuous heat Silvia was concerned the plastic might weaken and the bottles burst.

Silvia and Geber left the following morning. By mid-afternoon they arrived at the border fence. Silvia looked in either direction and could see no end to the steel bollards. They were as tall as palm trees and coloured orange from rust. That they had been spaced just far enough apart for her to be able to put her arm through to the other side seemed an especially cruel feature. Geber grabbed on to one of the steel bollards and attempted to scale it, but his inflexible leg arrested him. He suggested they continue west. He promised her they would soon find an opening.

Nighttime brought with it a chill that seemed to flourish under her skin, similar to the way a microwave cooked food from the inside out. Silvia and Geber lay on their backs and looked up at the stars. She tried to fall asleep, but something inside her gut forbade her relax. She listened to Geber's breathing. It was not regular; he was still awake. She wondered what he was waiting for and waited with him. In an instant he was atop her with his hands around her throat.

"No luches," said Geber. He squeezed tighter.

Silvia clawed at his face. When that didn't work, she struck her forearm against the glass bottle in her backpack until it shattered inside. The water seeped out the fabric, flowed beneath them, turned the dusty ground to mud. Geber tried to catch her arms underneath his legs. She fingered a piece of glass that had broken through and swung it at his throat. His blood splashed over her face and down her chest, drowning the image of Christ where it lay, still and somber, in the small divot above her breasts. Coughing and gasping for air, she crawled backward away from Geber. All the while she watched him to make sure he did not come after her again. His eyes blinked one after the other like a severed chicken's head, then suddenly stopped, so that one eye remained open and one eye shut.

In the morning Silvia wrapped Geber in a blanket and rolled him up against the wall where border patrol might find him. She took his backpack and left hers behind. Some hours later she came upon a bollard sawed off at the base and was able to squeeze between the adjacent two to the other side. Then Silvia clutched her necklace and whispered a prayer for her grandmother, and heard from Heaven the holy words of welcome, Hosanna! Hosanna!

#10 *Bambi, the Revelator*

THE REVELATOR'S VISIONS were always of a man named Bambi. He became that man; he *was* that man. The visions might occur at any moment. Roaming the streets of the city Carconrah. In flight over the fluctuate mountains of Alaam. On foot across the golden roads of Serasong. The Founderlings could not say what happened to the Revelator during these visions, for his vanishing was also their vanishing, and his reawakening, their reawakening. In the centre of the city, they congregated daily to hear his revelations. All but Fauna came to hear him reveal. She was jealous of the woman Constance, whom Bambi loved, and whose life it was the Revelator's duty to reveal.

Once Fauna asked, "Do you speak to her of me?"

The Revelator blushed for shame that he could not answer yes. And yet how could he explain that to speak Fauna's name in that world would be to befoul her? How could he explain that to speak her name or the name of the city Carconrah would be to invite the squalor and filth of that world into the immaculacy of this other?

On the day of his final vision, the Revelator met Fauna on the cresting peak of Mount Glasia. They made love on the mountain as it plunged into the valley below and flowed back up into itself, forever regenerating. At the moment of his climax, Fauna disappeared altogether, and then the world around him, too – first colour, then geometry, then space.

BAMBI CAME TO on the floor of his apartment. He was naked from the waist down, flaccid penis in hand, the dried seed of his fantasy spilled across his shirt. He rolled over and looked toward his lab. The table was flipped on its side. Around it lay scattered a broken blender, a single rubber eye dropper, and a latex glove with half the fingers pulled out the back. But where was the rest of it? His bottles of lye and naphtha? His bag of *Mimosa hostilis*?

"Connie!" Bambi stumbled about the apartment. He discovered his flasks and beakers and eye droppers smashed inside the kitchen sink. On the counter Constance had left him a letter.

Bambi

Today I came home to find you masturbating on the living room floor again. You disgust me. I can't be with somebody who disgusts me like you disgust me. I took everything and flushed your deems down the toilet. I recorded you masturbating and will post it online if you ever come near me. Have fun fucking yourself.

Con

Bambi shredded the letter into tiny pieces – then immediately set about putting it back together. It was stupid of her to blackmail him like that: now he would use her blackmail to blackmail her.

Constance darted by the opening into the living room. "Connie!" He chased after her. Nobody there. He rubbed his eyes. Wisps of snow followed his rough movements across them. He blinked them open and saw Fauna spread-eagle on the hardwood. She melted into the floor as he pounced to ravish her. These brief hallucinations would come and go for hours, until Bambi took another dose to end this terrible vision, to awaken him once again in Carconrah.

He returned to the kitchen and assembled the letter on a duct tape puzzle board. He held it up to read.

Bambi

The living room disgusts me like you disgust me and I can't find your deems. I came down the toilet masturbating with somebody who took everything. I will be online if you ever come home Today. You recorded me masturbating and Have fun fucking yourself near me. You flushed again. I post it on floor to disgust you.

Con

Close enough. Feeling hunger pangs, Bambi opened the fridge for something to eat and found it empty. Apparently, the only food left in the house were the leftover crusts in Constance's Domino's pizza boxes. He grabbed one and chewed on the end of it like a cinnamon stick. Suddenly he remembered the emergency supply of deems hidden inside their mattress. He scrambled to the bedroom and flipped the mattress up. He reached into the hole and pulled out a scrap of paper.

"Fuck, fuck, fuck, fuck." Bambi checked the drawer where they kept their money and the gun. Gone, taken. He dumped the laundry bin on the floor and recovered a T-shirt and sweats. He was going out, his first supply run in weeks. He inspected his reflection in the glass of his framed chemistry degree from New Mexico Tech. His eyes bulged from out his sallow face. He clawed his bangs down over them. The rest of his hair, however, remained wild and poofy, so that he had the appearance of a poorly manicured llama.

Bambi wandered shivering through the sultry San Antonio night along a highway which became and unbecame a road of Serasong. He was headed to the Walmart, which stocked most of the supplies he needed, and which, fortunately, adhered to a strict no-chase policy. This late at night, the loss prevention officer was an obese man named Charlie. His definition of "chase" included anything beyond a brisk walk.

A Founderling appeared, clinging to Bambi's arm.

"When will you be returning to us?" they asked.

"Soon, my child."

"We are missing you, Revelator."

Entering the Walmart, Bambi beelined past Charlie toward the backpack aisle. "Stop right there, punk!" Of course, the no-chase policy didn't void Charlie's obligation to pursue. Whether Bambi was speed walking or not, Charlie still had to follow him around.

Finding a backpack, Bambi proceeded to the household section. "Freeze, punk!" He grabbed four or five glass measuring cups to use in place of his flasks and beakers. Then coffee filters, rubber eyedroppers, a small blender, one-gallon pickle jar, spatula. Sodium hydroxide. No naphtha here, so he would have to get it from Lowe's in the morning – assuming he couldn't recover it from Connie, as well as the stolen root bark, when he went to her mother's mobile home to confront her.

Charlie was waiting for him in front of the entrance/exit doors. Feigning surrender, Bambi hung his head and held his hands out. Charlie produced a set of zip tie restraints and approached Bambi at a supercilious waddle. "Didn't think how you were getting out, did yah, punk?" Bambi almost felt bad it was this easy. As soon as Charlie had moved far enough away from the doors, Bambi ran around him and outside. And because Charlie's jurisdiction didn't extend into the parking lot, Bambi was immediately in the clear.

Constance's mother's place was about an hour's walk from the Walmart. Midway there, Bambi experienced that sudden and fearful nausea that signalled his total estrangement from Carconrah. No longer would Fauna or Founderling appear to encourage Bambi along his journey. It was now up to him alone to bring an end to the Revelator's vision, lest he be stranded here forever.

Ma Harkins met him on the front porch. "Con saw you coming and locked herself in the bathroom. Says she'll shoot you dead if you try anything." She waved Bambi in for a hug. "I just knew you'd come to fetch her back."

Bambi pushed Ma aside and entered the mobile home. "Connie?"

"I've got a gun," came her muffled cry from inside the bathroom. "It's loaded."

"I just want my bark. Just give me my bark and I'll go. And my naphtha."

"I'm uploading your video! It'll be on Pornhub any minute! I'm not bluffing!"

"Blackmail's illegal, you know!" he returned. "Now tell me where you put my bark or I'm taking your letter to the police!"

Ma Harkins addressed her daughter from the kitchen. "He's a better man than your father for coming back," she said. "Bastard never gave me a second thought."

Bambi banged on the door. "Where is my bark?"

He banged the door again and heard a boom so loud he had to wonder if he wasn't still Revelator after all. It was only when Bambi tried to raise his fist for a third time, and couldn't, that he realized Constance had shot him. He staggered backward into Ma Harkins, who caught him with a gasp.

"Con, what'd you do?" Ma wailed. "Oh, Bambi!" She stared down into his eyes.

"You are a vision," he said.

Ma fiddled with the heart pendant hanging over her chest. "Oh, Bambi, I – Oh, bless your sweet heart."

"No," he said, "you are –" But by then the blood had risen above his vocal cords.

AHEAD OF HIM the Revelator espied the outline of Carconrah as specks of light flickering in the distance. He might've simply flown there, but for the beauty of the road, unfurling from the horizon like gold poured out of a distant urn. Besides, it seemed to him such a long time since he had walked anywhere that he should enjoy a walk. He wondered what the Founderlings would say when he told them his last vision had been forgotten. The Revelator remembered his going out, but he did not remember his coming back in. It was as if he had vanished from Mount Glasia one moment and reappeared here, on a road of Serasong, the instant afterward.

At the Gates of Car-sera, the Revelator encountered a swarm of Founderlings.

"We have been expecting you."

"I have no vision to reveal," he admitted.

They led him by the arm into the centre of the city, to his usual speaking spot. The Founderlings patiently awaited him to speak.

"I have no vision to reveal," he repeated.

The Revelator watched a figure moving through the crowd. It was Fauna. He recognized her because she did not share the likeness of the others. When she appeared at the step below him, he turned his face in shame. Why had she picked today of all days to come and hear him speak? Fauna pressed a finger to his lips. "There is nothing left to reveal." And together they leapt into the sky above and, to the cheering of the Founderlings below, flew hand in hand into eternity.

#11 *Muscles Make a Shit Personality*

LIKE MOST PEOPLE who make New Year's resolutions but don't take them seriously until March, Otto Brecht arrived at Ultimate Club for his first visit two months after his initial sign-up date. A thick-bottomed brunette, of the sort commonly found in gyms, checked him in at the counter. "Welcome back!" Otto mumbled a reply and proceeded head down through the sickly atmosphere of sweat to the men's changeroom buried at the back. He found a locker in a spot out of sight, where he could change without fear of being seen, either by others or, worse, by himself in a mirror. He swapped jeans for gym shorts and one extra-large T-shirt for another. Though extra-large fit him like a woman's nightie, it was all Otto could do to hide his rail-thin body, which narrowed below disproportionately broad shoulders. Naked, he resembled the Tesla logo – or a comic rendering of a person entering a black hole feet first. That latter poetic description came courtesy of Ex-G, who had made the quip to He-Who-Shall-Not-Be-Named while they were all still friends.

After filling up his water bottle, Otto surveyed the open concept gym. Where to begin? There were four sections to Ultimate Club: free weights, cardio, machines, and stretching. Otto proceeded to stretching. On the way, he passed by a tattooed giant deadlifting a steel bar so loaded with plates it bowed in the middle. When the giant dropped it, a loud boom echoed throughout the gym.

"UHHHHHHHH!"

His miniature cheerleader raved behind him. "Fucking sick, bro. New PR." He sniffed, rubbed his little red nose.

Steroid Lennie meet Cocaine George. Otto chuckled at this, his imagining of a joke Ex-G might make. Though they were long broken up, she lingered on as a character in his thoughts, always making asides, popping up at random. Otto glimpsed himself in a mirror and heard her speak again. *Hey look, Casper the ugly ghost!* Whatever possessed him to think wearing white would be a good idea?

Stamped in large block letters on the padded floor of the stretching area was the adage All Bodies Are Beautiful. Otto crouched down on the capital A of All and commenced his stretching routine. One benefit of his irregular body shape was flexibility: he could fold and contort himself like the most agile ballerinas. He snaked his arms behind his back and shook hands between his shoulder blades. He grabbed his feet and pressed his nose to the firm foam. All Bodies Are Beautiful – To Somebody, Somewhere. An important addendum. The problem was finding the person for whom Otto's thinly fleshed skeleton was a kink, for no attraction to him could be anything but a perversity, a peculiar preference forged in traumatic early childhood. Somewhere, Somebody. If only people were more open about their sexual quirks, then the world would be a much less lonely place.

"UHHHHHHHHH!"

"You fucking got this, bro."

Finished stretching, Otto continued to free weights. He picked up two puke-green-coloured five-pound dumbbells from a small caddy and carried them to a rare section of wall without a mirror. He performed some arm curls, then hiked them over his head. Up and down, up and down, he repeated this movement until his shoulders burned and his arms vibrated like bridge cables from the strain. He found a vacant bench and lay on his back. A female snickered behind him. He withdrew the weights to his chest and sat up. Was this that Somebody, Somewhere? Ex-G was similarly hostile to the men she liked, using snickers and sarcasm to probe and prod, to challenge, to entice. For most of the six months they dated, he honestly believed Ex-G hated He-Who-Shall-Not-Be-Named.

Otto believed it right up until the moment he opened his Snapchat and was assaulted by a video of Ex-G down on her knees in front of him.

Otto turned to confront the snickerer. He met the woman's chestnut brown eyes for an instant, then dropped his own to the floor in submission. Blush seared his cheeks; his nostrils flared; he breathed deeply to cool his blazing insides. He watched her bleach-white Nikes stride in the direction of stretching. He watched until they were out of sight, until he could not help but raise his eyes and steal another glance at this most beautiful creature. Dressed in marble yoga pants and a matching sports bra, she appeared a Greco-Roman sculpture half come alive. She was both Apollo and Aphrodite, with masculine arms and legs and shoulders, her femininity displaced rather favourably to bust and buttocks. A belly button piercing set with a blue jewel dangled like a hypnotist's timepiece between washboard abs. She bent over to tie her shoes. Otto groaned as her ass inflated the Spandex like a sat-upon balloon, expanding the fabric see-through, revealing a seam running along her crack, a thong, also blue.

"You like that, buddy," growled a deep voice in his ear. Otto startled. The tattooed giant's right hand grabbed him like a shoulder pad. "That's my bitch. I get to fuck that every night." He bared teeth of dirty quartz. "If I catch you eyeing her up again, I'll twist you like a fucking pretzel and serve you with a load of hot cheese."

Otto thought it odd how hypermasculinity naturally curved toward the homoerotic, as if love were not a spectrum but a sphere. The giant slapped Otto hard on the back, then snuck up behind his "bitch," as it were, and, while she was still bent over, cupped her ass. Always the ass with these macho types.

"Fucker!" she cried, snapping upright, elbows cocked. When she saw it was only her boyfriend, she made a face that was – well, Otto wouldn't exactly call it *pleased*, but neither did she criticize him or make any indication that what he had done irritated her.

The tattooed giant laughed. "Don't be afraid to sweat a little, babe."

Ignoring him, she looked at herself in the closest mirror, flexed her abs, fingered her jewel. The tattooed giant walked around her once, twice, pissing a territorial circle with his pheromones, before lumbering off to the machines. *Muscles make a shit personality.* That was the first thing Ex-G said about He-Who-Shall-Not-Be-Named after their introduction.

And yet . . .

Into Otto's field of view slipped Cocaine George, the tattooed giant's cheerleader. "Don't worry about Hain, bro," he said. "He's all talk." He introduced himself as Ty. "You might call me the resident watchdog. I'm here to make sure everybody's having a good time, using the equipment safely, wiping it down, et cetera." Ty's designation of himself as watchdog was certainly apt. At hardly five feet tall, if he dropped on all fours, he would closer resemble a steroid-injected Pitbull than a human being. "First time? Thought so. Dumbbells are a dead giveaway. So what brings you to Ultimate? You looking to bulk? Guy like you loses any more weight, and you'll have those CrossFit pussies tossing you around like one of their medicine balls."

Otto indicated Hain. "I want to look like him."

Ty mlemed. "You've got a tough journey ahead." He eyed Otto up and down. "Important thing is you've got the wide shoulders. I mean, shit, yeah, I can see it. Might be a decade from now. Five years if you're lucky. With body types like yours, it's really hard to tell."

Otto had honestly thought he could get halfway to Hain's size in a couple months, given enough effort. "Any advice on how to speed it up?" he asked.

"Without taking steroids and opening a line of credit at Don's?" Ty laughed at his own joke. He completed a quick circuit in place, watchdogging, preparing a bed on the rubber floor. "Look, bro, I used to be a scrawny guy like you. It takes dedication to get to where I am. Question is, do you have what it takes? Are you willing to bend the knee at the altar of Almighty Iron?"

The Snapchat video flashed in Otto's thoughts. He nodded rapidly, both in answer to Ty's question and to shake the memory once more to the back of his mind.

"Now, I'm no personal trainer," Ty continued. "I'm just a guy who loves the Iron and wants to give back for all the Iron's done for me. Plus I see something in you that reminds me of me. You've got a real desire for the gains."

"I don't have very much money," Otto admitted. The break-up with Ex-G had cost him five thousand dollars, or half his savings, for damage deposit and first month's rent for his new apartment—

and then new furniture to stock it, new appliances, new dishes, cutlery, a new TV. She hadn't exactly taken everything: he simply let her have it.

"Like I said, I'm no personal trainer. But, yeah, I mean, I'm not gonna do it for free." He sniffed sharply. "How about this: anytime you want me for an hour, you flip me a twenty, and I'm yours. I'm here six hours a day, most days anyway. I don't mind taking an hour away to train a fellow bro." He extended a fist.

Otto pounded it.

"Nice, bro. Sick. Right off the bat I've got two pieces of advice. Call them a signing bonus. One, colour weights are for girls." He pointed to the two rows of black rubber dumbbells in the free weights section. "Thems for the boys. And number two, I wasn't kidding about the Don's. From now on it's high fat, high protein, high calorie. Usually I'd recommend lean bulking, but with you we better go full dirty. Fast food only. Five thousand calories a day. You hear me, bro?"

With that last instruction Ty headed off like a bloodhound on the trail of an unsanitized treadmill. Passing by his tattooed friend, he raised a hand for a high five. "Hainsy making gainsy!" Their hands collided with a loud clap that drew everyone's attention, and seizing on the opportunity to peacock, the two men began jostling each other. But their audience quickly lost interest; they preferred a different spectacle: themselves, moving in the mirrors.

While no one was looking, Otto grabbed his clothes from the changeroom and slipped out the front door.

FOR MOST OF HIS LIFE, until Ex-G told him otherwise, Otto considered his scrawny figure a blessing. He was the rare genetic type who could eat to excess and remain unchanged. Food passed in and out of him as if he were a tube of toothpaste rolled up from the bottom: no matter how much he ate the night before, he always unfurled flat and empty after his morning dump. He often caught overweight men in restaurants plaintively watching him plow through cheeseburgers and French fries, themselves forking lettuce leaves that for all their efforts seemed to add as much to their stomachs as a baker's dozen donuts. *If it wasn't for your cock, you'd be one ugly mothafucka.* Ex-G may have been evoking Schwarzenegger, but the sentiment was real. However balanced these jabs were by compliments to his sex, over time the sheer amount of them transformed Otto's conception of self such that he no longer saw what he saw, but what Ex-G saw, whenever he looked at himself in the mirror – that is, one ugly mothafucka with a giant redeeming cock.

A few visits later Otto had tried to slip Ty a twenty for a session and was refused.

"Not until you get your eating under control," Ty said. "Five thousand calories a day. And a week's worth of receipts to prove it."

Otto tried explaining to Ty his problem. "It won't matter how much I eat. I've been one hundred and twenty pounds since I was fifteen years old."

"Then you have to eat more. I mean, it's not rocket science, O." Recently Ty had taken to calling Otto O instead of bro, saving time on the utterance. "Have you heard of the forty percent rule?" he continued. "Whatever you think is your one hundred percent is actually your forty percent. That's some Navy Seals shit for ya."

Starting at his current maximum intake of three Big Macs, Otto did the math. Three Big Macs (3) / 40% (0.4) = x / 100% (1), and so x (0.4) = 3, and, therefore, x = 7.5. For supper that evening, after finishing his day at H&R Block (it was tax season, so the work was steady), he stopped at his neighbourhood McDonald's. He asked the teenage cashier behind the counter if he knew how many calories were in a Big Mac.

The teen screwed his young oily face up. "Like a thousand or something."

Otto ordered seven Big Macs. He carried the burgers on a plastic tray to a booth in the back. There, he looked up the nutrition facts online. 572 calories, 31g fat, 26g protein – he didn't have to do the math this time to know that if he finished all seven, and factoring in the calories from breakfast and lunch, he would make Ty's quota for the day. He pocketed the receipt for proof, flipped open the lid of the first Big Mac, and began.

The trick to overeating, Otto knew, was to gobble up as much as possible as quickly as possible, before the stomach signalled the brain it was full. He finished one sandwich and then another in quick succession. He swallowed large bites without chewing. The important thing was getting it all down, getting it all in. Let the bile take care of the rest. He broke his personal record at four Big Macs. But this was no cause for celebration. With three sandwiches remaining, his previous maximum still loomed ahead of him. The fifth burger Otto demolished in two bites. *Bruce! Bruce! Bruce! Bruce!* McDonald's Special Sauce splattered his face like Miss Trunchbull's chocolate blood and sweat. Shreds of lettuce decorated his lap like a Jackson Pollock. Picking up the sixth, he heard chatter and whispers and, languidly looking up, saw the entire McDonald's crew gathered at the front counter to watch. Their curious, amazed expressions shot like bolts of electricity into his fading will. He attacked the sixth furiously, tearing it apart, stuffing it down, throwing his head back in defiance of his constricted esophagus. He swiped the empty boxes to the side, leaving number seven alone in front of him. His body heaved. The crowd gasped. He was going to puke! Out came the cellphones, red eyes aflame.

"Beppp." A burp. Just a burp.

And in that newly created space, Otto crammed the seventh and last Big Mac.

There was no applause. The spectacle of gluttony having reached its end, the McDonald's crew simply returned to their jobs.

Meanwhile, Otto collapsed against the bench back and lapsed into a legitimate food coma. And he didn't wake until hours later when the teenage cashier from earlier, instead of politely nudging him, sopped over his runners with a mophead.

"SEVEN BIG MACS?" Ty scoffed. "That's nothing, O. I used to eat bags of chicken nuggets like they were Doritos. Thirty nuggies a pop." He snatched the twenty from Otto's hand and took off toward free weights. Otto hesitated. Ty whistled to him from across the gym. "Yo! Come on!"

Otto joined Ty by the bench press.

Ty held up three fingers. "Three most important lifts are."

Otto waited for him to continue. "Are you ask –"

"Bench, squats, deadlifts. Repeat after me: Bench."

"Bench."

"Squats."

"Squats."

"Deadlifts."

"Deadlifts."

"The Iron Holy Trinity." He crossed himself, then kissed his biceps. "Today we're doing what I call Chest Explosion. I'm gonna get you so pumped you'll be walking out of here with double-Ds.

I'm talking guys'll-be-stopping-you-on-the-street-corner-to-ask-for-your-number-sized titties. We'll start with the bar."

Otto reclined on the bench. He grabbed the cold steel with his middle fingers wrapped around the markings and did ten reps.

"How was that?" Ty asked.

"Pretty good."

Ty added twenty-five-pound plates. "Again."

Otto barely managed four reps. Instantly his T-shirt permeated with sweat. Ty found him some paper towel, which Otto used to wipe his glistening forehead. Ty added ten pounds to either side.

"You're adding more?"

Ty motioned to the bench. "Again."

Otto lay down. Sucking back a deep breath, he lifted the bar out of the holds. It fell to within an inch of his chest. "You fucking got this, O!" Otto pushed with all his might, but the bar kept falling. Like a hydraulic press, no effort of his could prevent its relentless coming down, called into communion with Almighty Iron, the centre of gravity, Earth's core.

"Help," Otto squeaked. "Help." The bar rubbed up against his T-shirt. A second more and he would be crushed.

Ty dropped next to his ear and whispered in it. "Think about Hain's girlfriend's juicy ass in your face. You want a girl like that, don't you, O? I swear if you lift this bar one time, you'll have a hundred girls like that just begging to dig their nails into your chest. All you got to do is lift this bar one time. Just one time."

Otto squeezed his eyes shut, gritted his teeth, and gave it one last attempt.

Give it up, buttercup. Ex-G had said that right before … right before He … before He-Who …

The bar changed direction.

"I'm not even helping you," Ty said, dancing his pinkies underneath. "That's all you. That's all you. All you, O!"

The bar clanged into the holds. "UHHHHHHHHH!" Otto didn't mean to cry out; it just happened that way. He wobbled to his feet.

"Fucking sick." Ty turned him toward the mirror. "You see that, O? Looking deisey."

Though common sense told him it was impossible anything had changed in the two weeks since he started eating more and going to the gym, Otto swore he could see the added weight.

"That's the pump," Ty explained. "The edification. If lifting's the agony, then pump's the ecstasy. You'll learn to love the pump. To live for the pump."

A moment later, after Otto wiped down the bench and bar, he peeked at himself again. Where was the pump? Gone! Vanished! His muscles had deflated like helium balloons walked to the car on a cold winter's day. No wonder everybody here was always looking into mirrors. All it had taken was the one time, and Otto was hooked. Who would've thought vanity to be the most addictive vice in the world?

"Don't worry." Ty jabbed him. "You'll get it back."

LIKE ANY GOD, the Almighty Iron offered in exchange for Otto's undeviating commitment not only the fleeting reward of the pump, but the lasting reward of limitless gains. Gains were the holy mark of the faith, the sign of its adherents. Only the most strident followers received gains in abundance, gains overflowing. For that reason Otto's life came to resemble that of an ascetic. His monkish regiment consisted of waking early, gym, shower, eat, work, gym, shower, eat, sleep, repeat. Outside of this routine he did very little else, remaining celibate so as not to be led astray, reading only the holy text of *Iron and the Soul*, lest he be tempted or have his faith shaken.

And because he performed these sacred rituals with such verve and devotion, over the years, his reward was great. Otto's weight goal had always been two hundred pounds, which was the optimal for a man of his height, six foot four. He achieved this, remarkably, in two years' time – with Ty's help, of course. Their relationship might have begun as a financial arrangement, but it quickly transformed into a friendship. Soon they became exclusive workout partners. They spotted one another. They broke PRs together. They shared in the gains. Otto hadn't thought Ty could get any larger, but he did, even surpassing Hain for sheer brute strength. Whereas Ty could bench and squat entire sets of three plates each, and deadlift four, Hain maxed out at the same weight, barely capable of completing a single rep. In fact, since Otto arrived, Hain had actually shrunk a bit. (The Iron giveth and the Iron taketh away.) Stretch marks appeared on his shoulders and along his biceps and over his pecs. As for Hain's girlfriend, whose name he learned was Valentina, Otto had caught her more than once checking him out clandestinely in the mirrors, through the maze of reflections. Now she was the one whose eyes fell in submission.

Fucccckkkkkkk. That was the last thing the character of Ex-G said to him, the day he reached his target weight. Because in service to the Iron god, he had become one, and for his first godly act, eradicated that annoying pop-culture conjuring bitch inside his head. It had been a remarkable coincidence that enabled him to do so, one of those rare confluences of life that a more superstitious man might credit to divine intervention. To celebrate Otto's achievement of the "Big Two-Double-O," as Ty called it, he and Otto had gone to Fleabags for drinks. Ty started them off with shots of Glenfiddich Scotch. "I don't drink much," he said. "But when I do, I go all the way. Yeahhhh. We're getting fucking wasted tonight, O."

Beers followed, then more shots. In a little under an hour, they downed four shots and three pints and pulverized two orders of nachos meant for four.

"I fucking love you, bro," Otto said.

"No, no, no," said Ty, sloshing beer from his fourth pint all over the table. "Enough, O. I fucking love *you*." He got up from his chair on the outside of the table and slid in next to Otto in the booth. He buried his head into Otto's chest. His arms wrapped incompletely around him. "I've always wanted a brother. And now I've got one. Iron be praised!"

"HeylookisBeastbackMountain!" The shrill laughter of Ex-G tore through the intimacy of Otto and Ty's broment like a wrecking ball through cellophane. Otto swung his head to confront her, expecting immediate recognition. Instead, he was returned the blank foggy-eyed stare of somebody too drunk to be standing. On the split ends of her hair extensions was congealed the splash-back of a recent trip to the toilet bowl. He could smell the vomit on her breath, as well as the familiar oaty musk, whose taste he also remembered from when they used to kiss.

Her friend, a girl Otto didn't recognize, tugged at her arm. "Come on, Trina."

Ex-G extended a hand to Otto to shake. "ImTrinawhatsyourname?"

"O," he said.

"JustO?Wowloser."

"Trina, pleeeassse."

Otto stood up. Ex-G licked her lips. Her eyes zeroed in on his armour-plated pecs. She dragged a hand down his abs. Her arms slid behind his back and massaged his lats. "Wowyoureso*fuckeen*hot. So*fuckeen*hot." Her friend grabbed her arm again. Ex-G shoved her back. "Backupstalker!"

"Fine." Her friend sauntered off. "Fuck you." She wagged a middle finger over her head as she left.

Ex-G stood up on her tiptoes and whispered in Otto's ear, "Takemehomeandfuckmybrainsoutmuscleman."

Ty tried to intervene. "I don't know, O. She seems pretty wasted."

Otto left with her anyway. He made her pay for the cab and carried her in his arms upstairs to his apartment.

She giggled, hiccupped. "Igotnowhereelsetogo!"

In the living room Otto ordered her down on her knees. He pulled out his cock, and she began to suck him off. When he felt himself about to come, he pulled out of her mouth and played with himself.

"You want it?"

She stuck her tongue out. "Uh-huh."

"Tell me how much you want it."

"Iwantyourcum."

"Say, 'Give it up, buttercup.'"

"Whaaa?"

"Just say it."

"Giveitupbuttercup?"

And in the second before he came, Otto saw in Ex-G's eyes the light of recognition, the strange specificity of his request having rattled her to sudden consciousness, so that he was able to finish on her familiar face, rather than the face of a stranger. She fell back on her elbows, wearing an expression of incomprehensible shock, and crawled away from him to the bathroom. She didn't need to be told where to find it; she had been here once before, in the beginning. Otto put his feet up on the coffee table and turned on the TV. When Ex-G had collected herself, she called a cab.

"Bye, Felicia," Otto said to her, on her way out the door.

SOME MONTHS LATER, on a Friday, Otto finished at the gym at the same time as Valentina. Hain and Valentina used to arrive together and leave together, but lately she had been staying longer than him or even coming alone. Otto asked Valentina if she wanted to go for a drink. Two hours later he was fucking her in his apartment. He remembered what Hain had said to him that first time Otto saw her.

"Say 'I'm your bitch.'"

"I'm your bitch! I'm your bitch!"

When it was over, Valentina dressed in her marble gym clothes, becoming once again the half-stone goddess whom Otto's touch, like the breath of Minerva, had earlier brought to full life. He dropped to his knees, grabbed her ass, and suckled on her belly button ring. She pressed his face into her abs and moaned. "Stop it, I have to goooo."

But she didn't go just yet.

Swaggering into the men's changeroom the following morning, Otto heard somebody crying. The sounds were coming from the mirrorless spot where he used to change.

"She dumped me, bro. She fucking dumped me." It was Hain.

Otto poked his head around the corner. Hain was bent over, face buried between his knees. Seated beside him, Ty alternatively rubbed and clapped him on the back.

"You're all right, bro. You'll be all right. Don't let her get you down." Seeing Otto, Ty dipped his chin hello. "Pull yourself together, Hainsy. Come on. We'll take it out on the weights. Let the Iron heal you."

"What's going on?" Otto asked. He tried to hide the quaver in his voice, not knowing what to expect, if Valentina had told Hain anything.

Hain sniffled. "Nothing, bro." It was the first time he had called Otto by the epithet. She hadn't told him a thing. "Just got some creatine in my eyes," he said, chuckling. "Shit stings." Hain's forced cheer rapidly devolved into body-wracking sobs. "What am I going to do, bros? I can't let her see me like this. How am I going to work out with her around? I'll have to switch gyms!"

"Switch gyms? Are you nuts?" Ty pounded himself on the chest. "This is our house. This is our sanctuary. You and me and O, we're the deacons here."

Hain's lips trembled. "Does that mean I can work out with you guys?"

"Of course you can," Ty said. "Fuck that bitch."

"Yeah, fuck that bitch," Otto added.

And he did. Twice.

With Hain added to their crew, Otto found himself in the dicey situation of having both to console Hain over his breakup and to give him hope that he and Valentina might get back together, while simultaneously being the sole reason for their not getting back together and continuing his sexual relationship with her on the sly.

"Did you see that, O?" Hain swatted him on the arm. "She just smiled at me. What do you think that means? Should I smile back?"

"I don't know, bro. What do you think?"

Of course, she was smiling at Otto, not Hain. But Hain's proximity was the perfect cover for Valentina's secret, open communications. Every glance thrown Otto's way, every sexy wink, every smirk and smile, every show of her tongue – they were every last one of them drunk up by thirsty Hain, who was so drowning in hope he had gone blind from it. Ty, however, remained suspicious. After all he was a watchdog, with a keen sense of things amiss. Otto tried to tell Valentina to cool it.

"I don't want Hain to find out," he said.

Valentina snickered. "Why? Are you some fucking pussy?"

"You're right. It's not about Hain. It's Ty I don't want to find out."

"Wouldn't want to kill the bromance? Don't worry about Ty. He's totally gay for you."

But Otto *was* worried. He was worried about both of them: Ty, because he was the only friend Otto had left since dedicating his life to the Iron, and Hain, because of the potential roid rage. (Post breakup, Hain had started juicing again, confiding this to Otto and making him swear to keep it a secret from Ty.) When Valentina told Otto that she had decided to switch gyms, to the ladies only TNAFitness, he felt great relief. Still, he would miss seeing her in her marble attire and bleached Nikes, in that sweaty state of partial undress which had first attracted him to her. She broke up with him soon after the move. He took out his anger for the breakup by dogpiling on her with Hain. Hain went along with it under the assumption Otto was offering his sympathetic support. Again, it was Ty who suspected something was up. He confronted Otto about it one evening on their way into the changeroom. Hain had gone there earlier because he wanted to shower, whereas Ty and Otto typically waited until they were home.

"What do you care about Valentina anyway?" Ty held one nostril shut and blew out the other into the cleaning wipe bin. "I mean, O, that was three *years* ago."

Otto realized Ty was thinking about the time Valentina had snickered at him and Hain threatened to cover his soft pretzel with cheese. "It's not about that," Otto said. "I'm just looking out –"

But he was not looking out well enough. From behind a row of lockers a twenty-pound kettlebell came swinging at him like the wrath of their Iron god. All Otto was able to register, before the weight knocked him clean into another dimension, were the familiar tattooed fingers wrapped around its handle.

Several years later Otto would learn that Hain, while showering, had overheard a man talking to his friend about "some ho" he met on Tinder named Valentina, and how she used to date a six-foot-four Chad from Ultimate with a ridiculous one letter name: O. Naturally, Hain decided the only recourse for this betrayal was to bash Otto's head in. And if Ty hadn't been there to stop his second swing, he might've actually succeeded.

OTTO AWOKE in the hospital choking on a large something crammed down his throat. He grabbed at the tube and, gagging, pulled it up and out. Loud beeping noises from the adjacent machines drew a crowd of nurses into his room. The oldest one placed a hand on his chest. "Sit back. Be calm." Otto tried to sit up anyway and was surprised to find his superior strength thwarted by this diminutive elderly women. One look down at his body revealed to him the awful truth: he had lost everything, all his gains, all his muscle. He was scrawny Otto again. Mr. Black Hole.

"Where –" Otto degenerated into a coughing fit. The uncomfortable sensation of the ventilator tube lingered inside his throat like a hard bong hit. A younger nurse graciously brought him some water.

Eventually, he managed to ask. "Where am I? What happened to me?"

"This might be difficult for you to hear, Mr. Brecht, but you have been in a coma for the last fourteen months."

The room began to spin. The alarm on his heart rate monitor whined. A doctor appeared swiftly with a sedative, which, when injected, delivered Otto temporarily out of this nightmare and back into the infinity of nothingness where he had spent, apparently, the past fourteen months.

A week later Otto was released. He returned home to his apartment and found his key did not work in the lock. He checked in with the landlord at her office. She informed him sadly that, having received no rent payment from him and being unaware of his situation, she had sold all his stuff after four months, as was policy, and moved somebody else in.

Otto was flabbergasted. "Is there nothing at all left? Nothing?"

The landlord, embarrassed, admitted she had taken a few of his things for herself. "If I had known," she started to explain, then abruptly rose and went to retrieve the objects from her conjoining apartment. She returned to the office with a Ninja blender, an exercise ball, and a weight scale. "I truly am sorry."

"Keep the ball," Otto said, and booted it against the opposite wall. It bounced back toward her desk and barrelled across it, shattering her picture frames and knocking the computer monitor to the floor. She didn't react, however, seeming to accept this outburst as justified.

Otto left the office and wandered through the front courtyard to the street. He set the Ninja blender down and took out his keys, his wallet, his dead cellphone, and set them down, too. Then he stepped on the scale. The screen illuminated blue and rapidly counted up from zero to one hundred and twenty pounds. One hundred and twenty on the dot. Same as before. Same as always.

#12 *Hair, A Fable*

REBEKA SHED LIKE A DOG. Her black hairs fell out in bushels and clumps, in screwy singles and knotted pairs. She left hairs everywhere she went as if her life were a labyrinth she hoped one day to follow back to the beginning. They tagged along on the straps of her handbags, hitched a ride on the bottoms of her heels. She found them regularly in her food. Prepared fresh, days old, it didn't matter: her hairs would be there, curled up like Egyptian cobras, waiting to snap at her uvula. If her hairs were arrows, her clothes were Saint Sebastian. She couldn't put on a pair of socks without them tickling her feet. Vacuum cleaner after vacuum cleaner lay siege to their territorial claims and suffered one-by-one ignominious defeat. Her hairs clogged the shower drains weekly, the toilets, too, when she tried to flush them. Combing them, she was surprised every time to look in the mirror and discover that she wasn't, in fact, bald, that there were still many millions more of them holding on.

IN THE BEGINNING Sean loved Rebeka's hairs. He loved running his fingers through them, the smell of them still wet out of the shower. The sight of them fallen over her naked breasts never failed to arouse him. Nor did the swinging back and forth of her ponytail when he and Rebeka went out for a jog. If he laid them on his bald head just right, he looked like Joe Jonas. He could hardly cum unless he pulled on them during sex. Hugging her, Sean buried his face in her hairs and breathed through them like a filter. Sometimes when he did this, a solitary hair might break free and escape down his trachea, but he never minded reaching into his mouth and pulling it back out. Balled in his armpit, bowed around his penis, threaded like a thong along his butt crack – Sean was amazed at all the places he had found her hairs over the years. On the subway he might feel somebody grazing the small of his back, might even make a face at the man or woman behind him, only to reach back later when he could and find the culprit: Rebeka's hair.

THE NIGHT SEAN BROKE UP WITH HER, Rebeka waited until he went to sleep, then combed her hairs. She combed and combed and combed, and distributed what came out like paratroopers all around the house. She may have been dumped, but her hairs would carry on, carry on. She sprinkled her hairs like fairy dust over the TV and his video games. She floated them into impossible-to-reach corners. She wrapped them like twine around the knobs of his PlayStation controllers. In his books her hairs became ribbon markers; draped over his collectibles, they were spider webs. She unloaded whole handfuls into his laundry bag and toolbox. All the while she laughed to herself thinking of the many years they might continue to torment him. Not to mention all the ways they would constantly remind him of her, beautiful black-haired Rebeka, the woman he had lost.

IT SEEMED PARADOXICAL TO SEAN THAT, with Rebeka moved out, he would be finding more of her hairs now than ever before. Somehow, too, these hairs were different, their ends sharper, their habits perverse. Without Rebeka around to rule them, they had gone rogue. Her hairs metamorphosed into worms inside his food and beetles under his covers. They poked and prodded his private parts. Shampooing his scalp, he found her hairs inexplicably amongst the suds like they were attempting to usurp his own. At the source of every itch, hair. The root of every tickle, hair. When he could take it no longer, Sean spent an entire day scouring the apartment for them. He swept out every drawer and cupboard. He plucked them like weeds from every crack, corner, crook. But this action seemed merely to embolden them. One hair embarked on a suicide mission to his tonsils. For days Sean exhausted himself trying to clear the unknowable something from his throat. He worried throat cancer had developed from his smoke-heavy college years. He visited the doctor. Reaching in with tweezers, the doctor removed the slimy black corpse. Afterward, the doctor remarked she had never known a hair to be so resilient.

REBEKA MET FRANCISCO AT THE GYM. He approached her at the squat rack to ask how many sets she had left and ended up with her phone number instead. They became lovers, then boyfriend-girlfriend. Francisco told Rebeka how much he liked top buns, so she tied her hairs up for him. When a girl walked by with pink streaks in her hair, he mentioned how sexy girls were who added a little colour. Rebeka made an appointment with a hairdresser and dyed her bangs green. Then Francisco decided he liked blondes exclusively. He begged Rebeka to see the hairdresser. He promised never to ask her to change her hair again. She relented and booked the appointment. Four treatments later, her hair was yellow blonde.

She prepared dinner with her new hair down, hoping to surprise him when he came home from work. Halfway through eating, Francisco clutched at his throat and bolted to the bathroom. Rebeka heard him gagging into the toilet. The next day he presented her with a box of hairnets. She broke up with him, bought electric clippers, and buzzed her hair off.

FOR MONTHS SEAN HAD BEEN LIVING HAIR-FREE. Whether the hairs' sudden departure was due to any effort on his part or whether they had capitulated all on their own, he could not say. At first he cherished his newfound freedom. Gone were the days of phantom tickles, of creepy crawlers in the night. His vacuum cleaner glided smoothly across the apartment floor, his meals down his throat. Then something strange happened: like a white noise abruptly silenced, once Sean became conscious of their absence, he couldn't help but long for their return. Yes, he actually *missed* them. He missed their death-defying acrobatics, their improbable hiding places and supernatural fecundity. He missed the pinpricks and the entanglements and the shock of finding them in his sandwich. But mostly he missed them on Rebeka. He missed their secure feel between his fingers, their lavender smell just out of the shower.

VERY SLOWLY REBEKA'S HAIRS GREW BACK. They sprouted from her skin like crowded radicles, then spread across her scalp like strawberry vines. She treated them gently with conditioner and stimulated them with tender massage. After a year she measured her hairs at six inches. They would take three more years to reach the length they were before. Until she had to grow them back, Rebeka never fully appreciated their magic. Never again would she act independently of their mutual consent. Her hairs were alive; she and they were symbiotic partners. They lived apart from her and were a part of her just the same. When they had grown sixteen inches, Rebeka ran into Sean walking downtown. He complimented her fancy new hairdo, and she agreed to a catch-up date later in the week. They hugged goodbye. As Sean walked away, Rebeka spotted one of her hairs trailing like a kite tail from his shirt collar. She smiled to herself imagining all the little, obscure places it might plant itself when he arrived back at the apartment. She hoped it would survive the journey there.

#13 *Old Friends*

I MET COLE LACHANCE at a Calgary Flames game. It was the last game of the 1988–89 regular season, our championship year. We were playing the Edmonton Oilers. Because it was sold out, I had bought a single seat from a scalper in front of the Saddledome. Sometime earlier Cole had bought the seat beside mine.

Because we had both come alone, we kept each other company during intermissions. We talked hockey and beer and women. Cole knew more about all three, so I listened most of the time. Nevertheless, he had a way of talking that made it feel like he was always adding to something I had already said.

Calgary won the game four to two. Rookie Theo Fleury scored the game-winning goal. Cole said before puck drop that if we won this game, we would win the Cup.

And he was right.

I SAW COLE ONLY TWICE after that: once at Ranchman's for the Stanley Cup Final and again, fifteen years later, when I drove him across the border into Montana in the trunk of my car.

After the game we had exchanged numbers. I waited a month for Cole to call before eventually calling him.

"I'm busy all next week," he said, "but what about the week after that, for the Final?"

"That works," I said.

Game six was in Montreal; the Flames were playing the Canadiens for the Cup. I asked him where he thought we should watch it.

"Let's do Ranchman's," he said.

Ranchman's was a cowboy bar, and that night Cole dressed the part. Red and yellow plaid shirt tucked into Wrangler jeans. Black felt hat worn straight over his forehead. Buckle won for calf-roping shining like a jewel above his crotch. He looked bona fide, but in Calgary that look was easy to fake. Anybody could be a cowboy with two hundred bucks and a trip to Lammle's. The belt buckle was another thing. He or somebody he knew had to have won it – or else he had paid a lot of money for it at a pawn shop.

Everyone at the bar seemed to recognize him. When he walked in, the bartenders greeted him by name. Two waitresses stopped him on his way over to me.

"Freddy." Cole extended his hand to me like a pistol, quick and from the hip.

"Cole," I said, shaking his hand.

"Hope you're not too comfortable," he said.

"Why's that?"

"We're moving."

I followed him to a booth in the corner with a reserved sign, which the waitress removed when she delivered my drink from the other table. How anyone could reserve a booth at Ranchman's for the Stanley Cup Final seemed incredible to me. I had waited an hour at the door and all I got was a two seater beside the entrance to the kitchen.

"Same as usual?" the waitress asked Cole.

"Two of the same," he said. "Do you drink whiskey?"

"I drink anything," I said.

The waitress returned with two whiskeys and two beers. Cole instructed me to take the shot and then chase it with beer. We clinked our shot glasses together.

"To the Cup!"

Presently the waitress returned with two more shots. One more round, and I was buzzed. She continued to bring us shots until we'd had four each. Then it was beers for the rest of the night.

"That was one hell of a game we saw," said Cole.

"Oilers without Gretzky are shit," I said.

"I'm telling you, Freddy, this is our year."

"Montreal could win. Push it to seven."

"Over my dead body." Cole leaned over and spit a glob of tobacco I hadn't known he was chewing on the floor. "And yours if you ever say anything like that again."

We ordered burgers for the first period. Thanks to a goal by Patterson, the Flames were up one to nothing going into the second. Already the bar was abuzz with talk of our first Stanley Cup.

"Four to two!" Cole cried.

"What's that?" I asked.

His eyes were cloudy, clairvoyant. "We win it four to two."

Not even a minute and a half into the second period, Montreal scored. Conversation in the Ranchman's hushed, was replaced with the hollow knocking of shot glasses and beer mugs, and demands for more beer, more whiskey, anything to buck the sobering truth of a tie game, which was that it could tip either way. Plumes of cigarette smoke poured against the ceilings like a busy day at the rigs.

It's only game six, I thought.

"There's not going to be a game seven," growled Cole, reading my mind.

Three minutes later Lanny McDonald returned us to the lead. Drinks ordered in worry arrived in time to be drunk in celebration. The floor became slippery with beer foam, the counter wet with whiskey, as we lifted our glasses in toast to the captain.

The second period ended with Calgary up by one. Cole suggested we order two jugs for the third. He grabbed the arm of a waitress passing by. She swung her head around ready to snap, but smiled when she recognized him.

"Another round?" she asked.

"Two jugs of Canadian." He winked at me. "It'll be like we're drinking their blood."

Puck drop, third period.

For that final twenty minutes the whole of Calgary remained at a standstill. Only the flashing lights of TV screens and the voices of announcers could be seen and heard – that is, until Gilmour scored and roused the city back to life.

Three to one!

But we didn't allow ourselves even a second of celebration. No one dared say what we all were thinking: the Cup was ours. When Montreal scored again, we were grateful to have said nothing. In sports, ritual and superstition reigned. A gaffe, a gesture, a glance – any of these might sway the hockey gods against us, and those to blame would be dealt with violently.

"Coming to centre ... Passes into Robinson ... He's stopped at the Calgary line ... The net is empty down there ... For Mullen ... And for Gilmour ... Gilmour has a shot to win it all here ... HE SCORES! Gilmour scores! With 1:03 left! Gilmour! And Calgary leads four to two!"

Ranchman's erupted in cheer. Beer catapulted into the air like champagne. Our neighbours embraced us, and we our neighbours. For that final minute and three seconds, the bar crowd remained in a singular embrace. And when the timeclock reached ten, we cried out in unison ten, nine, eight, seven, six, five, four, three, two, one – the Cup was ours! The Cup was ours!

Cole and I grabbed our half-full jugs of beer and followed everyone out into the streets. We flooded Macleod Trail and began the pilgrimage north toward the Saddledome. Car horns and fire truck sirens heralded our approach. With every bar we passed, we grew in number. When we finally entered the Stampede grounds, we were thousands, and there met thousands more already gathered.

"I swear to God," said Cole, gripping the small Flames patch sewn onto his breast pocket, "I'm going to frame this shirt."

"I can't believe we did it," I said. "I thought I'd never live to see it."

"Come with me," Cole said, and stole through the crowd. I chased him all the way to the eastern end of the Saddledome, to a red door. He set his jug of beer on the cement. He glanced around us, pulled a small tool out of his wallet, and jammed it inside the lock.

"What are you doing?" I asked.

I kept watch while he worked. If there were security, they were too focused on the crowd to do anything about us. It took Cole about five minutes to get the door open. He beckoned me in ahead of him.

"You won't regret it," he said.

The door led into a fire escape. Using only the light from the exit signs, we climbed the stairs to the top. There, he picked another lock, admitting us into what looked like a mechanical room.

"Where are we going?" I asked.

Cole continued on without answering me or checking to see if I was still behind him.

We stopped next at a narrow stairwell secured behind a chain-link door with a bolt and padlock. These again proved useless against his talent. When he was through, he propped the door open for me and said, "After you."

I ascended the stairwell. At the end was a ladder leading up to a hatch.

I turned around. "After you."

Cole laughed. He handed me his beer jug and cowboy hat. He climbed the ladder and opened the hatch. A gust of wind rushed down from above. Cole climbed out and reached down first for his hat, then for the jugs of beer. After he had gotten everything from me, he hopped over the hatch and vanished.

Slowly I scaled the ladder. When I got to the last rung, I peeked my head out of the hatch and found myself looking across the bowed, concrete surface of the top of the Saddledome. It appeared black as the sky above, like a dark pit viewed against the lights of downtown. I glimpsed over my shoulder and saw Cole, his silhouette, standing on the southern edge of the arena roof, gazing down upon the Stampede grounds where all the thousands of fans were congregated.

"You got to see this," he called to me.

I hesitated. I worried that the hatch might swing shut behind me and trap us.

"I'm drinking your beer if you don't come and get it," coaxed Cole. He dangled my jug over the edge. "Maybe I'll just pour it out."

I shoved my Flames jersey into the space where the latch went in, so that in the off chance the hatch did swing shut, at least it wouldn't lock. Then I jogged over to Cole. He released my jug to me intact.

"Bet you've never seen anything like this before," he said.

Below us the fans swarmed about like fire ants. Their voices – the songs, the laughter, the hurrahs – arrived at our ears a collective, muted buzz. I peered over the edge, got that sick feeling in my stomach like I was already falling, and staggered back.

"I assume you've been up here before?" I asked.

"Twice. Once with my brother, once by myself." Cole chugged the rest of his beer. He wound up as if getting ready to throw his jug off the roof. Then he just set it down beside him.

"Let's check out the other side," he said.

The north side of the arena faced downtown Calgary. The Calgary Tower glowed in the skyline like an eternal torch; yet its flame was eclipsed now by the Petro-Canada Centre West and the new Bankers Hall, and no longer burned bright above the rest of the city.

Cole took his cowboy hat off and set it on his heart. "Damn beautiful city from up high."

"Ugly as piss from the street," I said.

"The prairies through and through." He adjusted his belt buckle.

"Did you win that?"

The question had been on my mind since Ranchman's. If he had won it, that would explain why he had been given so much attention from the bartenders and waitresses. Rodeo men were famous in Calgary the way movie stars were in Hollywood, though I didn't recognize him.

"My father did," he said. "This one's from Cloverdale. He's got hundreds of these things. Boxes and boxes of them. He won the Stampede twice in the sixties, for bareback and cattle-roping."

"Did you ever compete?" I asked.

"When I was younger, in junior rodeo. Not that I wouldn't have been able to go national if I tried. But my brother was that much better than me." He spat. "Also, horses never liked me much. Bulls neither. Whatever they smelled on me drove them wild."

"Your brother," I said, "did he ever win the Stampede?"

"I'm sure he would've," Cole said. "But he got kicked in the head by a horse at Snake River. And that was that."

"Sorry," I said.

"There are worse ways to go."

"Like falling off the top of the Saddledome?"

Cole laughed. "Just high enough to shit your pants before you hit the ground." He put his cowboy hat back on and straightened it over his forehead. "Let's get back to the action."

We left the same way we had come in. In the crowd we met a group of fans who supplied us with beer, and we celebrated with them the rest of the night.

Cole and I caught the CTrain from Stampede station at six in the morning the next day. We were headed in opposite directions, he south to Chinook, I north to 7th Street. He waited with me on the northbound platform for my train to come first.

"So long," he said.

The last thing I remembered of Cole was seeing a tired cowboy, tipping his hat as the train pulled away.

WHO CAN KNOW THE REASONS why we lose touch with some friends and not others?

I couldn't recall the precise moment I quit trying to meet up with Cole. The last time I remembered calling him was four years after that night. I had been cleaning out my apartment, about to move in with Denise, who would become my wife, when I found his name and number in an old book of contacts. I dialled the number; an elderly woman answered. She had never heard the name Cole Lachance. With that final effort I abandoned the idea of ever seeing him again, except perhaps in passing. Still, he endured as a faint image in my memory, and, in a somewhat exaggerated form, as the supporting character in the story I told of the time I had drank beer on the roof of the Saddledome the night of our championship game.

Shortly after we were married, Denise and I moved south to Lethbridge. She had received an appointment with the university as a professor of art history. I took an assistant management position at Maple Leaf Pork in the department of Food Safety and Quality Assurance. We had two children, Marley and James, two years apart. We settled into a comfortable existence in that hot dusty town. For my children Calgary was always the big city. In time it became that way too for my wife. But for me it remained home, and I took every opportunity to return my thoughts there.

In the spring of 2004, the Calgary Flames advanced to the Stanley Cup Finals for the first time since 1989. Fifteen years. Marley and James were nine and seven, respectively, and in my opinion old enough to appreciate the occasion. I convinced Denise to let me take them to Calgary for game six. With the Flames up three to two in a seven-game series, the game was a potential Stanley Cup Final. If they won, it would be our first Cup won on Calgary soil.

We drove up the night before and stayed with Denise's parents. Denise came along for the visit, but she would watch from home with her mother and father. She didn't think her presence at the game worth the money. The tickets had cost me four hundred dollars apiece.

On her way to drop us off at the Saddledome, Denise, at my request, made a detour down "the Red Mile," a stretch of 17th avenue near the arena, where Flames fans gathered in the tens of thousands to watch the games and celebrate. Neither the kids nor Denise had seen anything like it before. Nor had I. Nor had anybody in the country for that matter. Marley and James pressed their faces against the windows and pointed out the funny costumes.

"Look at him!" Marley cried.

"Come look over here!" said James.

Denise was more alarmed by the crowd than excited by it.

"Are you sure it's safe?" she asked.

"It'll be fine," I said.

A girl on the sidewalk exposed herself to the men driving the Ford truck in front of us. They honked their horn encouragingly.

Denise frowned. "Now I know why you wanted to come this way."

She dropped us off at the entrance to the Stampede grounds. The kids and I walked to the Saddledome from there.

"Wow!" James said. He was seeing the arena up close for the first time.

"Guess what?" I asked.

"What?" Marley asked.

"I've been on top of there."

Marley and James stared at the Saddledome in awe. Neither bothered to ask how I had gotten on top, content to imagine the circumstances. I had scaled the walls; I had been lowered out of a helicopter; I had built it.

As we waited in line to be admitted, I thought about Cole. I surveyed the crowd on a hunch he would be here. I wondered if I might see him inside, perhaps on the scoreboard between whistles, cheering loudly in his cowboy clothes. Or maybe on the kiss cam with a wife I hadn't met, reined in, settled down.

Exciting though it was, the first period ended scoreless. During the intermission, I escorted Marley and James to the washroom. Afterward, we all got refills of pop. I would've killed for a beer just then, but I had made it a rule never to drink in front of my kids.

Shortly into the second period, the Lightning went on a power play and scored. (Where was that beer when I needed it?) But we fans never faltered in our cheers, in our raucous confidence. I regretted not bringing earplugs for the kids; the noise in the arena was unrelenting, as loud as a fighter jet they would claim on the news. Later, when Chris Clark scored for the Flames, Marley and James covered their ears against the sting of nineteen thousand cries of celebration.

Another power play goal by Richards returned Tampa Bay to the lead. Everyone within earshot cursed the referees.

"You suck, Bettman!" cried out one fan in his frustration.

For a time it seemed the Flames would not recover. Chance after chance led to nothing. Then, with two minutes left, Nilson scored on a turnover in the Tampa end. We could relax now, more assured of our inevitable victory.

During the second intermission, I went with the kids to buy popcorn and pizza. We arrived back at our seats just in time for puck-drop.

A lot happened in that final twenty minutes, but to no result: we were headed into overtime.

Most fans stayed put while the Zamboni cleaned. We were afraid that in moving we might inadvertently trigger a chain of events that would rob Calgary of their rightful Cup. If none moved, then none were culpable. I was, however, obliged to make another washroom trip. I rushed the kids in and out and back to our seats.

"Dad," Marley whined, "I'm tired."

"It'll be over soon," I said.

Waiting for the game to resume, Marley balled up her jersey on the armrest and rested her head on it. I ruffled her hair and glanced overtop her at James. His eyes were drooping, but for my sake he tried his best to remain engaged.

The first overtime period was unwatchable. If we scored, the Cup was ours; if they scored, we would have to go through it all again two days later. Every so often, after a stunning save or an unsuccessful two-on-one, I would glance over at my kids, wanting them to share in the turmoil. Marley had fallen asleep, and James was cuddled up against her, himself passing in and out of consciousness. How could they fall asleep at a time like this? Yet I also envied their unconcern.

With first overtime come and gone, the crowd allowed themselves to unwind. It seemed we were in for a long night. The man in the seat next to me commented to his girlfriend, "Sometimes these can go to three, even four extra periods."

But no one could expect how soon it would actually end. Thirty seconds into double overtime, Martin St. Louis, an ex-Flame, snapped the puck past Kiprusoff. The red light flashed behind home net like a warning come an instant too late. The game was over.

We tarried in shock and disbelief. Only when the players had filed off the bench, their shoulders slunk, heads bowed, defeated, moaning already at the thought of returning once again to Tampa Bay, that murky harbour at the opposite end of the continent, did everyone accept that we had lost.

I woke my kids.

"Is it over?" Marley asked dreamily.

"Did we win?" James said, blinking his eyes.

"We lost," I answered. "But there's always game seven."

MY FAMILY AND I RETURNED to Lethbridge the following evening. And who should we find waiting there for us but Cole Lachance himself. His face, hands, and hair were stained with sand. It was obvious from the amount of dust covering him that he had slept outside the night before.

"Freddy." He reached out to shake my hand, the same quick hip snap I remembered.

Denise and the kids huddled behind me. Dirty and dressed in cowboy clothes, he appeared a disturbed outlaw come to repay an ancient debt. How had he found out where I lived?

I shook his hand cautiously. "What are you doing here, Cole?"

"Just visiting an old friend," he said. He smiled at Marley and James. "Are these your kids?" He smiled at Denise. "And your wife?"

"Everybody, this is Cole," I said. "Cole, this is Denise, Marley, and James."

They said hello from where they stood sheltered behind me.

"Why don't you take them inside," I said to my wife.

Cole was probably harmless, but I wasn't going to take any chances with my family. No man showed up out of the blue without wanting something, and I was anxious to find out what that something was. Although perhaps it was true what he said, that he had merely stopped by to visit an old friend. There were often nights when I recalled people from my life with whom I wished to reconnect. Many times it had been the very man standing in front of me.

Cole clapped his hands together. "We had them beat, Freddy. We had them bastards beat."

"I was at the game," I said. "I thought I might see you there."

"Did you see that goal in the third period? The one they didn't count?"

"Not while the game was on."

"Bullshit." Cole spit some chewing tobacco off the deck. Half the glob missed its mark and splattered on the wood. "Sorry about that." He whipped out a handkerchief as if thinking to clean it up, but didn't.

"So what are you really doing here?" I asked.

"What? A guy can't say hello to an old –"

"Cut the bullshit, Cole."

"Okay, okay," he said. "You're right. I wish that were the only reason. It's one of the reasons. But it's not the only one."

"Is it about money?" I asked.

"No, nothing like that."

"Then what?"

"I need a ride."

"Where?"

"South to the border," he said. "And then across it."

"To Montana?" I had never known anyone, unless they had family there, to visit Montana for pleasure. There were only ever two reasons anyone north of the border had for travelling to that state: to shop or to run. And Cole didn't strike me as a bargain hunter.

"What's going on?" I asked.

Cole opened his mouth, but nothing came out. Then he began to sob. "I fucked up, Freddy." He wrung the cowboy hat in his hands. "I've made an awful mess."

I tensed up in my chair. "What happened?"

Cole wiped his face clean of sand and tears and sweat. He glanced at the door leading from our deck to the kitchen.

"Do you have anything to drink?"

"I can't let you inside," I said.

"I understand." He brought out a tin of chewing tobacco from his back pocket. He spit the rest of the old batch out and stuffed a fresh pinch against his bottom lip. His fingers were shaking as he did it, and he missed getting it all inside. Flakes of chewing tobacco stuck to his lips like blueberry pulp.

"What day is it today?" he asked.

"Sunday," I said.

"Would've been Thursday, then."

"What happened Thursday?"

Cole looked askance. "I suppose it doesn't matter," he muttered to himself. Then, "You'll know the story soon enough."

I waited tensely for him to start.

"About a month ago," he began, "I found out that a good friend of mine was sleeping with my wife. Not my wife like you and Denise. But we were living together for eight years, so that's what I called her." He paused to lick the tobacco off his lips. "I couldn't tell you how long it had been going on. But I had caught them. Course they didn't know it." Cole leaned forward and grasped the air as if he were strangling a ghost. "Sarah was the only girl I had ever felt anything for in my life. And, Freddy, I couldn't look at her. Our love had turned to vomit. I couldn't see her without seeing them, and it made me sick. It made me wretch, just looking at her. Just seeing her.

"Anyway, every year he and I went hunting –"

"Cole."

"– and I got in my head that if I was going to kill him, that would be the time."

I shook my head. "Cole, Cole."

"The plan was I would take him to a spot where there was a lot of brush. That way the cops might believe it was a mistake." He gestured off to my right, gazed absently in that direction. "So when we were out there, I waited until he had gone about a hundred feet or so ahead of me. And then I shot."

Cole stared down at his feet. His hands twitched in his lap.

"Did you kill him?" I asked.

"I don't know. I didn't have it in me to check."

"Why didn't you go to the police?"

"Because I left him," he said. "I got scared and ran. I knew they wouldn't believe that I would just leave him like that."

"Are they looking for you?"

"We were in deep country. I doubt anyone has found him yet, if he's dead. If he's living, he would have a hell of a time getting out. But I guess it's only a matter of time before someone finds out something."

There was a moment of silence.

"So will you do it for me?" Cole pleaded. "Will you help me?"

"I can't," I said. "I just can't."

"Don't make me beg, Freddy."

"Please don't. Begging won't change my mind."

He nodded, made to speak, and nodded again. Eventually, Cole asked me if I knew the quickest route to the border.

"Go south on the 5, until Magrath, then south again on the 62," I said. "How are you going to get there?"

"Hitch." He shrugged. "Walk."

I saw him off my property.

"This never happened," I said.

Cole offered me his hand again, and I shook it.

"It would've been nice to have watched the game tomorrow," he said. "Be together for one and two."

"You think we're going to win?"

He grinned. "When have I ever been wrong?"

COLE WAS TEN MINUTES OUTSIDE MAGRATH when I picked him up.

I had only a vague understanding of what made me decide to do it. All I knew was that I had stayed awake most of the night thinking about him and remembering back to the championship game and the gift he gave me with that memory. And then that afternoon, coming home from the slaughterhouse, I had been watching the pre-game show in the living room, my wife and kids in the background going about their routine as usual, not even caring that in a mere hour, at six o'clock Mountain Time, a game would begin which might never again be seen in their lifetime, or at the very least a decade or two – and I realized that I couldn't enjoy it without him.

We pulled off onto Township Road 50 to listen to the first period. On the Lightning's second power play in twelve minutes, Fedotenko scored off a rebound to put Tampa Bay in the lead.

"This is just what I'm talking about," Cole ranted. "Bettman and his black-and-white bullies. I'd like to see those calls on replay."

The first period ended with a score of one to nil. In Tampa Bay, the Zambonis applied themselves like Band-Aids to the lacerated ice surface; in Magrath, a possible murderer and his friend strategized. It was during the first intermission that we decided Cole would hide in the trunk. We both agreed it would be safer that he not be seen at the border with me, lest the police suspect correctly he had fled south and catch us together on camera. At the same time we decided on my reason for crossing: I was going to Cut Bank to visit Henry Moore, a friend of mine who was just diagnosed with prostate cancer. Everything about the story was true, except that Henry lived in Edmonton.

The first half of the second period was uneventful. During the lull I thought about the story I had told my wife. I promised Denise that I would come home from the bar as soon as the game ended, win or lose. I realized that if I were going to keep hidden what it was I had really done, I would have to get to the border while the game was still on to give me time enough to cross and then cross back.

I started the car.

"What are you doing?" Cole asked.

I explained to him why we had to leave.

"All right," he said. "Let's hope the signal holds out."

Save for a quiet crackle underneath the announcers' voices, we had received the game clearly thus far. Minutes after leaving Township Road 50, however, the radio station became overwhelmed by static. The sound of the game disappeared as within a sandstorm, with the same suddenness and ubiquity – and at the worst possible moment, too: Fedotenko of the Tampa Bay Lightning had just scored his second goal of the night.

It was the last play either of us would hear.

Ten kilometres from the crossing at Del Bonita, I pulled over so that Cole could get in the trunk. We waited for a semi-truck to pass, and then, when the road was clear, I helped him climb in. He wrapped himself inside a black and red emergency blanket Denise had made me get in case I got stuck out on the road in winter.

"Thanks again, brother," Cole said.

"See you on the other side," I said.

The highway leading to Del Bonita was flat and grey, the fields adjacent to it gold, like a film negative of the Yellow Brick Road. I tried my best to avoid any bumps in the pavement, imagining Cole knocking around in back. I drove slower than usual. But not so slow as to draw suspicion.

"You doing okay back there?" I shouted.

If Cole had heard me, I didn't hear him answer.

"We're coming up on it now," I said.

The semi-truck that passed us earlier continued left to the oversized checkpoint. I pulled forward. The border crossing looked like a converted acreage, with the road penetrating what had once been the car port of some old, repurposed ranch house. I half-expected to be approached by a senior in overalls and a straw hat. Instead, a young uniformed man with beady eyes and a buzz cut approached the car.

I rolled down my window.

"What brings you to Montana tonight?" he asked.

"I am visiting an old friend of mine," I said. "Henry Moore. He has cancer."

"Passport."

"It's prostate."

"Your passport."

"Oh, sorry." I handed him my passport.

He opened it, closed it. "Why are you crossing this late?"

"Because of the game," I said.

"What game?"

"The Stanley Cup Final."

"What is that?" he asked. "Hockey?"

"Calgary Flames."

"Did they win?"

"I don't know," I admitted. "I was listening on the radio, but the signal cut out."

"So you're crossing late because of a game that you didn't finish listening to?"

"I – I honestly thought I wouldn't lose the signal."

"Wait here a moment."

The border agent walked by the front of my car to his booth. He lifted his phone off the receiver and dialled a number. While he talked, he watched me from his post.

Panic set in. He didn't believe me. He was calling in backup. He would find Cole in the trunk, arrest us, and when they found out what he had done, we would both go to prison. Did this qualify me as an accessory? Would I, too, go away for life?

Some minutes later the border agent returned.

"Bad news," he said.

"What's that?" I asked.

"Well, I called the Canadian side to see if they knew about your game. Sure enough they were watching it."

"What's the score?"

"Two to one for the other guys."

"How much time is left?"

"It was in the final minute when I called," he said. "It should be over now."

I shook my head. "I really thought we had this one."

"Sorry to disappoint."

The border agent stepped back from my car and waved us on.

#14 *Opposite Ends*

SHE GOT THE NAME AZZA because she was first to arrive. Otherwise, she would've been Zara.

Their mother picked their names to begin with the first and last letters of the alphabet. Azza and Zara were proper twins' names, with just the right similarities and differences. Everybody confused them anyway. When they weren't calling Zara Azza or Azza Zara, they jumbled them into entirely new names like Zaza, Arza, Azar, Zarza. Their father had coined the latter name, Zarza. Over time it became his idiosyncratic way of referring to them both. It was "Zarza! Dinner!" or "Zarza! Bedtime!" The girls liked the name so much they made a character out of her. Zarza was their ideal imagining of themselves. They concocted for her a boyfriend who resembled Harry Styles, their main crush at the time. To name the boyfriend, they wrote out the alphabet, found the middle letters M and N, and thus was born Nicky Miles. They filled journals with the adventures of Zarza Shadid and Nicky Miles. These were always variations of the same story. Zarza and Nicky would visit some gloomy, stormy place, a swampland or a castle, and be captured and imprisoned there by a raving beast or bitter queen, and then have to escape. And when they were finally free, Zarza and Nicky would share a romantic kiss.

It wasn't until their father found their journals, and infuriated by the abundance of kisses, confiscated them, that they abandoned these earlier fantasies in favour of a fantasy all their own, which began with them running away to California at the age of eighteen.

They shared a bedroom in the basement suite their family rented and would lie awake at night and brainstorm ideas.

"We can buy a Volkswagen van and drive there ourselves," Azza might say.

Then Zara, "Or we will convince some cute guys to take us on a road trip and then ditch them in Santa Monica."

"Or we could steal a motorbike and ride it through the desert."

"Or we could buy two one-way tickets to LAX."

"And then we can be in movies together."

"And then we can live in a mansion with lots of boys and have parties every night."

"We will be the most famous twins in the world."

"More famous than the Olsens."

"More famous than the Kardashians, except we'll be twins."

But all their scheming was pointless without money. At fourteen years old, they had few options for work; and, besides that, their strict father forbade them to apply at Dairy Queen or McDonald's. He would only allow them one way to make money: babysitting. Using birthday money from their Uncle Hassan in Syria, they paid for and took the required courses. Then they printed flyers advertising their services and distributed them around the neighbourhood. The very next day they got two calls from two different families at opposite ends of the block. Both wanted the girls for Friday night.

"I don't want to do it alone," Azza said.

"I don't want to, either," said Zara.

"But we should, because it's double the money."

"We can always talk to each other on the phone."

"We can just put the kids to bed early and talk the whole time."

Because she was oldest, Azza picked first. They had always made decisions this way, deferring to the twenty-one-minute gap between them. Azza picked the McCameron family with nine- and seven-year-old girls and a four-year-old boy. The other family, the Eremitas, had only two children, aged one and two years, both boys and both still in diapers. Persons versus poop – that was the trade-off.

The McCamerons lived in a well-manicured dark blue bungalow enclosed on one side by a box hedge and the other by a high white fence. Coming up the front walkway, Azza could see the three children perched like watchful cats on the sofa set against the bay window. They attended to her all the way up the front steps, even to the point of squashing their cheeks against the glass, until Azza rang the doorbell and scattered them loudly into the house.

Mrs. McCameron answered the door. She invited Azza in, then lined her children up in the living room and made them introduce themselves one by one.

"My real name is Georgia," the oldest girl said. "But everybody calls me Peaches because of my hair."

"Not *everybody*," the middle girl said. "I'm Heather, just."

The boy ran up to Azza and, through a forced smile of clenched teeth, said, "My name is Carson. Want to see my Hot Wheels track?"

Mrs. McCameron ushered Carson aside. "You can show it to her later, okay?"

A toilet flush preceded the appearance of Mr. McCameron, rotund, dressed in apple-sack jeans and a loose Henley shirt. "And you must be Zaza," he said.

"Azza," she corrected him. Then, finally greeting the children, "I'm Azza."

Mr. McCameron made a face at his wife. "Oh, I was kind of hoping we'd get the nice one." He winked at Azza. "I'm only kidding, child."

Mrs. McCameron showed Azza where they had written down the emergency contact numbers and gave her instructions on what snacks the children were allowed and what time they were to be put to bed. Then the McCamerons left on their date.

Azza ran straight for the phone and dialled her sister. Peaches and Heather hopped up on the island counter nearby. Carson, meanwhile, ran squealing to the basement.

"Who you calling?" Peaches asked.

"Her boyfriend," said Heather, all long and drawn out.

The call went to voicemail. To spare herself the embarrassment of being left unanswered in front of the girls, Azza muttered, "Wrong number," then hung up. She retreated to the living room.

The girls followed.

"Aren't you going to call again?" Peaches asked.

"Azza's got a boyfriend," Heather sang, "Azza's got a boyfriend."

"I don't have a boyfriend," Azza snapped. "I was calling my sister."

Peaches: "Mom says you're twins."

Heather: "What's it like having a twin?"

Azza had been asked the question hundreds of times before, and whether with Zara or without, she always answered, "Having a twin is like having the best best friend in the world."

"I wish I was a twin," Heather said.

"They'd call us Peaches and Cream."

Just then Carson dashed into the living room and ejected a box of toys across the damaged hardwood floor. Unprompted, he proceeded to show-and-tell Azza every last action figure, Hot Wheel, and Lego man.

"Hey Carson," Peaches said.

"Whhatt?" he groaned.

"Azza's a twin."

"Yeah," Heather said, "there are *two* of her."

Carson's eyes widened. "You have a clone?"

Peaches: "Not a clone, stupid. A *twin*."

"What's the difference between a twin and a clone?"

All three children looked at Azza.

"Twins are born," she answered, blushing. "Clones are made in a lab."

After a combative game of Apples-to-Apples, which Carson won by tantrum, Azza put the children to bed. Peaches and Heather went without an argument, Carson only when Azza promised to read him to sleep. Once she was alone, Azza tried Zara again. This time Zara answered.

"Why didn't you pick up earlier?"

"Can you hear that?" Zara asked.

Azza couldn't hear anything.

"It's the baby. He's talking in his sleep."

"What's he saying?"

"Pff, bah, uh, ff, heh." Zara burst out laughing, and Azza, too.

When they were back home and in their bedroom, Azza and Zara presented their earnings from the night.

"Forty dollars!" Azza was amazed, then swiftly envious. She pouted. "They only gave me twenty."

"Then we'll put twenty dollars each toward California," Zara said. She slipped a twenty between the pages of their copy of *The Breadwinner* and handed the book to Azza to do the same.

"I can't believe they paid you forty dollars."

"Langston did."

"Who?"

"Mr. Eremita."

Henceforth, Azza and Zara babysat for the McCamerons and Mr. Eremita on a weekly basis, always on Fridays. Occasionally they picked up a babysitting gig with another family in the neighbourhood, but these were usually Saturday one-offs or the odd weekday emergency replacement. And they never booked anybody else on Fridays in case of a call. Every so often Azza and Zara would flip through the pages of their books and count the myriad twenties stashed between them. In three years they had saved twenty-five hundred dollars. It might've been more, except that their parents, upon learning how flush they were, started to demand Azza and Zara contribute toward school supplies, clothes, extracurriculars, all things usually provided.

One evening the McCamerons sat seventeen-year-old Azza down on the couch and told her the bad news: now that Peaches was twelve, Azza would no longer be required as a babysitter.

"But," Mrs. McCameron added, "you're always welcome to come by and visit. I know the girls would love to see you."

Zara, of course, continued to babysit for Mr. Eremita, sometimes two, three nights a week. It got to the point Azza was so lonely at home, she actually accepted Mrs. McCameron's invitation to visit the girls. She went every Friday like she used to, or whenever Zara was gone.

At the McCameron's place, Azza would complain about Zara

to Peaches and Heather, who, because they were still very young, were easy sycophants. (Carson never bothered with them anymore, too busy playing *Fortnite* on the TV downstairs.) Though relieving in the moment, the grudge sessions with the McCameron girls often left Azza feeling ashamed, not validated. Every insult directed at Zara, it seemed, was an insult directed at herself – because in every way they used to be the same, in every way that counted. There was a time when she might've gone to Zara with her feelings, might've admitted to her sister, *I am lonely without you, I feel like half myself when you're away*; but something had changed between them lately. Their similarities had shrivelled to surface level, skin deep, a curiosity, nothing more. Azza suspected it was the money. Since being let go by the McCamerons, she had been forced to withdraw some of her contributions from the California fund. A twenty here for a trip to the mall. A twenty there for lunch with friends. And yet she still expected Zara to pay in.

"But it's *my* money."

"And California's *our* dream," Azza reminded her. "Besides, I've paid in just as much as you."

"But you've been taking money *out*."

"If you would let me babysit for Mr. Eremita, then maybe I'd be able to put some money *in*."

One Wednesday before supper, Azza noticed a rash forming on Zara's cheeks. In minutes it had spread over her nose and up her temples and down her neck. She became feverish. Their parents rushed her into the car to drive her to the hospital.

"I don't want to go," Zara said. "I'm supposed to babysit for Langston."

Azza offered to stay behind and go in her place. Their mother handed her a house key out the passenger side window. She watched her family zoom down the street to the stop sign at the McCamerons' end of the block, then speed left toward the hospital. Azza went back inside, ate the half-prepared supper, and did some homework.

At six forty-five she locked the door to their basement suite and walked the alley route to Mr. Eremita's house.

Mr. Eremita owned the smallest house on the block. The house appeared shrunken on its standard sized property, like a cotton shirt accidentally dried. Azza entered through the rear wooden gate. Other than for a new swing set gleaming in the centre of the large circumscribing yard, she could see no obvious signs of children. There were no sounds coming from the house, no faces pressed against the windows in wait.

Azza rang the doorbell.

"Open!" shouted Mr. Eremita.

She went inside. She kicked her shoes off on an empty doormat. Mr. Eremita came around the corner and startled at the sight of her. "Oh! You cut your hair. It looks – good." For some reason she had expected him to be taller than her or, like Mr. McCameron, larger, but skinny Mr. Eremita stood at eye level, and, with his young shaved face and low fade hair, gave Azza the impression not of an adult, but of a new boy at school, perhaps a few grades older, perhaps come back from college to visit a favourite teacher.

At his response Azza almost laughed. He had mistaken her for Zara. She decided it might be fun to pretend; it wouldn't be the first time she had done it. "Yeah, I like it short like this, don't you?" She stroked her hair as she might if it were a fresh cut.

Mr. Eremita smiled, his smooth cheeks inflating. He was duped.

"I made tacos again," he said, disappearing into the house. "They were out of avocados, though, so no guacamole."

Azza listened for the familiar noises of children: pattering feet, high voices, the dull plastic collision of toys. But there was only the radio, playing "What Do You Mean?" from somewhere inside. She turned the corner confidently – and bumped into an open closet door.

Mr. Eremita glided out the kitchen. "What was that?"

"Nothing. I –"

He caressed her shoulder. Azza froze. "You're extra jittery today." He leaned down to kiss her. Azza flinched.

"Azza?"

She tried to break free and run, but Mr. Eremita seized her by the upper arm. His rough fingers gripped to her flesh like Velcro.

"Let me go!"

"Where's Zara?"

"She's in the hospital."

He acted concerned. "What happened?"

Azza wasn't buying it. "Let me go. Or I'll tell."

"Tell what? What's there to tell?"

"You tried to kiss me."

"Not at all," he said. He swung her in close to him. Close enough that she could smell his man's breath, a hint of alcohol, the sour stench of decades lived. "I was leaning down to whisper that I knew it was you. Obviously a bad joke. A stupid joke."

"Where are the children?"

A pause. Then, "They're asleep in their rooms."

"Let me go."

"Look," he said, "your sister and I, the reality is, if you say anything, you'll ruin both our lives. If you tell. Do you realize that? I love your sister very much. What we have is special, rare. A rare thing. Do you know how rare a thing our love is? Because your sister does. And, bec*au*se," his voice cracked, then nosedived low, "because I don't know what I'll have to do if I don't think I can trust you. And I'm having a hard time thinking I can trust you."

Azza felt faint. "No, Mr. Eremita," she begged. "Please, I won't say a thing."

"Good," he said. "Because if you do – it won't matter which one of you I see next – I'll, I'll have to – I'll kill you."

He released her. Azza ran out the back door, tripped over her own feet, and fell flat on her face in the yard. She burst into tears imagining he was behind her, chasing her, that this had been her one chance to get away and she had failed. But when no hands grabbed her to drag her back inside, she scrambled back upright and ran all the rest of the way home.

Azza showered for a long time in the locked bathroom, which was the only door besides the entrance to the basement suite that locked. She brought with her a chef's knife just in case, and set it within reach on the privacy window ledge. While the hot water tranquilized the touch-memory of Mr. Eremita, Azza was terrorized by prognostic visions of a final, violent encounter with the man. She saw him throwing aside the shower curtain. She saw herself reaching for the knife and swinging it at him, saw herself stabbing him in the neck and chest. When she imagined this, she also conversely felt the phantom sensation of a knife sliding into her.

Finished showering, Azza listened at the door of the bathroom. Her heart jumped at every house creak, trying to distinguish between the movements of their landlords above and what might be somebody pacing in the living room, hearing Mr. Eremita everywhere at once, in her parent's bedroom, in the kitchen, shifting on the couch. Her hair had almost dried before she dared venture out. She emerged with the knife pointed in front of her, squeezed inside both hands. She took it to her bedroom and hid it under her mattress, in a spot where she might easily unsheathe it, if he were to come in the night, or be let in by Zara. Stupid, naïve Zara.

Azza tore through her sister's chest of drawers, looking for any proof of their affair. Not that she didn't believe Mr. Eremita, just that she couldn't accept Zara would keep something like this from her. That was what offended Azza most: the secret. Did Zara not think her trustworthy? After she had successfully kept so many other secrets over the years? Secrets like the time Zara stole a Chanel purse from Marjorie in eighth grade and pawned it for California cash. Or when on vacation Zara met Jake at the park and he took her into the woods and showed her his penis. (She never told anybody about that but Azza, and they still joked about it from time to time.) Or how about when she broke the TV while vacuuming and Azza agreed to take the blame for it, because their father always went lighter on her, the eldest. Then again, neither Azza nor Zara had ever been in love before.

Was this the sort of behaviour Azza could expect from her in California?

When the family returned from the hospital, Azza pretended everything was fine. Zara asked her how babysitting went with Mr. Eremita, and Azza shrugged and said it was pretty boring, uneventful. Zara pressed her for more, but Azza feigned fatigue.

"He didn't think you were me?" Zara asked.

"Nope."

"Not even for a second?"

"Not even for a second."

This seemed to satisfy Zara, her nervous curiosity.

Now there were two secrets, one for each of them.

As for what had prompted their visit to emergency, it turned out Zara was showing all the symptoms of lupus, an autoimmune disease.

"If you have it, doesn't that mean I'll get it, too?" Azza asked.

"There's a higher chance," Zara said, "so you'll have to be careful."

But Azza didn't get it. She remained healthy as she had always been. Zara, however, continued to experience flares every couple months or so. Though her case was mild in comparison to others, the doctors advised her to work less, to rest more. This meant no more babysitting for Mr. Eremita. Zara begged their father to allow her just one day a week, but his word was final. And in the end, she submitted. Their mother wondered why Azza would not go in her place. Azza lied that she wanted nothing to do with children anymore. Besides, she and Zara had more than enough put away for California. Three thousand two hundred dollars the last time she counted.

On the day of their eighteenth birthdays, Azza and Zara went with school friends to the Saanich Fair. They rode the Zipper and ogled boys. They bought elephant ears and petted the cows and horses. They might've stayed for the concert and the fireworks, but after a long day in the sun, the party had wound down by six. Their father picked them up. Azza and Zara were quiet the whole ride home. He asked them what was the matter. They said it was nothing, and he let it go.

Back in their bedroom, Azza removed two brand new suitcases from their hiding place behind her wardrobe. She handed one to Zara and opened hers on her bed. She began to pack.

A moment later Azza noticed Zara hadn't moved. "Why aren't you packing?"

"I'm not going."

"What do you mean you're not going?"

"I'm going to stay."

Azza started packing for her.

Zara wrestled her clothes back. "I mean it, Azza. I'm not going."

"Why? Because of–" She almost said it, but stopped herself.

Zara's eyes steeped in a shallow pool of tears.

Azza angled her head toward her suitcase to hide tears of her own. "We'll talk about this more tomorrow," she said. "But *I'm* still packing."

In the morning Azza called a taxi. Then she told their father about Mr. Eremita.

Their mother's wailing woke Zara, who had slept in.

"How could you disgrace us? How could you disgrace us?"

One look at Azza and Zara knew. She ran out the door after their father, screaming his name and Langston's as she ran. Their mother gave chase.

In the suddenly silent basement suite, Azza held their books one by one above her suitcase and flipped through the pages. Landed atop her things, the twenty-dollar bills seemed much more than there really were, like millions of dollars lay piled underneath them, and this fantasy of limitless wealth provoked such a rush of adrenaline that she could hardly zip the suitcase up.

#15 *Tilikum, The Killer Whale*

ON FEBRUARY 24, 2010, Tilikum swam onto the shallow deck of Shamu Stadium at SeaWorld Orlando for a relationship session with Dawn Brancheau. Though witness reports differ in their explanation of how the orca seized her, some say by her drifting hair, others by her arm or shoulder, almost as soon as the session began, Tilikum dragged Brancheau off the deck into the deep centre of the tank and, over a period of several minutes, mauled and drowned her. Thus she became the third victim in a killing spree beginning twenty years earlier with Keltie Byrne. A championship swimmer and student at the University of Victoria, Byrne had been similarly "pulled" into the performance tank at the now defunct Sealand of the Pacific, and drowned. Between these two, Tilikum also killed Daniel Dukes, a twenty-seven-year-old homeless man. (Dukes had hidden on the grounds of SeaWorld beyond closing time and attempted a midnight swim with the whale. Employees discovered his body the next morning draped naked over Tilikum's back.)

All three killings occurred within an approximate decade of each other, as if to suggest a mad internal clock at work. This is especially true in regard to the trainers Byrne and Brancheau, who were killed twenty years apart virtually to the day, February 20 and February 24 respectively. Certainly it could be argued that this periodicity was coincidence, to use a phrasing often reserved for serial murderers, merely crimes of convenience which happened to concur. Using the same comparison, an argument could also be made in favour of the timely explosion of a murderous desire kept too long at bay.

But the question remains: if Tilikum found pleasure in killing, then why did he not take every opportunity presented him to kill? Perhaps it is not, as some have suggested, that he was naturally violent, or even psychotic, but that, when confronted with the inescapable reality of the pen, he saw no other recourse for rebellion against his condition *except* violence.

TILIKUM WAS BORN in December 1981 in the North Atlantic. For just under two years, he lived with his mother as part of an East North Atlantic transient whale pod, until his capture by Don Goldsberry on November 9, 1983. Seven years previous, in 1976, the state of Washington had passed legislation banning the capture and sale of orcas around Puget Sound. This move was mainly a direct reaction to the discovery of four orca carcasses washed ashore, which Goldsberry and his crew had attempted to sink by tying anchors to their flukes and stuffing rocks inside their abdomens. Forced to look elsewhere, Goldsberry turned his sights to the waters off Iceland. There, he would capture Tilikum, as well as Nootka and Haida, all three of which would be sold, after a year of holding at the Hafnarfjördur Marine Zoo, to Sealand of the Pacific in Victoria, British Columbia.

In the fourteen years before Tilikum, Nootka, and Haida arrived, seven whales had died while under the care and custody of Sealand. (Rare is an orca who survives longer than a decade in captivity, in large part due to their susceptibility to disease, often of the lungs.) As an attraction, Sealand was relatively limited, boasting a single performance pool circumscribed by a floating dock one hundred feet long by fifty feet wide and enclosed by a net thirty-five feet deep. Behind the performance pool sat a concrete "module" about one third the size. Trainers of Tilikum closer to the time of Byrne's death praised him for his quick learning, eagerness, and sociability. Unfortunately, Nootka and Haida did not share the trainers' opinion. The two female orcas regularly bullied Tilikum through the act of "raking," using their teeth to scrape, to bite. This negative behaviour was only exacerbated by the deprivation-chamber-like setting of the module, where the orcas were packed fin to fin for fourteen hours at night to avoid possible release by saboteurs. At one point the relationship between the whales was so poor that Tilikum refused to enter the module, even at the risk of starvation, for it was there that they were also fed. Of course, the strained relationship was only one of many explanations for his reluctance. With the second-largest brains on the planet, orcas are intelligent mammals with highly developed insula, the part of the brain that regulates self-awareness and emotion. It is not hard to imagine the terrible cost to such a mind when deprived of light, sound, space, and sleep,[1] day in and day out, for years and years.

1 Cetaceans, which include species such as dolphins and porpoises, sleep on the move, resting one half of their brain at a time, while the other half carries out the diving and breaching motions required for breathing. Thus, for them, sleep requires generous space to carry on uninterruptedly.

The general belief is that when Keltie Byrne slipped on the deck and fell into the performance pool, Tilikum reacted to the stimulation with a perverse excitement. Though local media reported the cause of Byrne's death either misleadingly as a drowning or inexactly as a frenzy, witnesses Corinne Cowell and Nadine Kallen in the film *Blackfish* place sole responsibility on the orca with "the flopped over fin," that is, Tilikum. According to them, Nootka and Haida simply swam circles around the two. But there were reasons both financial and litigatory to deny such testimony. And, ultimately, it was this calculated obfuscation that led to Tilikum being sold to SeaWorld for one million dollars, instead of rightly released or euthanized.

For SeaWorld, acquiring a male orca was important for their incipient captivity breeding program. Over the years Tilikum would assist in the conception of, by some estimates, twenty-one calves. (Some sources report his genes as being found in fifty-four percent of SeaWorld's orcas.) At the same time he participated in the daily shows, but mostly in a limited capacity: perimeter pec waves,[2] photos at the underwater port, wetting audiences in the splash zone. Though SeaWorld never admitted to Tilikum's violent history, they nevertheless discouraged their trainers from performing water work with the whale.

The day he attacked Dawn Brancheau, Tilikum was denied food after failing to respond to Brancheau's whistle to end his perimeter pec wave. Was this denial of food, as some have suggested, the objective reason for his fatal assault? Perhaps it was one reason, but not the only one; the starker realities of Tilikum's day-to-day life must also be taken into consideration. In the wild, orcas swim for hundreds of kilometres, eat fastidiously, and are in the constant presence of

2 When an orca performs a circuit of the pool and waves his or her dorsal fin for the crowd.

friends and relatives, sometimes in pods of twenty or more. They are polyandrous and have varied sex lives. Comparatively, Tilikum's life at SeaWorld was like that of a prisoner in solitary confinement, including allotted time for exercise/performance, the minimum daily requirement of food, and spurious social encounters. (Not to mention frequent masturbation by a foreign species, recalling to mind the more cartoonish depictions of alien abduction.) Put a human being in similarly deprived conditions and it is easy to understand why some prisons make their bedsheets out of paper. It could be argued that Tilikum's attacks were just that: misguided attempts at suicide. Many species of animals have been reported to have "committed suicide," though, with the possible exception of elephants, only cetaceans may be intellectually capable of the act, due to the aforementioned insula. The link between violence and suicide has been well-documented. According to Hentig (1948), they are, in fact, "complementary phenomena." It is not out of the realm of possibility then that Tilikum, having no option for suicide, embraced suicide's complement, murder, for the solution to his problem of living. This might even explain the bizarre draping of Daniel Dukes over his back, as if Tilikum were saying, here, look what I've done, I have made no attempt to hide it, do with me what you will.

RETURNING TO VICTORIA, I check in to my room at the Oak Bay Beach Hotel, then walk Beach Road to the Oak Bay Marina, formerly Sealand of the Pacific. Tomorrow I will fly to Orlando and meet my girlfriend Helen and our five-year-old daughter Nella at SeaWorld. After my overnight on the mountain with Richard, I am thankful for the extra day.

At the entrance to the marina stands a statue of an orca: head-twisted, mid-breach, its saddle splattered in seagull shit. Whether this is a leftover relic of Sealand or a memorial to its demise, I cannot tell. (Later, the clerk at the gift shop will direct me to it when I ask her for further information.) Either way, the statue is obviously of little importance to the groundskeepers. They seem content to relegate the duty of cleaning it to the rain, which is doing a poor job. I park my car and proceed first to Marina Restaurant and Dockside Eatery for an early lunch. I ask for a spot on the patio where I can overlook what used to be the location of the performance pool, since converted to docks to accommodate additional moorings.

When Sealand of the Pacific was still in operation, the colour scheme was blue and white, as in the style of modern Greece. Now the buildings are painted a significantly less dynamic beige and wood brown. All that remains of the vibrant old pattern are the matching blue sail covers and the white sailboats moored here today. I peer over the railing into the murky green water and sigh. I cannot begin to imagine what it must've been like for Tilikum to inhabit such polluted waters. Victoria is infamous for being the last major coastal city to stop pumping raw sewage into the ocean. Cognizant of this fact, I am perhaps more surprised that Tilikum survived long enough to kill than I am that he killed at all.

I ask the young server if she knows anybody I might speak to who was around during the time of Sealand and Tilikum.

"I don't know," she says. "That was a long time ago."

"Not too long ago," I say.

"Before I was born."

Five minutes later she returns with an apology: there is nobody from that era still working here. I thank her for her trouble. She refills my empty water glass and floats to the next table.

I wander the docks, hoping to run into somebody, anybody old enough to remember, even vaguely, Sealand of the Pacific. Ideally,

I would want to speak with a person who attended one of Tilikum's shows. But the docks are vacant, the sailboats are vacant or appear vacant, and I am alone. It is at this point I stop in at the gift shop and am pointed toward the statue. I pass by it on my way back to the hotel.

In my room I transcribe the notes from my notebook to my computer. If I were any less of a procrastinator, I might attempt a draft of the article now. I certainly have enough material to work with. But where to begin? And for whom am I writing this article? Who is my audience? Helen would tell me there is no audience for articles on suicide. It doesn't matter how good the stories are, no one wants to read about people (or orcas) forced to the limits of their tolerance of life, who do not then step back from the edge. And I will say the article is not about suicide: it is about choice.

But the article is about neither, really. It is about me. This trip – it is a trial of my life without her. I have taken this week off to contemplate things. The time has come for me to decide what sort of life I want to commit to. Resigning is to commit without serious consideration, and I do not want to resign. It would not be fair to Helen. Or especially Nella.

I call down to the front desk and order a cab. I need a drink and would rather not have one at the hotel bar. When I am in the cab, the driver asks me where I want to go. I tell him anywhere downtown. He drops me off in front of the Strathcona Hotel. Before I leave, he gives me his phone number to call when I want a ride back later in the night. I wonder if I have overtipped him.

Adjacent to the hotel lobby is a dive bar called Big Bad John's. The floor inside is covered in peanut shells. There are so many that even with loud country music playing overhead I can hear them crunching underfoot. Bras hang from the ceiling like paper cranes over the bed of a dying Don Juan. Notes to lovers and friends tattoo the walls, which are also tacked with foreign currencies and faded Polaroids. I order a pint of Phillips Blue Buck at the bar and take it to a table in the corner. Each table has its own plastic bucket of peanuts. I drink, deshell peanuts, munch, crumble the husks onto the floor. Most of the clientele here are older, like me. There are middle-aged women in groups of three or four, looking around, hoping to have their glances reciprocated, and an equal number of solitary men too intimidated by their numbers to approach them. I realize it's for reasons as simple as this that so many of us are alone.

"Can I sit here?" The woman who asks this question sits before I answer. She sets her drink down. Dark eyebrows curved inquisitively, she looks left, then right. I guess correctly that she is searching for her own bucket of peanuts and offer to share mine. She laughs. "Was I that obvious?"

She tells me her name is Irene.

"Are you local?" I almost say resident.

She nods. "And you?"

"Transient."

"Hmmm." Irene withdraws her hand from my peanut bucket to her lap. A phone screen illuminates her round face from below the table line.

"A stupid joke," I say, recovering. "I'm writing an article about orcas. Transients are one type of killer whale. Although I suppose they're called Bigg's now. I was trying to say that I'm not from here."

"Oh, I love killer whales!" She sets her phone right-side up on the table and leans toward me. I pick up the smell of cigarettes wafting off her jacket. "Tell me something else."

I think for a second. "Did you know orcas live in matriarchal societies? And sons never leave their mothers' sides. They stay with them until the end of their lives."

"Orcas and elephants," Irene says. "Two of the smartest animals on the planet, and they both live in matriarchies." She gestures to the ceiling with crossed fingers. "Soon, one day soon."

For the next two hours we drink, eat, tell our life stories, talk politics. With some careful maneuvering, I avoid mentioning my girlfriend and our daughter. After every drink, we step outside for a cigarette. I am stumbling by our third trip to the curb. I lean on her shoulder and grab her waist. I justify these physical contacts as necessary for balance. I do not see her kiss coming until it is too late. Because it is already in progress, I permit myself this brief infidelity. Passersby hoot at us.

When eventually I manage to pull away, she asks me back to her place.

"I can't," I say. "I shouldn't. I have a girlfriend. We – we have a little girl."

"I didn't know."

"I didn't tell you."

Irene scoffs. "Unbelievable. *Men*." She flags the nearest cab, and is gone from my life as abruptly as she entered it.

I call the cab driver from earlier. He is there within minutes. I don't have to tell him where to take me. He remembers. Neither one of us says a word the entire ride back. He must know that I am drunk, but for whatever reason I feel the urge, for his sake, to pretend that I'm not, merely brooding over the events of the night.

We are passing in front of the marina when I ask him to stop.

"You want off here?"

"Here is fine," I say.

The fare is fourteen dollars. I give him twenty dollars and tell him to keep the change. He thanks me profusely; I have made his night. But I am trying to buy forgiveness when it must be given.

And, anyway, he isn't even the right person to give it. The marina gate is locked. I manage to scale the fence and drop down on the other side. I wander to the end of the docks. I have needed to pee for a while now and unzip my pants to do it. It feels a sacrilegious act, all things considered. And yet I am only human. Midstream, a wave arrives that bucks the particular spot where I'm standing, and I think how appropriate it would be if I fell – at the exact moment I lose my balance. The icy ocean water sobers me instantly. I scramble back onto the docks and crawl on my hands and knees away from the edge. I spit repeatedly to clear the dirty water from my lips.

Tonight has been a disaster. I am thirty-three years old, the same number of years Tilikum spent in captivity before his death in 2017. I want to go home. I want to be with my family again. Tomorrow I will tell Helen everything that happened, and if she forgives me, I will ask her to marry me. My mind is made up. I cannot wait to put this awful chapter of my life behind me.

#16 Release, the Sequel to "Hard Time"

BEFORE I TELL YOU THE STORY of how I got out, I want to clear the air on all that don't-drop-the-soap-in-the-shower bullshit. Like a prisoner was ever in fear of getting raped chasing after a bar of soap. Take it from me, bent over is not the time to worry. The time to worry is when you're standing up. Standing too close to the wall. It's a slippery business, rape. You need to brace the rapee up against something. Not that I know how to do it, I only know how it's done. And then there's that whole thing about prisoners tying bars of soap around their wrists. You think any of us have the patience to be drilling holes in here? Pun intended. Not to mention if they gave us even six inches of rope there'd be a suicide party worse than Jonestown. The bastards need us alive. How else are the fine folks of Kansas going to get their license plates?

So no. Nobody's getting raped bent over in a shower. And nobody's tying soap bars to their wrist. And if you want to know the truth about rape in prison, it's that, eventually, everybody has their turn against the wall. And the less you fight it, the better it will be for everybody in the end.

Now back to how I got out.

In prison there are only two ways you're leaving. Three if you count in a body bag. But typically, you escape or you're paroled. And because you can never be too certain which one will work out for you, you have to give equal attention to both. I knew a guy named Theo spent thirty years doing everything possible for a ticket out on good behaviour. Running Bible club. Making buddy-buddy with the COs. Volunteering for every shit-cleaning, bootlicking, ass-kissing project the Warden dumped on us. During the Single-Ply riot, Theo offered himself up to be our ransom for the TP we wanted. Ended up with a nasty scar on the neck for that one. Then came his parole hearing. CO after CO after CO affirmed his upstanding record. Every pastor, priest, teacher, imam testified to his wonderful character, his loving kindness for his fellow inmates. Theo helped. Theo listened. Theo prayed and baptized and saved. Theo was the best goddamn prisoner we ever had. Those were the Warden's words. The fucking Warden! But in the end Theo's request was denied. Turns out it doesn't matter how nice and kind you are when you're a child molester. Poor Theo. He never had a chance. They took away his bedsheets soon after for fear of suicide. But Theo found a way around that. He started telling anybody and everybody what he had done to end up here. And got shanked shortly thereafter.

Same thing happened to Pineapple. Except where Theo pinned all his hopes on parole, Pineapple pinned all his hopes on escape. And since this story of mine is about finding a balance between the two, it's best you hear examples of both.

Pineapple was called Pineapple for two reasons. First, because his name was Dale, like Dole with an A. But the second and main reason was that he had hard dry skin that scabbed and peeled off in big brown flakes like pineapple scales. To me they looked like the rotten communion wafers they handed out during service. And I was right, because one day they caught Pineapple mixing them in. Been doing it for years apparently. Anyway, because of his skin condition, everybody steered clear of Pineapple, even the rapists. This gave him a lot of privacy to plan his escape. He acquired a Shawshank starter kit and chiselled his way into the vent above his cell. He crawled around in there for a while. Dropping flakes on the other prisoners. Searching for an exit. Eventually, he found one, and got so excited he decided right then and there to escape. Poor Pineapple. He dropped into the control desk, strangled the CO to death, then tried to buzz himself out. Problem was you had to hold the buzzer to keep the door unlocked. So he kept going back and forth buzzing and trying the door and buzzing again. When the COs found him, they beat him paralyzed. He's been shitting himself in solitary ever since. Used to be Theo cleaned him up. It's me who does it now.

But I digress.

My name's Robert Crawley. I'm five foot two, one hundred and sixty pounds. Shaved head. Stubble like cracked pepper. Mouth like a gummy horse. And I killed my father thirteen days shy of my eighteenth birthday. Don't know who I heard it from that I'd get hardly a slap on the wrist that way, but I woke up one morning and thought, well, shit, it's now or never. So I took a crack at the old man. And cracked the back of his head open. He beat me for so many years I learned the best approach is to sneak up on the person from behind. Take them by surprise. Imagine my surprise when they tried me as an adult.

"Life!" Judge Faartz ordained.

"Jesus!" Mom wept.

"Fuck!" I hollered.

Judge Faartz added six months for that one. Bringing my sentence to a total of six months plus life. No possibility of parole, either. Life plus six months. Meaning I wasn't getting out alive or dead. Meaning if Mom's Rapture ever came, the cops would be right there by my graveside waiting with Ghostbuster-grade handcuffs to float me back in. Needless to say I spent the next fourteen years doing pretty much anything I wanted. Because why not? Wanking every night. Telling off COs. Shanking pedos. All that run-of-the-mill sort of stuff. Although there was that one time I spat on Officer Oink for rough-handling the love of my life. *Delilah*. My Delilah. But I never killed anybody. I never raped anybody. And I got along well with the other prisoners.

Then 2007 passed, and the Great State of Kansas decided I was thirteen days away from knowing what in the hell I was doing.

I still remember when my lawyer Colonel told me the news. Colonel prefers to be called Doc or Dr. Bailey. But I call him Colonel on account of he's always dressed in white. White suit. White shirt. White shoes. Mom hired him straight off the billboard. 1-800-Doc-Bail. Hundred bucks an hour, lowest rate in the city. *If he don't get your client out, we pay you!* As the jingle goes.

"Your sentence has been commuted. That means –"

"Don't patronise me, Colonel."

"Let me put it simply then," he said. "In one year's time you'll be eligible for parole. Congratulations, Robert. You're getting out."

I jumped across the table to hug him. "Glory! Glory! Hallelujah!"

"No touching!" shouted a CO. A bunch of them pounced on me, but I held onto the Colonel like he was Delilah in another flesh. They struck me a few times in the back until I let go. Spat up some blood on his fancy white suit. Oops.

Mom got the bill the next day. Three thousand bucks plus six hundred for the suit. They always get you with those hidden fees, I told her. That white devil tricked her into signing a double or nothing deal courtesy of the jingle. Of course, it seemed pretty reasonable at the time.

Mom took my hands. "Let us pray for deliverance from this debt."

She closed her eyes. I took the opportunity to check out some of the New Guys' mothers and sisters and girlfriends. Hell, these days even the grandmas had me growing in the pants.

"Dear Lord, I pray that my son Robert stays in prison –"

"Hey!"

"– just as long as it takes me to raise the money to pay back this debt. But I thank you for providing him an opportunity for release. Amen."

Next visitation Mom claimed Jesus had come to her in a dream.

"And He was holding a book with the title 11," she said. "And He handed me the key to the lock on the book. And I opened the book and found a zero written on every page. Don't you think it sounds like prophecy?"

"He's telling you to declare bankruptcy, Momma." Clever one that Jesus.

"Bankruptcy?"

"Just make sure you move all your junk to Marcy's first," I said. "The stamps and coins. All the shit they might mistake for valuables."

"Mind your language, Robert."

"Shit, piss, cunt."

"Robert!"

They denied me my first parole hearing and my second. Two years I wasted doing nothing when I could've been planning my escape. Same mistake Theo made, except I should've been smarter than him and wasn't. Like I said, you have to find a balance. You can't rely on the sympathy of judges and COs. And especially now there are so many women on the board. One look at me and it didn't matter how good my record was. No woman wants ugly on the street.

I found that balance in Pineapple. Poor paralyzed Pineapple. In exchange for a clean record, I agreed to hose him down twice a week. The COs were more than happy to arrange it, having been stuck washing him themselves since Theo died. I figured while I was in there, I could squeeze Pineapple for information. Work out the kinks in his failed escape plan. Because they fed him the same food day in day out, I got used to the smell of his shit pretty quickly. Soon I could stroll in there without a tickle. I always started with a blast of water to his face to wake him up. Moaning and groaning, he'd say hello. Pineapple was all but blind and dumb at this point. Only so much silence and darkness a man can take before it takes him, too.

"Uhh, Uhhhhh." *Hey, Robert.* It was a while before I understood him, but the words were there for anybody who cared to listen.

I fingered the nozzle. "You ready?"

Pineapple nodded. As he was nodding up, I took aim and got him in the nostrils. He sputtered and coughed. "Uh uhhh!" *No fair!* Nostrils, ear holes, asshole, mouth. That was the game we played: nostrils, ear holes, asshole, mouth. I'd chase him around like a carny after a circus seal and every miss he'd get a point and every hit I'd get a point. And by the end he'd be squeaky clean.

"My count is twenty-five to two. Final score."

"Uhhhh-uhhh uh *uhhhh*."

I rolled my eyes. "Fine, twenty-five to three. Either way it's a goddamn blowout."

Pineapple peeled off a scab and set it on a stream of water running down the drain. Years of darkness had worsened his condition to the point where he looked more sewer crocodile than human. Never fazed me. But nobody else could stand the sight of him.

For weeks I had cozied up to Pineapple with the intention of asking where he hid his chisel. A chisel was any prisoner's Holy Grail. Worth ten times more than cigarettes or a pass to the conjugal. The story of his escape I got out of him without even asking. He explained the route he took through the vents and the problems he encountered along the way. The mechanics of the buzzer. The timing of the CO routes. Meanwhile, all the guards listening in heard was "uhhhhh" and variations thereof. But Pineapple never revealed where he kept his chisel. Didn't even hint at it. That chisel was his closest secret. Pineapple guarded it like his asshole, which counted for double points.

I propped myself against the squeaky-clean toilet. Pineapple seal-walked next to me and folded himself into what might pass for a casual recline. "You know what, Pineapple?" I asked.

"Uhhh?"

"Much as I love hosing you down every Tuesday and Saturday, I feel I'm meant for greater things. Love and power and such." I splashed some water from the toilet bowl over my face. Pineapple had made me work for it today.

"Uhhh'h uhhh uhhh uhh uhhh?"

"No, that *was* my sentence," I said. "But not anymore. Been eligible for parole for three years now."

Pineapple asked me why I was still here then.

"They don't like the look of me. Can't stand my look. You understand that more than most. It's these gums. These god-awful gums. With you it's skin, with me it's gums. And I suppose my lips, too. They're thin and too red. Hell, you've seen them! It's the small differences that make all the difference, Pineapple. One hiccup in the womb and whole worlds close to you. You think I'd be in here if I didn't sicken everyone who looked at me? Give me a nice smile and I'd be president. Give me a thick set of lips and I'd be sucking on pussy instead of sucking back vomit at the sight of you. No offense."

"Uhhh uhhhh."

"I guess what I'm saying is, Justice is the type of bitch to put her hand over her eyes and peek between the fingers." I leaned in and whispered, "I guess what I'm saying is, I'm breaking out of here and I need your help."

Pineapple made a wide sweeping gesture to his legs and around the room.

"Your chisel, Pineapple," I continued to whisper. "I want your chisel."

He shook his head and tried to crawl away. I grabbed him by the socks and dragged him back.

"Listen, Pineapple. I'll make you a deal. No, a promise. You help me with this, and I'll tell your story. I'll blow the lid wide open on the way they've mistreated you in here. How's this for a headline: Disabled Prisoner Spends Days Wallowing in Own Feces. Warden Says, 'Never Again.' What do you think of that, buddy? Imagine buzzing around the yard in your own motorized wheelchair. People will be lining up for rides for days. You'll be the most popular prisoner in all Lansing!"

And with that I rested. No matter if it was all a ruse. I just needed him to tell me where the damn thing was. He owed it to me as far as I was concerned. For all the joy I'd given him the past couple months. For every half-digested cornbread and oat I swallowed back to spare his feelings.

He sighed. "U uhh uh uh uhh uhhhhh uhhhhhhhhh."

"You're a saint, Pineapple. A real saint." Without thinking I kissed his forehead. Beyond pretending now, I dove into the toilet and thrashed my head around inside it. I must've flushed four times just to be sure I got all of him off me. When I resurfaced, I saw Pineapple had tears in his eyes. Tears of affection. Tears of his loneliness broken through. Even in the dark I could see them streaming down his cheeks. Damn that hit me hard. Must have been decades since anybody touched him. Touched his skin.

I found the chisel screwed inside the fourth showerhead just like Pineapple said. Made sense now why the damn thing had the water pressure of a diabetic's squirt. I took it back to my cell and stuffed it in my mattress along with all the other contraband. Toothbrush shiv. An unopenable History of the Bikini *TIME* magazine. Ciggies for trade. Then I waited for lights out.

Soon as it was dark, I leapt from my top bunk and woke Juan, my cellmate, below. Juan was what we in prison call a whimperer. I liked whimperers. Whimperers were easy to manipulate. In the pecking order they were one step above bitches, who themselves were one step above rats. Juan was given life for being the driver on a robbery turned deadly. Drivers invariably end up bitches or whimperers because driving is bitch or whimper work.

"Get up, muchacho. I need your help."

He snorted. "What do you need?"

"I need you to prop me up while I chisel this vent."

"All right, homes."

Juan held me aloft while I chiselled away at the vent. I felt a bit like Michelangelo suspended there above his head. Doing God's work. But instead of ropes: Juan's tiny fingers trembling against my shoulder blades. Wasn't long before he started whimpering, and it was the perfect cover for all the chiselling I had to do. Five nights in a row we did that. I gave him a break every hour or two. Juan even thanked me for them.

Finally, I popped the vent out. With a boost from Juan, I scrambled inside. Among my contraband I also had a keychain flashlight. I shone it ahead and crawled. I followed Pineapple's roundabout directions to the CO desk. It might've been a lot quicker but for the skeleton of Benjamin Franklin – the prisoner, not the patriot – blocking the way. Whose disappearance was never solved, but whose discovery by Pineapple explained the dead possum smell Lansing put up with for that year and a half back in the mid-'90s. I located the CO desk, and then headed back to my cell. Unfortunately, it was too tight to turn around, so I had to make a loop.

And that was when I passed over George. Ol' Georgie. George "John Wayne" Holcombe. Ex-fiancé of my Delilah. Delilah used to come to visitation to see me. But of course she had to sit with George to keep up appearances. Affairs are complicated in prison. It's a lot of glancing and lip biting and mouthing words. George was a minor offender given two years. I conned him into starting a riot, to keep him in and keep her coming. But it worked out one way and not the other.

Long story short I needed to know where she lived for when I got out. And it seemed fate that I had to pass over his cell on the way back to mine. I knew just how to do it, too. One night George admitted he had this recurring nightmare about leprechauns. He hated leprechauns. Leprechauns scared the shit out of him. In the nightmare he was trapped in a house of leprechauns. It was a normal house, and they were a perfectly normal family aside from being leprechauns. And George was their full-sized human baby. They would spoon feed him. Say gootchy gootchy goo. Many nights I woke up to him screaming just that. Lucky for me, Robert Crawley, Irish as Irish be, the leprechaun's voice was my easiest impression. In another life it'd be the voice I grew up with.

I beamed the flashlight into his face. "Gootchy gootchy goo," I said. "Gootchy gootchy goo, Georgie."

He screamed.

"Shhhhhhher! Keep 'er down, Georgie! Keep yer goddamn trap shut!"

"Anything you want. Please, I'll do anything."

"But we want yer soul. I're be waitin' fer you at hoame, Georgie. Gootchy gootchy goo."

"No, no, no." He grabbed what remained of his hair and pulled out large chunks of it. I could tell he was on the verge of a nervous breakdown. About to plunge off a cliff into his vanishing place. I got straight to the point.

"We need a soul, Georgie. It's yer soul er another."

"Anyone," he pleaded. "I'll give you anyone."

"We want Deliler. Give us Deliler."

"Take her. She's yours!"

"We need 'er address."

"50 SW 93rd Street. Please."

"Is that Warkerersa er . . . ?"

"Yes, Wakarusa."

"If we find out yer tellin' lies, Georgie, wer'll be back fer blood. Gootchy gootchy goo!"

"I promise. She's there. She'll be there!"

Easy as that. I turned off the flashlight and crawled back to my cell.

In two weeks' time I had another parole hearing, so I figured I'd give them a chance to deny me again before trying Pineapple's way out. Day of, Colonel dressed me in my brand new used white suit. Dry cleaned, bill still attached. The cleaners had gotten my blood down from crime scene photograph to ketchup stain. Like a bit had fallen out the back of a hot dog onto my shoulder. Colonel led me into the hearing room. I smiled at Judge Faartz and the day's lottery of female doctors, psychologists, and bureaucrats. Every last one turned white at the sight of me. Like my suit colour was contagious. Go figure. I hadn't said.a word yet and already my case was lost. But that wouldn't stop Colonel from whooping after his three thousand bucks.

"Let the record show that my client Robert Crawley has an exemplary record."

"Mm," I said.

"He has served twenty-five years for his first crime, which was his only crime."

"Mm."

My churchy encouragement spurred Colonel's oratory. His voice soared. "This is the third time I've brought him before this boarrrrrd. Must I bring him three years morrrrre? Are we not called upon, ladies and gentlemen, to show him the mercy of our Lorrrrrd?"

"That's right! Preach!"

Judge Faartz fumbled for his gavel. "Order! Order! The court demands Mr. Crawley save his hallelujahs for the pews."

Colonel didn't look back at me. Just waved his hand as if signalling a barking dog to shush. "My client offers up his apologies." He continued, "What I mean to ask is, Your Honour, is there nothing my client can do to gain your approval? If a perfect record and twenty-five years does nothing to persuade you, then it behooves me to ask the court, what will?"

Judge Faartz thought about it for a moment. He whispered to

the woman on his left and woman on his right. They shook their heads. Ugly loses again.

"This court denies Mr. Crawley parole on account of the lack of respect he has consistently shown these proceedings. It is hard to believe he has learned anything in prison at all, and I am not convinced that, if released, he will not continue in a life of crime. This hearing is adjourned."

Two burly COs appeared behind me to escort me out. Batons already drawn. They knew me well. I rushed at Judge Faartz. Not that I would actually do anything. But I wanted to see him cower. Emasculate the man in front of his harem. He squeaked like a caught mouse. Before the guards could beat me, I pissed myself, which made them back off. Then I straightened my tie and walked out of there with my dignity. What was left of it running down my leg.

That night Juan boosted me into the vent for my escape. I gave him my *TIME* magazine as a parting gift and he whimpered so loud for gratitude I could hear him all the way to the control desk. Once there I waited for the CO to leave on a bathroom break. Unlike Pineapple, I was no killer. But for that one time, which was really thirteen days away from counting. If you haven't killed before, I'll tell you: in the moment it really fucks you up. Body and mind. The soul part comes later. It's the adrenaline that does it. Does weird things to your body, adrenaline. Things you can't plan for or expect. I had a hard-on for hours after killing my father. Nothing sexual about it. Another guy told me his eyebrows fell out. Just all at once fell out like leaves off a tree. Poor bastard had done everything he could to hide his DNA. Shaving his arms. Wearing a hairnet. A beardnet. But in the end eyebrows was how they caught him.

Pineapple had the right idea dropping down into the control room and buzzing out. But when he killed the CO, he lost his goddamn marbles. There's nothing too obvious to miss on the other side of murder. It's why the prison is bursting with us. Why they're always running out of cells. My plan was to stab my toothbrush shiv into the computer chair and then jam the chair under the counter with the shiv pressing against the buzzer. Pineapple might've used a pen, had he been thinking straight.

This next part might be hard to believe, but I swear it's the way it happened.

About two hours in this big Black CO appeared out of nowhere and pulled out his big black cock, and the CO at the desk started sucking him off. They were lovers, I guess. He used the best technique I'd ever seen. I didn't want to watch, but I was amazed. I couldn't look away. Witness to a master craftsman at his work. With ten thousand hours of blowjobs behind him. And after they went skipping to clean off, I realized this blowjob was a divine gift. Providence. Because to keep their secret, they would have to keep my secret. Because in the end it didn't matter about rights or marriage or any of that equality crap. Because when you're this far south, a faggot is a faggot is a faggot.

I dropped into the control desk, stabbed the shiv into the chair, and jammed it under the desk. Then I ran out the control desk and out the front door. The Black CO must've been the tower guard, because the watchtower was empty. Another blessing in a night full of them. Either way I ran zigzag just in case. A bunch of us had watched a guy get blown away once running for the fence. We cheered him on from our cells all the while the bullets were whizzing through him. And still he kept going. Until his head exploded and his momentum with it.

I stripped naked of my prison clothes and sprinted into the wheat fields. I was free! Free! And I knew just where I was going first. At the highway a kind trucker picked me up. Truckers will pick up anybody for a good story. Doesn't matter if you're a prisoner or a prostitute or a prig, but you better have a good story. And naked me told that trucker the best story he had heard in years. He gave me a spare set of clothes and dropped me off at Delilah's. Door-to-door service courtesy of America's lifeblood.

I fell asleep in the fields out front to wait for morning. There was something I needed to tell her, and I planned on doing it first thing. The sun woke me bright and early. I crouched in the tall grass and waited for Delilah to come down the drive.

Then I saw her. She had me weeping at the sight of her. I sprang up and ran to her.

"Delilah!"

The look of surprise on her face told me just what I needed to know. That she never could've believed I would be here. My Delilah. Like I was the last person she expected to find waiting outside her door.

So it made sense when she pepper sprayed me. That was just like her. Her sense of humour. The taser didn't land as well comedically, but I let her zap me once or twice anyway. Tell you the truth, I lost count. But if she was having fun doing it, then I was having fun taking it. She ran screaming and crying back inside her farmhouse. Meanwhile, I lay there twitching on the ground, trying to shake off the electricity, with a big smile on my face thinking how excited she must be to have me back.

I never did get to tell her all the things I wanted. To tell her that I loved her. That it wasn't just about her tits and ass, but the small something in her soul only I could see. I wanted to tell her she had stopped me obsessing about Catherine, the cunt, which was what no woman had ever done before. Or ever could. And it was too bad because ten minutes later, I heard sirens coming down the road and realized if I didn't leave now, then I'd never see her again. They'd drag me back to Lansing and throw me in solitary next to Pineapple.

Sometime in the future I'd be back. Until then I was on the lam. A proper fugitive like I'd always dreamed. With enough stories to get me anywhere. Halfway around the world if I wanted. The next trucker who picked me up didn't even ask where I was going. I started talking as soon as we set off. "If there were a prettier girl in all Topeka, I had never seen her."

#17 *A Deserted Island*

KATSUMI DID NOT EXPECT to survive the night. The last thing he remembered was a sucking feeling, of Akeru Maru's ghostly hands dragging on his legs, as if begging *don't let me go, don't let me disappear,* as she sunk a hundred feet below him, a thousand feet below him, and so on toward the distant nadir of the middle Pacific Ocean. The ship might've succeeded in taking him down with her, but for his life jacket. Katsumi did not know how to swim, nor had he ever tried to learn. He was like the sailors of old that way, preferring a quick death by drowning to the slow deaths of thirst, exhaustion, attack by shark. But Captain Hara had ordered they put on life jackets, and so he did. Then followed the mad moments of the sinking, during which time he could think of nothing beyond his immediate survival. And then there was the sucking feeling, and before he could foresee to take the life jacket off, a sweeping vanishing into darkness.

Katsumi awoke in shallow water, his heels dropped in the sand like anchors. He paddled back toward the shore and crawled out of the ocean on his hands and knees. From this prostrate position he surveyed the small island that had captured him in the night. It was not much larger than his apartment in Nagoya, about two hundred square feet. A ring of sand surrounded the peak of this volcanic bump, and in the middle grew a stand of stunted coconut palm trees. He counted five total. Katsumi removed his life jacket and hung it on a palm branch. Then he took off his wet shoes and socks and lay them out in the sun to dry. Fortunately, the wind and waves had smoothed the rough surface of the rock, so he could walk barefoot across it without cutting his feet. Hoping to find something useful or perhaps someone else washed ashore with him, he performed a circumnavigation of the island. But there was nothing. No debris. No persons living or dead. Nothing.

Katsumi's immediate concern was securing fresh water. He could not imagine surviving longer than tomorrow without it, considering his significant exposure to the sun. Later he might construct a shade from the palm leaves; but, for now, he worked instead to carve a hole in a coconut for the water inside. Breaking through, he tipped the coconut upside down and drank. A pleasurable quiver swept through his body at the first sensation of its sweet liquid on his lips. When it was empty, he cracked the coconut in half on the rock and scraped at the young meat with his teeth. He did this until his jaw hurt and his gums bled and he could eat no more.

Next, Katsumi set about turning the perforated surface of the rock into various rain catches and desalination basins. He scooped out the desiccated remains of sea moss and green algae from four evaporated tide pools. The largest two he left empty for rainwater collection; the smaller two he filled with ocean water. Overtop the smaller pools he laid palm leaves. He presumed as the water evaporated in the heat, a portion of it would condense in droplets on the leaves. He waited three hours before checking them. On their underside he found drops like morning dew waiting to be drunk. He licked the palm leaves dry. There was not much water, perhaps a teaspoon for each leaf, just enough to satisfy him while he decided his next step.

But just what would his next step be? He did not expect a rescue anytime soon. They might go searching for the wreckage, but he had watched Akeru Maru sink. Everything had happened so fast: the rogue wave punching a hole in her hull, the ship careening, life jacket orders, cries of abandon ship, Captain Hara retreating to the helm to lock himself in, lest he be tempted to leave her behind, and all the cargo going down with her. What little flotsam remained on the surface would evade spotting and slowly migrate the Pacific, perhaps join the Great Garbage Patch, perhaps years later wash up in the Philippines or on the Oregon Coast, like the pieces of the wreckage of MH370 on Reunion. And until that time: The Mystery of Akeru Maru. What had happened to the Akeru Maru? Was it aliens or a miniature black hole? No, not a mystery at all. A random sinking. No reason for it but a phenomenon of waves. No reason for it but physics and bad luck.

For every day that passed, Katsumi placed a shell inside one of the tide pools not used for water. He selected only the most elegant, intact, and colourful for his counting of the days. Commonly he picked Cowrie shells, but every so often he stumbled upon a Hebrew Cone or a Spider Drupe. One afternoon he counted the shells. He set them in groups of five and one group of four. He had been on the island twenty-four days. Twenty-four days without rain. Twenty-four days without seeing a single ship on the horizon or even a plane flying overhead. How long could he go on like this? How long could he survive eating coconuts, drinking coconut water, licking leaves, obsessively shell hunting? What was the point? Katsumi raised his fists above the shells. But the world had not yet broken him, and so he could not break the shells. To preserve something simply for its elegance, that was how he imagined his survival.

He pushed the shells back into the tide pools and returned to the beach to pick one for today. He spotted a Banded Tulip shell and was about to grab it when he noticed antennae poking out the front. A hermit crab squeezed itself out the tiny opening, freeing first one claw, then another, then one leg, then two legs. Katsumi ran back to his tide pools and found his biggest shell, a Shark's Eye. He returned to the beach and set the shell some distance from the hermit crab. Then he stood back and watched. Five minutes later the hermit crab fully emerged, dragging its vulnerable red Fibonacci tail behind it. The crab backed itself inside the Shark's Eye and crawled off.

Katsumi knew from his university days the term for this exchange: "trading up." If only there were another island he might "trade up" to, then he might also be spared the suffocating death of a hermit crab stuck in a shell too small for its body. And yet a hermit crab would never allow itself to die in such a way. Once it outgrew its shell, it would go out in search of a new one. Hermit crabs did not rationalize one death over another. They acted in one direction – survival. In the same way, Katsumi could choose to stay on the island or he could choose to swim; there seemed an equal probability of survival with either choice. The only difference was that one felt like resignation and the other like fighting. Katsumi picked up the abandoned shell and lobbed it into the ocean. He would fight.

But first he needed to learn how to swim. He practised by paddling around the island in his life jacket. In the beginning it took him what felt like hours to complete a single circuit. Soon he learned to kick his arms and legs in unison, and was able to cut his time in half. Katsumi ate four coconuts a day for energy and to build up his fat stores. He weaved palm leaves together for a satchel, in which he would carry his carving stone and three coconuts for sustenance on the impossible swim west.

One evening a storm struck the island. Katsumi spent the night clinging to the palm trees in his life jacket while waves battered him and washed away the satchel and the chisel rocks and the last of the coconuts. Halfway through the night, the ocean calmed and the rains he had long been hoping for came. Cupping his hands, he drank from the sky until he vomited, then drank some more. This late answer to his supplications seemed to Katsumi an endorsement from the gods. In the morning he set out for land wearing only his life jacket.

He swam for two days without stopping. On the second night he was awoken from his sleep by a splash. He saw the top of a shark's fin, watched it slide along the surface of the water, then slip just under it. The attack came swift and violent on his left side. He used whatever energy remained in him to beat the shark back with his fists even as it tore his flesh. Eventually, the shark retreated. Against the incredible pain, Katsumi kicked his right leg and skimmed his right arm to hold his head above the surface of the water. He might die of blood loss, but he would not drown.

Moments later, when the shark returned for another attack, it did not find Katsumi there, only a shell.

#18 *Bundy Vibes*

WHEN DUSTIN INVITED HER to his island cabin for their second date, Elizaveta agreed without a second thought. Their first date had been a dream. Candlelight dinner. Bordeaux wine. Ocean walk. They had stopped to sit on driftwood and nestled into one another and brushed icy fingers together. He kissed her goodnight at the door. She invited him upstairs, but he declined – a gentleman. Elizaveta told her best friend Yelena about their plans and was returned a stern warning not to go. Yelena didn't like it one bit. The whole thing stunk of something sinister. A setup for an "accidental drowning." Reading the text conversation, Yelena said she got Bundy vibes from the dude. It was not the first time.

"Which part?" asked Elizaveta.

Yelena snatched Elizaveta's phone and scrolled up. "*I can't wait to watch you dip your toes into the hot tub.* Um, foot fetish much?"

"Was Bundy a foot fetishist?"

Yelena scrolled some more. "Or what about this one: *We can skinny dip in the nude.* The nude, Liza, the nude. What kind of sociopath uses the word *nude?* And it's a redundancy."

Elizaveta supposed it wouldn't be the worst thing to save the island excursion until they got to know each other better. But she was a week out from her period and worried that if Dustin suggested next weekend instead, she would again have to say no, and then perhaps he would stop asking her altogether. So it was now or never. Sex on a deadline. Saturday was going to be a full moon, too. She confirmed it on Google Calendar. She had never had bad sex during a full moon.

The plan was to meet at the harbour Friday around five o'clock, boat over to the island, dinner, hot tub, skinny dipping, hot tub, sex; then Saturday, explore the island, relax, maybe get some reading done (Yelena had lent her *Normal People*, in case you don't get it right the other way, she said), sex; then return early Sunday morning for breakfast by the bay.

Elizaveta left directly from work. She took the bus to avoid paying for two nights' parking at the harbour. She proceeded down the slanted jetty toward the security gate where Dustin said he would meet her. In front of the gate, a vagrant type wearing a red and black Hadlock cap fumbled through a pile of garbage bags. He was whistling. Whatever the song, it seemed composed for the purpose of signalling a dog from out of the woods. Elizaveta fled while his back was turned. She called Dustin from the parking lot.

"Where are you?"

"Here." "Here." "Look behind you." "Look behind you."

She recognized Dustin's chiselled face squared inside the Hadlock cap. Night and day compared with the GQ fashionista she met on Tuesday. She pictured him naked. It helped.

Elizaveta joined Dustin by the gate. "What's with the garbage bags?"

"Supplies," he said. "I don't get out there very often."

Together they carried them to where he had moored his boat: a two-person dinghy, originally bright orange but covered in a Theseus' ship's worth of black patchwork. Underneath the wooden seats, a Big Gulp cup rolled in and out of sight with the waves.

"Are you sure everything will fit?" she asked.

He shrugged. "We'll make it work."

Loaded up, the dinghy floated half a centimeter above the waterline. Elizaveta sat at the bow under a pile of bags. The added weight made her legs go numb, and the cold ocean water spilling into the dinghy her feet. Would mobility return to these appendages in time if they capsized? Probably not.

With one hand on the tiller and the other tossing Big Gulp servings of ocean water over his shoulder, Dustin piloted them toward the island. He attempted to carry on a conversation with her over the noise of the engine.

"----------."

"What??"

He laughed. "--------------! -------.-----."

Elizaveta pointed to her ears and shook her head.

Half an hour later, they arrived at his dock. Dustin hopped out to tether the boat. He removed the bags from her lap. "Like I was saying," he said, assisting her onto the dock, "the otters get under the deck, and that's what the smell is."

"Smell?"

"Similar to moldy bread. But don't worry. You get used to it."

Presently the circulation returned to Elizaveta's legs. Her feet, however, would need a minimum hour in the hot tub for a full recovery. To be honest she couldn't wait to "dip her toes" in the warm water – even if it did mean letting Dustin watch. And perhaps that had been his plan all along: get her feet wet, get her to take her socks off, then convince her to let him suckle on her toes. God, it grossed her out to think somebody might actually be into that.

He handed her the keys. "Why don't you go on ahead and take a look around? It will take me a minute to unload the rest of these bags."

"Should I turn on the hot tub?"

"Go ahead."

"It's my toes," she said. "They're freezing."

"I've got some slippers in the cabin. If you want to wear them while you wait. It takes an hour or two for it to heat up."

Landed crookedly atop the seaside rocks, the cabin looked to have been time-warped from the homestead west and dropped on its foundation from twenty-five feet up. The only modern feature were its glass windows; otherwise, it was all moss and rot and warped log siding. Elizaveta noticed a small shed installed in back amongst the trees. At least she prayed it was a shed. A wide deck supported on splitting columns extended beyond the front of the cabin.

And then she saw it – the hot tub as promised, above ground, anachronistic. Its laminated sides glimmered in the retreating sunlight.

Arriving at the deck, Elizaveta slammed into the awful smell Dustin had warned her about. It was atmospheric. A fog. She could taste the otter stank, feel its animal heaviness in her lungs. She would have to get used to it. She had no choice.

The hard top cover lay slanted on the hot tub. Elizaveta grabbed an edge and dragged it off.

"Jesus Christ!"

Dustin dropped the bags he was carrying and ran toward her. "What's wrong?"

She pointed a trembling finger at the hot tub. "It has no head!"

He peeked inside at the dead raccoon. Evidently, it had entered the hot tub in search of fresh water and drowned. Dustin scratched behind his ear. "I swear I thought I locked it up."

"I'm going to be sick." Elizaveta looked around for a place to sit. She might've dropped on the decking, but it was slick with grime. "Where is its *head*?"

Dustin chuckled. "Good question." *Bundy vibes*. "I'll grab the pump from the shed and empty it out. Shouldn't take more than thirty, forty minutes to clean up."

"Are you crazy? You know how many diseases those things have?"

"Actually, the raccoons on the island are fairly clean, disease-wise," he said. "Nothing a quick spray down and some chlorine won't sanitize. We'll be dipping nude in no time."

"Nude? I wouldn't dip into that thing inside a submarine!" She groaned. "And for God's sake stop saying *nude*."

Dustin took the keys from Elizaveta and sulked toward the shed at the back. She had offended him. But he deserved it. No, he didn't deserve it – he was trying. After the first date, Elizaveta had set her expectations too high. Crack rock high. Never again would any hit be as euphoric as the first. All downhill from here. If she could give one piece of advice to the men out there, it would be this: make just enough mistakes at the beginning: women like a steady incline.

Elizaveta glimpsed at the decapitated raccoon. Its purple-pink insides were feeling outside the opening for the missing head. Devoured whole. What ungodly monster lay coiled in the bottom of that black entrail soup?

Dustin returned from the shed wearing Wetland overalls and long rubber gloves. He set the pump and hose down beside the hot tub. "Here goes nothing." He reached his hands in to grab the corpse. Floating, its fur had flared outward, giving the sorry raccoon a semblance of shape; hanging in the air, the hairs clung shockingly flat to its deflated remains. Elizaveta looked away. She heard some bushes rustle nearby.

"Shouldn't we bury it?" she asked.

Dustin dropped the hose into the hot tub and started the pump. "Why?" Black water spewed out the opposite end across the deck. "Shit!" He redirected it to flow off the side onto the brush below.

Elizaveta asked for the keys again and went inside the cabin. Besides the otter smell, more concentrated inside than out, the interior was actually quite nice. Cozy even. The open concept living room/bedroom/kitchen layout reminded her of the bachelor suite she rented many years ago in university. Futon bed doubling as a couch. Mini-fridge and standing sink. A zigzagged chest of drawers. In one corner stood a tube TV with antiquated rabbit ears, and across from that a wood-burning stove enclosed inside a magic circle of split logs. In the opposite corner a white curtain hung around what she assumed was a shower head and drain. She threw it back. A common toilet bowl. She closed her eyes and exhaled in thanksgiving. She lay toilet paper on the seat, then sat down to pee.

"Found the head!" Dustin called from outside.

No way was she getting into that hot tub.

No fucking way.

Elizaveta found the slippers slid under the chest of drawers. They were pink and designed with bunny's eyes and ears. An ex-girlfriend's perhaps? She hung her socks over the shower curtain rod to dry and put them on.

She poked her head out the door. "Do you mind if I start a fire?"

"Go ahead," Dustin said. "Matches are . . ." He set his rag down and his rubber gloves beside it. He squeezed a garbage bag. "I'm pretty sure it's this one."

She tore it open in front of the futon. Amongst the contents were flyers, glow sticks, mosquito coils, batteries, and, yes, waterproof matches. She ripped pages from a Best Buy Black Friday Blowout flyer, built a teepee around them, and lit the fire. Toxic ink smoke billowed into the cabin. Even when she closed the glass door, it continued to steam out the sides.

"Dustin!"

He stomped over to the wood-burning stove and opened the damper. The smoke vanished up the metal chimney. "What were you thinking?"

She apologized. "I –"

"If you don't know what you're doing, then don't do it. Shit."

"I want to go home."

"I didn't mean it."

"I want you to take me home."

"Let me make it up to you." He folded his hands. "Please, Eliza," he begged. "Please."

Elizaveta crossed her arms. She looked out the windows across the bay to the distant flickering city lights. It was already too late to leave. Searchers would never find them in the dark. But she wasn't just going to let him get away with snapping at her like that. And dammit, he did look kind of hot in those overalls.

"How *exactly* are you going to make it up to me?"

"I can give you a foot massage," he said. "I give really good foot massages."

She sighed. "Fine. But if you try anything more, I'll kick you in the teeth."

"Try what?"

"And you have to shower first."

"I'll go shower now." Dustin paused in the doorway. "Hey, did you know it's a full moon?"

"That's tomorrow."

"Then I guess you won't have to lock me up tonight."

"What?"

He smiled, half chuckled. "I said I guess you won't have to lock me up tonight then."

"Because you're a werewolf?"

She stared at him. Did he actually expect her to laugh at that? What she wouldn't give to find a funny man. A genuinely funny man. So rare these days. Dustin left. A minute later Elizaveta heard the swishing sound of a shower coming on around back. She checked her cellphone. X for bars. She texted Yelena anyway. *Worst date ever. Headless raccoon in hot tub. Confirmed foot fetishist.* Perhaps a satellite would pass over in the middle of the night and beam it off.

Dustin returned from showering. As he changed into pajamas inside the curtained bathroom, Elizaveta asked if there was anywhere on the island with cell service.

"There's one spot in the woods where you can get reception. I tied a blue ribbon around the tree. But it's a ways in." Dustin emerged shirtless. He grabbed her right foot off the ground and pivoted her so that she lay lengthwise on the futon. He settled in across from her. He dropped her heel in his crotch and pressed his fingers into her arch. She edged back.

"Are you relaxed?" he asked.

"I'm relaxed."

Elizaveta closed her eyes. She imagined herself in a cabin much like this one but modern, with state-of-the-art amenities, a working hot tub, and, instead of a wood-burning stove, a true fireplace, cobblestone with a proper brick chimney. The crackling fire made this vision come alive in her thoughts. Dustin kneaded her heels; she moaned. She imagined, too, she was with somebody much like Dustin but with all the personality and charm of the man she dreamed to meet one day, funny, eccentric, who would rather squeeze her ass than pick the lint from between her –

"Dustin!" She wrenched her foot out of his mouth.

"Please, Liza," he begged. "Please. Do this for me and I'll do whatever you want. I'll eat you out. Would you like that?"

She guffawed. "After your mouth's been all over my foot?"

"All right, I get it." He beckoned to her. "Give me your left."

His pajama pants were hiked up by a hard-on. Elizaveta wanted to see it, his cock. She wanted it, this extension of him. She would let him inside her and close her eyes and go back there. She would return to the modern cabin with the bubbling hot tub and the blazing fireplace and the quiet, brooding, dominating lover who danced an orgasmic lead.

"Just fuck me, Dustin. Fuck me and then let's go to sleep."

He obliged.

It was better than expected.

It was good because she wanted it to be.

IN THE MORNING THEY AWOKE to find the dinghy gone. Sunk, stolen, swept away in the tide, set loose on purpose – whatever had happened didn't much matter to Elizaveta. What mattered was getting off this island, with the exception of swimming, by any means necessary and at the earliest convenience. Dustin's stoic confidence when faced with their stranding seemed proof that he knew of other ways off. She broke the bad news over breakfast. Marmite toast. On their first date she had told him it was her favourite, and he remembered. Biting into the salty treat, she almost changed her mind. Almost.

"I want you to take me home."

Dustin set his plate down on the floor. He shook his head. He went to say something, then said either that or something else. "If that's what you want."

"It's nothing personal," she said. "It's just …" She bit into her toast, chewed and swallowed. She wished he had made her hard-boiled eggs or something. The Marmite was just so damn *good*.

"I thought it would be romantic," he said.

"It was a nice thought. But come on, Dustin. First we almost sink coming across the bay. Then the raccoon in the hot tub. And now the boat? At a certain point you have to admit the weekend's beyond redemption. Right? Don't you agree?"

Dustin started dressing. "I'll head into the woods and call Carl. See if he will pick us up."

Elizaveta suddenly felt awful. If she could go back ten seconds and give him a second chance, she would. But it was too late for that now.

"Should I come with you?" she asked.

"Whatever you want." He knelt to tie his boots. He yanked on his shoelaces garrote-style. He wrapped them once around his ankle and tied them. Dustin the foot strangler. Bundy was never a foot fetishist; Elizaveta knew that much for certain.

"Whatever you want," he said again.

"I'd like to come."

Elizaveta dug through her overnight bag and found a pair of yoga pants and an athletic shirt. Meanwhile, Dustin paced the deck outside. When she emerged from the cabin, he took off ahead of her. She followed mutely behind. She dared not burden him by asking him to slow down or wait up. The trail ended before the cabin was out of sight. Only unbroken wilderness ahead. Dustin pushed forward into the thick woods. Not long afterward a branch he had moved out of the way snapped back and lashed Elizaveta across the cheek. She stifled a cry.

"Are you okay?" he asked.

"I'm fine."

"Don't follow so close." He touched the spot where the branch struck her. "There's going to be a welt."

She ran a finger over it. She could already feel the bump. "Are we almost there?"

His tenderness evaporated. "You didn't have to come."

An hour later they found the tree. Dustin hollered upon its discovery. Even exhausted Elizaveta joined in the celebration. She raised the roof. "Woot! Woot!" Dustin opened his arms for a hug. She allowed it. Her face sponged against the Superman sweat stain demarcating his chest. But at least he didn't stink. She hated when they stunk.

Dustin felt his pant pockets. "Shit!" The colour left his face. "I forgot my phone."

Fortunately, Elizaveta had brought hers. She handed it to him.

"What's the password?" he asked.

"Oh," she said. "It's 44444." She could always change it later.

Elizaveta leaned against a nearby tree and watched Dustin, contemplated him. How long did he spend wandering the woods before he found this spot? A capable outdoorsman. Handsome, too. Upper-middle-class property owner. Just decent in bed, but hey, it was their first time. Sure, there were hiccups: the foot fetish, his at times questionable fashion. Nothing a little therapy or positive reinforcement couldn't fix. Yes, she could work with a man like this. She could see herself with a man like this.

Dustin had been staring at the phone for some time now.

"Can't remember the number?"

"Your friend replied," he said.

"What?" Elizaveta lunged after her phone. "Why are you – You shouldn't –" She read Yelena's reply. *I'd be more worried if it was missing its paws lol. But seriously did you check? Serial killers love killing animals btw. Text me when you get this so I know you're still alive.* "Those were private messages," she said. "Do you usually go through people's phones?"

Dustin didn't answer. He looked sideways, through the trees, nowhere in particular.

"Dustin."

"You let me suck your toes," he said.

"That was a mistake."

"I trusted you with my biggest secret. And you betrayed me."

"Is it really a secret, though?" As soon as she said it, Elizaveta realized it was not worth the argument. She apologized. "Honestly, I sent that before you – before what happened last night, happened."

Dustin looked at her through not-quite-teary eyes and gestured for the phone back. "I'll call Carl, and then we can go."

She held his gaze for as long as would make it seem that she didn't want that more than anything right now, to be gone from this place. She wished she could just click her heels (for now, while she still had her feet – *God,* enough already!) and teleport inside her apartment, to finish off the weekend with Yelena and a bottle of wine. Or two. She handed him the phone.

Dustin called Carl. "Voicemail," he mouthed. Then, "Yeah, buddy, it's Dustin..I'm here at my cabin with Eliza, and my boat kinda fuckin' floated away. I hope it's not too much to ask, but could you come get us? We're pretty over it here, so," he glanced at Eliza, "so, yeah, if you could come get us, that would be really great. Peace. Bye."

They started back for the cabin.

"He knows my name?" Elizaveta asked.

Dustin pointed at a stump. "Watch out."

She stepped around it. "You told your friends about me?"

"I had high hopes."

There the conversation ended. For the rest of the return journey, Elizaveta and Dustin trekked silently, indolently, together and yet apart. Many times she wanted to say something to him but didn't. Quiet discomforted her. Blame it on the monkey genes. That irrepressible desire to whoop. Bears and cougars never spoke more than an occasional grunt and growl to each other. Why couldn't humans have evolved from them? Hard to have a foot fetish when your lover has three-inch claws.

Back at the cabin, Dustin prepared a supper of beans and hot dogs on the wood-burning stove.

"Do you mind stirring?" he asked Elizaveta.

"Sure."

He dug inside the chest of drawers, then flashed her rolling papers and a bag of weed. "Partake?"

"Oh God, yes," she said. She second-guessed herself, "Or wait." Did she really want to be high going across the bay? Oh, what difference did it make? She wanted to be high right *now*. Part of her, too, doubted the existence of this Carl person. Perhaps there was no "Carl." Perhaps there was no way off this island purgatory.

She should check her call history beforehand to confirm Dustin didn't stage the entire thing. Yelena would be proud.

"So what is it?" he asked. "Yay or nay?"

"No, yes, let's."

"Before or after?"

Elizaveta stared into the bubbling red and brown sludge. "Definitely before."

Dustin rolled the joint and lit it with kindling. They took turns stirring while the other toked. At one point they caught each other jointly licking their lips in anticipation of the meal and then couldn't stop giggling until dinner was served. Channelling the spirit of Oliver Twist, Elizaveta gulped it down and asked for more.

"What's the recipe?" she asked.

Through his laughter Dustin flashed bean-skin-armoured teeth. Elizaveta slapped a hand over her mouth to contain her last bite. He stood up and walked over to the pot.

"First," he said, snickering, barely under control, "you open a can of beans."

"Heinz beans?" she asked.

"The best beans."

"Go on."

"Then you chop up hot dogs. Chippity, chop, chop," he both demonstrated and described. "Drop them in, and voila. Bon appetit."

"What do you call this magnificent dish?"

Dustin eyed her very seriously and said, "Raccoon heads in a hot tub."

"That's not funny," Elizaveta said, laughing. "That's really not funny." But it was funny. It was *really* funny. She couldn't help herself. And once she started laughing, she couldn't stop. She laughed until the tears swelled her eyes shut, until all the world was a blur.

Suddenly Dustin cried, "The moon!"

They dropped their bowls and ran outside. The full moon hovered right overtop the ocean horizon. A giant bullseye. Close enough to throw stones at. Close enough to skip one across its moonglade and hear the dull thump when it hit.

Then Elizaveta saw it. "Look," she said, "the dinghy. Dustin! The dinghy!"

It must've floated in with the tide. Dustin stripped. Howling, he bolted down the dirt trail, over the rocks, and along the dock, "Oww! Oww! Owwwww!", and dove off the end of it into the freezing ocean water. Elizaveta took off everything but her underwear and joined him. She waded some feet out while he tugged the boat back to the dock and tied it. She watched the moon's reflection swirl in the beating of her arms. Swirl, reform, swirl, reform. He paddled over to her when he was done.

"Are you nude?"

She took off her underwear and lobbed it inside the boat. "I am now."

"It's not too late if you want to go back," he said.

"Let's go in the morning," she said. "I don't mind."

She had never had bad sex during a full moon.

#19 *Rachel*

I STARTED SEEING GETHSEMANE eleven years after the raid on Unity Assembly. The raid concluded tragically with the mass suicide of twenty-four men, women, and children, including the cult leader Dvita Hunter and his entire family. Fortunately, Gethsemane had been able to escape a week prior and thus avoid certain death. I presumed that the reason for her coming to see me, a therapist, was for help in dealing with the common problems associated with survivor's guilt – depression, nightmares, shame, sexual dysfunction – but, truth was, she desired therapy for the more complicated reason of Dvita's continued influence over her *being*.

"I was with him for so long I've forgotten who I was before. And it's difficult to imagine how I might make my way forward to her, to Gethsemane before Morphos." I vaguely remembered reading in the newspapers about "Morphos," Dvita's program of indoctrination, of cultic control, but asked her to elaborate. She replied, "Dvita said that Morphos is to the soul what decomposition is to the dead. It is the dissolution of the infinite within ourselves. And the reshaping of it."

I noted her actions while she provided this answer, how she clenched the chair arms and scraped the index fingernail of her left hand, uncoloured and unclipped, back and forth across the black leather (was it for the sensation or the noise?), how her mouth had twisted before sounding Dvita's name, and yet how her cheeks balled wistfully below her eyes as she finished her explanation. Gethsemane was an uncommonly tall and skinny woman, with the constitution of a tree: long limbs, burls for knees, hair like Spanish moss. The finger-scraping continued even after she finished speaking – scrape, scrape, back and forth, like branches against the siding of a house.

"I noticed you started with 'Dvita said,'" I replied. "I am less interested in what he thinks than what *you* think. What was Morphos to you?"

Gethsemane turned her head. Her eyes converged on the file cabinet in the corner of my office. I waited for as long as it took for her to respond. My experience taught me that sometimes, in response to a question, silence was not so much resistance as it was particularity, the answer being usually quite quickly arrived at by the patient, but the right words for its expression requiring further contemplation.

"Morphos is . . ." She paused, admitting another change. "Morphos was when I stopped being Rachel and became Gethsemane."

"Rachel was your birth name?" I hesitated before asking, "Would it be helpful if I called you Rachel?"

Gethsemane answered me in a parable, delivering it as Dvita might, with an affected spiritualism that was persuasive enough in its time to convince twenty-four people to cram into a five-by-ten unventilated locker and suffocate on each other's exhalations.

"A man was journeying over an immense snowy plain. When he felt he could not go forward any longer, he tried to follow his footprints backward to the place from where he had come. But no sooner did he turn around than he discovered them erased by the wind." She straightened a fold that, while she was speaking, had appeared on her pant leg. "No, I would rather you not."

FROM MY EXPERIENCE treating survivors of trauma and abuse, I learned there were typically two departures: the physical and the mental, the former almost always preceding the latter. First get out, then leave – that was how I worded it in an article I wrote for *Psychology Today*. A decade ago Gethsemane succeeded in getting out of Unity Assembly, but she had not yet left. She was still in her mind a member of Dvita's congregation, his wife and his disciple. Leaving was letting go, staying was holding on. Like a survivor of domestic abuse who continues to wear her wedding ring, Gethsemane held on to Dvita in countless different ways, the most significant of these being her name. Nevertheless, I knew that the key to initiating her mental departure lay buried somewhere in the story of her physical departure, which was why I began our second session with the question:

"What made you decide to leave Unity Assembly?"

Again, Gethsemane took some minutes to answer.

"I never did become pregnant in all those years," she said. "Dvita and I tried, and there was nothing medically wrong with either of us, but I never did get pregnant from him. Dvita blamed this on a wandering mind, *my* wandering mind. His theory of conception was that it required both partners' total presence in the moment, not only in body, but also in mind. And there must be some truth to that, because he was certainly right about me. I never did think about him once while I was with him. Even when we were intimate, and he asked me to look him in the eyes, I always looked right through him to some vision beyond. I looked at the man I saw on the street a month before. I looked at God. I looked backwards inside myself.

"But the other women, all of them became pregnant. I loved the children very –" Gethsemane croaked. She waited for the trembling of her chin to subside, then continued soberly, "But I loved Shiloh the most. Why, I can only guess. Looks-wise she resembled all the others, having Dvita's hourglass nose and ochre eyes. And like the others, she was quiet and introspective, but she could become boisterous during play or when encountering someone or something for the first time. Still, I felt a strange attraction to her, as if she were a child God had destined for me but was forced by my sexual incompatibility with Dvita to deliver through his second wife. When did I realize I loved her the most? If I had to guess, it was sometime during the summer of her eighth year, when she used to go daily to the fields and lie on her back in the tall grass. When I asked her why, she said she liked the way the stalks tickled her ears – she had very wide ears – and shoulders and toes when the wind blew through them. The other children were afraid of the fields. At night they told scary stories of beasts crouched in the grass, waiting to tear off their limbs or drag them away to be eaten. But Shiloh was never afraid, not even in the dark. She would often fall asleep outside, forcing me to search for her in the evening before bed, a difficult task considering how small she was, how easily she remained hidden.

"I decided I was going to leave Unity Assembly the day Shiloh began Morphos. Every child underwent Morphos at the age of thirteen. Mothers were exempt from participation. But as I was not her mother, I was required to participate."

She stopped there, apparently having come to the end of her answer.

I finished the note I was taking, then asked, "Was her name always Shiloh? Or was that the name Dvita gave her?"

"None of his children were named until they completed stage one of Morphos."

"Did you call the children something in the meantime?"

"We called them by their mothers' names."

"Did you call Shiloh by her mother's name?"

"I called her, I called her –" Gethsemane's face deformed. I recognized Dvita's demon moving inside her. She went silent.

"It's all right," I said. "You don't have to answer. We can come back to it another time."

But I wouldn't need to come back to it. Irrespective of its accuracy, the story of Shiloh in the tall grass was clearly avoidance coping, an attempt to divert me away from the real answer to the question why Gethsemane loved her above the rest. The bond between them did not begin in the fields; that was obvious to me now.

It began when Gethsemane named the child Rachel.

WHAT'S IN A NAME? My name is Natalie Begovin (née La Monta). Natalie Faith Begovin. Faith was the name my father used. My husband calls me Talie. My mother told me once if I had been born a boy my name would've been Nathan. Sally, my daughter, calls me Mawm, never Mum. My patients call me Dr. Begovin. Until Gethsemane, I never considered names as more than convenient identifiers, making no real difference to the person, meaningful only for others' use. Speaking through his character Juliet, Shakespeare expressed much the same opinion. But then neither Shakespeare nor I had been through so profoundly disturbing a program as Morphos. As Keith Raniere did literally with his initials, Dvita Hunter, at the end of Morphos, branded his disciples figuratively with a new name. Rachel became Gethsemane. "Rachel" became Shiloh. Before I could begin to help undo the psychological damage done to Gethsemane by Hunter's Morphos, whether during her own initiation or in her participation and perpetration of the program against others, she needed first and foremost to renounce her name. The problem was that Dvita's maxim of "Forever Forward" made it all but impossible to steer Gethsemane in the right direction – toward her past. She subscribed absolutely to the philosophy, and it would be no easier disabusing her of it than a Christian of her faith in Christ. This meant she would have to discover the name Rachel somewhere on her journey forward, and choose it for herself. I merely needed to travel some steps ahead of her, lay it on her path, and point it out to her as she passed.

Gethsemane was not my only client to have been involved in a high-profile tragedy like the one at Unity Assembly. Years prior I had treated a survivor from Columbine, who developed a rare case of cleithrophobia. The mistake I made then, however, which I promised myself never to make again, was that after our first session I went online and spent hours researching the massacre, discovering even his own story in my searches, and so entered our next session with preconceived notions of the event and his experience. (The irony is not lost on me that, in hoping to treat a person whose very phobia was being trapped, I had inadvertently trapped him inside the walls of my own assumptions.) But with Gethsemane I avoided the temptation. What few facts I did remember from the decade-old news story – censored, sanitized, and for good reason – were trifling compared to the savage reality of Morphos as elucidated by a person involved. Practicing therapists know the importance of presenting ourselves stoically to our patients; regardless of our feelings toward them or our visceral human reaction to their actions or words, we are to remain emotionally neutral. I attempted to maintain my composure during Gethsemane's confession, and generally succeeded, but it was not without incredible difficulty. In fact, I felt nauseated the entire time, constantly on the verge of a violent sickness. And though I could hide it well in my posture, by crossing my legs and using my left arm to crutch my weary head, I could not prevent the blood running from my face, nor my tremulous fingers from shaking the pen while I took notes.

"I was asked to fetch Shiloh the morning of her first session. I found her in the lounging area having breakfast and led her through the compound to the downstairs locker, where the other three women were waiting. Shiloh asked me many questions on the way. 'What do you think my name will be?' 'What sort of gifts do you think I'll get?' It appeared the older girls, those who had been through Morphos before, had lied to her that it was something like a birthday party. I couldn't imagine why they would be so cruel to her, knowing full well the terrible, contrary truth. But like Dvita said, nothing fills emptiness easier than cruelty, and ultimately that was the very point of Morphos, to empty you out, transform your body into a chrysalis for the emergence of a new self. I tried to answer Shiloh's questions truthfully without giving too much away. She pouted when I told her there would be no gifts. My heart broke for her, for her doomed innocence.

"We ushered Shiloh into the locker and stripped her of her clothes. Morphos starts at the surface, with the destruction of body-ego. To get to the yolk a man must crack the egg, as Dvita said. We began by mocking her. We struck first at the parts of her we remembered feeling most vulnerable about at her age. We jeered at her unformed breasts and teased her about the budding hairs above her vagina. We pinched the baby fat lingering on her stomach and her waist. We pulled on her wide ears, her most obvious feature. Even those parts of her that were truly beautiful, legs and shoulders, her skin, lips, and hair, we ridiculed them in ways as to make them seem ugly, telling lies about their shape, their feel, their colour. Then we beat her. We continued until her crying stopped, until our hits landed with barely a whimper in response. I wish I could tell you that I remained a passive observer, that my only sin was standing back while the other women cooperated, but I carried out my duty unflinchingly, and worse, considered myself noble for doing so. I honestly believed what we did was for Shiloh's eventual benefit. I had gone through the exact same process many years earlier, and, in my mind, emerged a stronger woman for it, without vanity, without fear.

"But everything changed the moment I spat on her. I had been spat on, too, by Dvita's second wife, and I remember how after all my resistance to their abuse, after how meekly I tolerated their violent beating, it was her spit at the end that finally broke me. Some children required two or three sessions to complete the first stage, but thanks to her I had only needed one. When I did it, I believed I was doing Shiloh a favour, by sparing her more suffering. I remember she looked up at me just before I spat. I expected to see in her expression the pleading whys of a daughter forsaken. Instead, I saw only rage. I watched the light in her eyes go out and return a blazing fire, fed from the hot centre of her heart. It was a rage I had seen before only in Dvita, during his worst tantrums. For the rest of my life, I will never forget that face, the snarling lips, her eyes like sulfur. It took us four more sessions to break her. All the while I was planning our escape, Shiloh's and mine, to happen during the day's respite between stages one and two. With every kick and insult, however, I pushed her farther and farther away from me, and deeper and deeper inside herself, so that when the time came for us to run away together, she rejected my offer of escape. In the end I left, and she stayed behind."

Though our session had officially concluded fifteen minutes prior, I was not going to send her away without discussing what she had just confessed. I could also clearly see now a path to "Gethsemane before Morphos," to Rachel, and did not want to forfeit this opportunity to lead her there. I excused myself under the guise of needing to use the washroom and went to apologize to Mr. De Vries, my incoming patient, for the delay. (Mr. De Vries and I had been seeing each other four and a half years, and he was not so much in need of therapy anymore as he was in want of judicious conversation.) I told him that I would not be able to see him for at least another hour. He was very understanding. I instructed my secretary Virgilio to push my remaining appointments an hour back.

In the five minutes since I left her, Gethsemane hadn't budged at all from her stiff upright position in the chair. Passing by on her left, I glimpsed the deep scratch she had made unconsciously in the black leather. She followed my eyes to the spot.

"Did I do that?" She checked her fingernails and, seeing the end of her left index finger was black, withdrew both arms to her chest. "Let me pay for that. Whatever it costs, I'll pay."

I assured her she would do nothing of the sort. "My mother used to tell me don't bring anything home that you want to keep perfect. And that's how I want you to feel here, to feel at home, to feel you don't have to be perfect." I might've said more to reassure her but worried it would have the opposite effect of seeming like I was trying too hard. "But I want to return to what you mentioned about *your* being spat on. You said it was Dvita's second wife that did it." I double-checked my notes before continuing, "That was Shiloh's mother, wasn't it? Last week you mentioned she was the daughter of Dvita's second wife. Is that true?"

Gethsemane nodded. "I'm the reason."

"The reason for what?"

"I'm the reason Shiloh stayed behind."

"What makes you think you're the reason?"

"Because I was conscious of that," she admitted. "I remembered her mother and so I – And so I . . ."

"And what about Shiloh's mother? What about her responsibilities? Where was she during all this?"

"I was more of a mother to Shiloh than she ever was," Gethsemane snapped. Knowing anger to be a common mask of sorrow, I wasn't surprised when after this outburst she began to cry. "And I let her die." She retracted her legs onto the black leather like a spider trying to squeeze itself into the darkest corner of a lighted room. "I left her there to die!"

I waited for a low point in the ebb and flow of her tears to ask, "And what if you had stayed? Do you think that would've made any difference?"

"I could've convinced her. I could've saved her. I tried to go back. But they arrested me outside the compound. They were already there. Dvita didn't know it, but they were already there. They had been watching us for weeks."

"If you had stayed with Shiloh, do you think you would be alive to tell me about her today? You are the only survivor, no?" After waiting some time for her to respond, I recited Dvita's maxim, "Forever Forward."

"Forever Forward," Gethsemane repeated like an amen.

"During our first session you told me the parable of a man walking in the snow. Do you remember that?"

"I do."

"He wants to return from where he came and turns around to follow his footprints, but then finds they were erased by the wind. I wonder, though, when he turns *back* around, won't those footprints too have been erased? So then how can he know which way is truly forward?"

Her body unfurled from the leather chair. "Because he remembers where he was going before he turned around. He doesn't forget that he turned around."

"Are you turned around, Gethsemane?"

She shook her head. "I am standing still."

"Even so, you may still be turned around. This is what I think: You are the man in the parable who has come to the end of his footprints, who can't decide if the way back is the way forward or if the way forward is the way back. I believe you want to honour Shiloh's memory but feel it is impossible to do without earning her forgiveness. Truth is, you must honour her *first*, and then forgiveness will come. That is where you are turned around. That is why you are standing still."

"But how? How can I honour someone I am responsible for destroying?"

"But you're not responsible for destroying her – Dvita is. He created Morphos. He put Shiloh in the locker. He is the destroyer. You are the survivor. Without you, without your memories, Shiloh is only a name on a list. And it is not even the right name."

I heard Gethsemane mutter something underneath her breath. I asked her to say it again; I had to be sure I heard her right.

"Rachel," she said. "Her name is Rachel."

AFTER THAT THIRD SESSION, I never did see Gethsemane again in person. I specify in person because a year later, *Dateline* and *20/20* produced independent specials on Unity Assembly, which were, in essence, long-form interviews with Gethsemane talking about her experiences and about the girl named Rachel, whom she loved the most. Some months before that I had written her a letter inquiring about her situation and her mental health, even going so far as to offer her a follow-up appointment at no charge but had yet to receive a reply. In any case I didn't take offense.

Then, just when I thought I would never hear from her again, Virgilio handed me a letter on my way out the office. "It's from *her*," he said.

I knew exactly to whom he was referring.

I took it to my car to open. It was February, and a dry snow was falling from the sky. As usual, frost had built up thick on the front windshield. After a long day at the office, I didn't want to expend the effort to scrape it by hand, so I started the car and let it idle with the defroster on max. I read her letter to the background drone of the fan, while the interior of the car heated to room temperature and the ice on the windows cleared.

Dr. Begovin,

I hope this letter finds you doing well. I don't know if you remember me, so I will summarize for you briefly the time we spent together as therapist and patient. Two years ago I came to you to discuss my involvement in Unity Assembly and my relationship with Dvita Hunter. We talked about my participation in his program "Morphos," and I admitted to you many of the terrible things I did. I want to apologize for quitting your treatment so abruptly. When I left your practice that afternoon, I was deeply ashamed. You were the first person I ever told my story to, and though I knew patient confidentiality would prevent you from sharing it with anyone else, my real fear was not the story getting out but facing you again. It wasn't until much later that I realized how much you accomplished for me just by listening nonjudgmentally and asking questions. By the time I had this realization, however, I felt too much time had passed to thank you properly in person. I am writing you this letter now to tell you one important thing, which I hope will please you. I believe it was the very thing you wanted for me from the start. I have resumed using my given name, Rachel. Everybody I know knows me as Rachel. Even the figures in my dreams have taken to calling me by that name. And when I hear it, I remember her, my daughter, and I find her forgiveness.

With love,
Rachel

P.S. Enclosed is a cheque for five hundred dollars for the leather chair. Don't attempt to return it to me, I will not accept it back. I want to put something new in your home. I want for somebody imperfect like me to sit in it.

#20 *Don't Let the Door Hit You on the Way Out*

THIS TIME, which Jaclyn promised herself would be the very, very last time, the fight had started over a missing remote. Because the manual buttons had quit working years ago, the Samsung could not be powered on without it. So no remote, no TV – and she was the last one to have it. And it was game five of Jamie's Blue Jays versus the Kansas City Royals. She apologized profusely, but this only seemed to enrage him further. When she tried to help him look, Jamie rose swiftly from the couch, elbow out, and caught her underneath the chin. Watch it, he said. Watch it. She ran to the washroom to spit the blood from her mouth and inspect the teeth marks in her tongue. Five beers and six innings later, Jamie came creeping into the bedroom with a dumb smile on his face, just drunk enough to feel guilty. Just drunk enough to explode if she didn't make up with him on the spot. He couldn't enjoy the game, otherwise. And they were winning. He opened with that. Jackie, we're winning. But she already knew that. She managed to slip by him to leave. Don't let the door hit you on the way out. She heard something breaking in the bedroom.

That night she stayed with her best friend, Amy. Jaclyn told her enough was enough and asked her help in getting out. Amy had a similar experience before with a man who stalked her at Shoppers Drug Mart. He used to send her Queen of Night tulips. He left his number in one of the cards, then showed up on her doorstep a day later when she didn't call. That she recognized him was the scariest thing. Harmless type, shy. Always the same boring conversation coming through the till. How's it going? Good, and you? It only got worse from there. He broke into her apartment one evening and poured Drano in her fish tank. He shit on her floor. So Amy disappeared. She said the only sure way to escape violent men is to disappear. One second you're there and the next second, gone. She insisted more than anything else that Jaclyn resist the urge to say goodbye. Whatever you do, don't pity him. Don't pity him and don't say goodbye.

They went apartment hunting the next day. Amy browsed vacancies like most people browsed the news, so she had a place already picked out for Jaclyn before they began. It was a little pricey but worth it for the 24/7 security guard. Amy paid Jaclyn's damage deposit and first month's rent to prevent Jamie from tracking her down through their joint bank account. What a mess it would be unravelling everything they had stitched together over the years. But one thing at a time. Jamie had been blowing up Jaclyn's phone with apologies since dawn. I'm sorry, baby. I'll never hurt you again. I was drunk. Excuses she could scroll up and find repeated a hundred times. Don't engage, was Amy's advice. Not even out of anger. An abuser's remorse is a ruse. It's a light at the end of the tunnel. He'll make you feel like you're heading to Heaven, but there's really only darkness on the other side. Jaclyn couldn't imagine what she would do without her.

Still, the hardest part lay ahead, of recovering Jaclyn's possessions, her irreplacables. Amy begged her to just let it go. Jaclyn tried to explain why she couldn't. Besides, she had a foolproof plan. Game six was on a Friday night, which meant Jamie would be out at the bar to watch it. She'd show up there midway through the game and be in and out in an hour. Amy made her promise. One hour. One hour and no goodbyes. Amy apologized that she couldn't go with her. If it were anything else, Jackie, but not this.

Jaclyn waited until the game came on the radio, then drove over to their place. Jamie's place now. She wasn't surprised to find everything in perfect order. He always tidied when she ran away. As if to say, I can be a good boyfriend. I can do all the things you want me to. If only you would let me. Soon the beeper went off on the stove to tell her the hour was up. She returned to the bedroom one last time to empty out her nightstand and made the mistake of checking Jamie's. In it she found his half-written letter of apology to her. Remember the time you twisted your ankle and I carried you on my back a mile to the car. You know I can be good. I quit drinking before, I can do it again. You are my life light. I am nothing without you. Without you I am nobody. Reading his words, Jaclyn pitied the small flame that still burned inside his heart for her. For a while she sat on the bed crying. Her phone buzzed. Amy asking, where are you? Jaclyn chose the kitchen to wait for Jamie to come home. Jaclyn, baby! She could smell his booze-breath from the door. He stumbled into the kitchen, eyes swollen from crying, and fell at her feet. I don't even care that they lost. I just want my baby back. She told him she had found his letter. She told him that she didn't feel right leaving him without saying goodbye.

That Amy told her not to, but that she had stayed anyway to say goodbye. Jamie slumped. His grip tightened around her legs. She almost fell over, he was squeezing her so tight. Jamie. Stop. Stop it. You'll put out the flame.

#21 *The Darién Gap, A Beginning*

ONE MONTH BEFORE THE SPRING EQUINOX, Sandra and her children, Michael and Maya, started the long journey south to Ushuaia in Argentina. There, they would join a hundred thousand others embarking by ship for Antarctica. It was a two-hundred-hour journey, give or take a night.

The year before Sandra had made the reverse trip to Prudhoe Bay in three and a half weeks. She might've done it in less time, but she always allowed her children one stop along the way, to sightsee. Her only rule was that the destination be within a night's drive, about eight hundred miles, of the highway. Along the Pan-American Highway, there were UN shelters; travelling off it, Sandra would need to find for herself a concrete structure thick enough to shield them during the day. Naturally, this meant committing some time to the search. As for her one rule, she didn't want to stray too far from the highway in case they ran into trouble.

Last year Michael picked Disneyland, and Maya picked Yellowstone National Park.

This year both Michael and Maya agreed they wanted to go home.

"Have you checked your maps?" Sandra asked.

Maya unfolded her map. She measured the distance from San Antonio to Baltimore using her thumb. "One hundred miles, two hundred miles –"

"It's one thousand five hundred miles," Michael said.

"That's too far," Sandra said. But she had already known it was.

"Five hundred miles, six hundred miles –"

"Maybe if you let me drive," Michael complained.

"If I let you speed, you mean." Though their Audi Q7 topped out at 140 mph, as a precaution, Sandra never drove faster than 100 mph. "Anyway, you're still too young."

"Then why did you teach me? Why would you teach me to drive and then not let me?"

Because if anything happened to me ... "No, you're right," Sandra answered in place of the truth. "I should've waited until you were older."

Winter road conditions necessitated careful driving for the first leg of their journey. Fortunately, most of the community had left earlier that month, meaning Sandra could follow their tires' grooves in the snow. Still, she remained vigilant. On this section of the highway, any accident would leave them exposed not only to the sun but to the frigid weather as well.

When the car touched pavement outside of Edmonton, Sandra felt relief like the seat belt sign coming off after a long bout of turbulence. Michael and Maya dozed through most of the early drive. In Prudhoe Bay, because the sun reached its zenith six degrees *below* the horizon, Sandra and her children had accustomed themselves to normal waking hours – that is, as normal as was possible in the half-light of Arctic winter. For the journey south, however, they would need to reverse their schedule, staying up through the night and sleeping in the shelters during the day. Sandra didn't mind if Michael and Maya took a night or two at the beginning to adjust. But then she would want them awake. Even if just to keep her company. To keep her from falling asleep at the wheel through the monotonous Midwest.

At a pop-up gas station in Calgary, Sandra and her children overtook the Dominguez family, who had left one night before them. Roger and Elena Dominguez had a four-year-old girl named Camilla and a baby on the way. How humans still managed to conceive with all that had happened amazed the few remaining doctors.

"Everything all right?" Sandra asked.

"All right," Roger said. He arched his hand over his stomach. "Elena, you know?"

"Do you think you will make it to Billings tonight?"

He shook his head. "Great Falls."

They talked for as long as it took to fill their tanks. Sandra wished the family safe travels and continued on to Billings. She regretted being unable to spend the night with them. But if she was going to surprise Michael and Maya by taking them home, she needed to make good time.

Home was a bungalow in Rognel Heights. She wondered what Michael and Maya would want to do when they got there. Play in Leakin Park? Walk along the Inner Harbour? Or might they be simply content to sit in their rooms and sort through the old toys they had decided in those mad hours of the evacuation to leave behind? Sandra knew what she would want to do, but this was not her trip. And her memories of home were not their memories. In her memories Sandra kept another home, a row house in Lansdowne, which she and Federico had rented for five years before buying the house in Rognel Heights. At that time, a decade ago now, Michael was three.

Outside Billings, Sandra asked him if he remembered anything about those early years.

"Bricks?" Michael answered uncertainly.

True, the row house was made of brick. But she had been fishing for a detail more sentimental. Like how they used to stroll along the Patapsco River together looking for frogs. She and Michael had done that almost every day of their last summer in Lansdowne. Did he really not remember that? Although perhaps it was better Michael had forgotten. Whenever Sandra thought of those days, she felt a sickening emptiness. Because in those memories, before the darkness, there was so much hope.

MAYA BOUNCED UP AND DOWN in the back seat.

"I want to listen to Raffi! Please, please."

"We'll put on Raffi now," Sandra said, "but then it's Michael's turn."

"I wonder if I'm growing," sang Maya. "I want to listen to that one first. Or I want 'Robin in the Rain.' Can you start at that one?"

Sandra addressed Michael in the passenger seat. "Can you find Raffi for your sister?"

"We listened to Raffi twice yesterday," he complained.

"It's only fair."

"It's only fair," Maya repeated.

Taking his time, Michael found Raffi's *Singable Songs for the Very Young* and put it on. He started at track four.

"Thank you." Sandra reached over to ruffle Michael's hair, but he evaded her hand. She turned the music up for Maya, and together they sang along.

One thing Sandra looked forward to doing in Baltimore was going through her and Federico's CD collection and picking out some new albums for the road. When the evacuations began, they hadn't known they would be leaving for good, so they packed like they would for any trip. A week's worth of clothes. A dozen books. The iPad. Whatever toys the kids preferred at the time.

Michael ejected the CD.

"Mom!" Maya whined.

"What are you doing, Michael?"

"No," he said. "No more."

Michael rolled his window down an inch. The deafening noise of their speed startled Sandra. She grabbed the wheel in both hands reflexively. Michael held the CD up to the opening. Maya squeaked. "Don't you dare," Sandra said. Michael let go of it anyway, then rolled up his window.

"Why did you do that?" Sandra demanded. "Why would you do that?"

Maya lunged forward from the back seat and yanked Michael's hair. "I hate you, I hate you, I hate you!" Michael grabbed her arm and twisted it. Sandra reached over and tried to pry them apart.

While Sandra was looking away from the road, a figure appeared in her peripheral vision, lit up by the headlights. No time to stop. Then – impact. An explosion of meat and metal. The Audi heaved up as whatever they had hit passed violently underneath it. Sandra glanced off the airbag and struck the driver's side window. *I can't see*. But she could hear the tires screeching as the car listed sideways. And she could feel the wheel in her hands. And, finally, she remembered her foot on the brake.

A moment later Sandra's sight returned. Lit up by the surviving headlight, the blood-splattered windshield cast a red hue on the interior of the van. She checked on Michael first. He was shielding his nose and rocking. Blood leaked through his fingers onto the deflated airbag in his lap. In the back seat Maya was still screaming, as if aware of some approaching horror her mother was not.

"It's all right," Sandra said. "We're stopped now. It's over now." She touched Michael's shoulder. "Let me see." He lowered his hands. The airbag had injured his nose and striped a friction burn across his forehead. Reaching behind the passenger side airbag into the glove compartment, Sandra retrieved the package of Kleenex and handed it to him.

"My seat belt hurts! It hurts!"

Sandra turned her attention to Maya. Maya's seat belt was stuck on auto-lock, pinning her against the seatback. Sandra found the buckle. "I'm going to undo it, okay?" Maya mewled as the seat belt came free. "I know it hurts," Sandra said, "but I need you to lift your arms up. Can you lift your arms up for me?" Maya raised her arms. Nothing broken. Good. Now to check on whatever they had hit. "You two wait here. I'll be right back."

With her first step onto pavement, Sandra realized she had sprained her ankle. A minor bout of dizziness hit her. She supported herself against the Audi to keep from falling. She felt her way to the back of the vehicle. Shining like Satan's eyes, the red brake lights illuminated in the near distance the inert corpse of – to be honest, she couldn't really tell what it was. She discerned parts of three legs and there were obvious intestines. She knew it was animal, mammal and large. But it was also hairless and overgrown with tumours, which covered all parts of it like a fleshy shell.

Sandra vomited. Then she returned to her children.

Sandra retrieved her map from the glove compartment. So far they had travelled two hundred miles. Including the seven hundred they had travelled yesterday, that meant they were six hundred miles from Baltimore. Or nine hundred from San Antonio. A night's journey either way.

"Grab your backpacks," Sandra said. "We have to go." She hadn't forgotten Maya's injury. "Maya, I can wear yours if your shoulders hurt."

A lot of what they had brought with them, Sandra realized, regrettably, they would have to leave behind. Like her books, for example. She had allowed herself that one indulgence: a box of books. Perhaps one day she would come back for them. But for now she gave any spare room in her suitcase to her children, to their own books, toys, and stuffies, which, after all, were of infinitely greater significance to them than her books were to her.

Sandra made her children cover their eyes as she led them past the animal.

Passing a road sign, Michael remarked, "That says Birmingham. Why are we going to Birmingham?"

"What's in Birmingham?" Maya asked.

"I'm sorry," Sandra said. "We don't have a choice."

Michael ran in the opposite direction, toward home.

"Michael!" Sandra dropped her suitcase and tried to chase after him, but the pain in her ankle prevented her. "Michael, stop, I can't – Michael!" She tried one more time to run and collapsed to her knees.

Maya tugged on her mother's arm. "Get up! He's running away!"

"I can't, Maya," Sandra said. "I can't." And she wasn't about to send her daughter in her place. All she could do was sit there on the pavement and wait for his fear of night to deliver him back to her.

Thirty minutes later Sandra and Maya saw Michael returning to them in the distance. They heard his crying long before they could make out his face. When he was close, Sandra reached out her arms and gathered him into them.

"I'm so sorry, Michael."

"I want to go home," he sobbed.

"I promise next year we will." Sandra peeked at her watch behind Michael's back. "But we have to go now," she said. "We don't have much time."

WHEN TRAVELLING OFF THE HIGHWAY, Sandra employed a set of three rules to make certain they would never be caught outside during daylight. Rule 1: When passing any city, reset the odometer. Rule 2: Stop for gas whenever the indicator passes the halfway point. And Rule 3: Find shelter a minimum one hour before sunrise. These three rules had never failed her. Even now it was because of the odometer that she knew her best option was to make their way back to Springville, eight miles behind them, rather than continuing north to Attalla, twenty miles ahead.

An hour into walking, Sandra stopped to rest. Though the pain in her ankle was severe, she held herself together for the children's sake.

"How much time do we have before sunrise?" she asked Michael.

"Why don't you ask her?"

She turned to her daughter. "Maya?"

Maya dug inside Sandra's suitcase and found her sun chart,

which listed the hours of dawn and dusk for every day of the year at every degree latitude and longitude in the New World.

"We have three hours and, and thirty minutes."

At their current pace Sandra knew they would be cutting it close. She didn't doubt they would arrive in Springville before sunrise. As for finding an appropriate shelter in whatever time they had left when they got there – that she did doubt.

She stood on her ankle and winced. "All right," she said. "Let's go."

Eventually, Sandra and the children arrived at the turnoff into Springville. Adjacent to the turnoff lay a strip mall with a Walmart Supercentre. She decided to comb the parking lot for a vehicle to drive the rest of the way into town. Spread out widely across the lot were six cars and a truck.

"Michael, why don't you go check on those cars over there, and Maya and I will check on these ones here?"

Without a word Michael departed for the shopping plaza to the west of Walmart.

Meanwhile, Sandra and Maya checked a Ford Escape parked at the Murphy gas station. No keys. She opened the gas cap and sniffed. At least there was gas to syphon. She and Maya continued to the Zaxby's, where Sandra had spotted the truck. Again, gas, but no keys. Sandra popped the tailgate to rest her ankle for a moment. Looking east she saw the violet light of dawn beginning to creep above the horizon. How easy it would be if the sun brought death to humans like it did to vampires, with a flash and then ashes, instead of with slow and inevitable cancers. That death she could not endorse, no matter how hopeless their situation.

A horn beeped in the distance.

"Is that Michael?" Maya asked.

Sandra and Maya hurried around the Zaxby's until they had a clear view across the Walmart parking lot to the honking car. Michael pressed the horn again and flashed the lights. Behind the Honda Civic rose a cloud of exhaust; he had gotten it running. Sandra waved for him to drive it over to them. She would watch how Michael did crossing the parking lot and, assuming he did well, let him drive them into town. She might even let him drive them all the way to Argentina, if the pain in her ankle persisted.

The Civic lurched forward and stalled. Michael started the car again. He pulled the rest of the way out of the parking spot but did not turn sharp enough and rolled onto a desiccated island. He chose to go over it instead of reversing off it, his front and back bumpers bouncing loudly off the curbs. He made the remaining journey across the empty parking lot without incident. But with mere minutes before sunrise, Sandra knew if there was any hope of finding shelter in time, she would need to drive them into town herself.

Sandra tried to open the driver's side door; it was locked.

"Open the door," she said.

"It's my car," he said through the window. "I'm driving."

"Michael, this is not the time."

He reached across the passenger seat and pushed open the passenger door. In any other situation Sandra might've fought obstinacy with obstinacy, planted herself outside the driver's side and waited him out. Unlike Federico, she had never forced Michael physically to do anything. Not that she found physical intervention reprehensible, just that she couldn't actually imagine herself wrestling Michael out of the front seat.

Sandra loaded their backpacks and suitcases in the trunk, then hobbled over to the passenger side. Because Maya wanted to sit with her, Sandra got in first and helped Maya onto her lap. Michael started the car and pulled out of the Walmart parking lot.

"How is the gas?" Sandra asked.

"Half a tank left," he said.

On the next turn, Michael stalled the car again.

"That's all right," she said. "Take your time."

In the east the sky glowed weakly orange. Soon the sun would reveal itself as a small orb hovering above the horizon. And then, from what she had heard, would come a terrible, intensifying headache, followed by nausea, vomiting, and, inevitably, death. Few people exposed for an hour survived longer than two years afterward. Those exposed for two hours or more, all of them had died within a year.

The Civic sputtered and coasted to a stop.

Before Michael could start the car again, Sandra took the keys from the ignition.

"What are you doing?" he asked.

"Into the back," Sandra said to Maya, helping her climb over the centre console.

"Give me the keys," Michael said. "I can do it."

Sandra went around to the driver's side. Michael locked the door. She put the key in the lock and turned it. Michael locked the door as it came unlocked. They went back and forth like this until she succeeded in opening the door.

"What are you doing?"

She pushed Michael out of the driver's seat and into the passenger seat.

"You never let me do anything!"

She started the car.

"I wish Dad was alive instead of you."

Sandra turned on to Main Street and sped into town. The devastating force of Michael's words she directed through her injured ankle into the gas pedal. Later she might wonder about them, even cry about them. For now she had to drive. Passing by churches and schools, Sandra noted their size and potential. They had enough time to survey their options but not enough to explore them. Once she had decided where they would spend the day, that's where they would spend it, so she wanted to be sure.

Left of the intersection of Murphees Valley Road and Highway 174, she spied a building surrounded by a barbed-wire fence. Above the front entrance the signage read Alabama National Guard. It would do. Sandra turned into the neighbouring fire station. Her rear-view mirror flashed momentarily as she swung the car around to face the building. The elongated shadows of a grove of trees appeared like oil stains on the pavement in front of them.

"Mommy, my head hurts."

Just then the odd sensation behind Sandra's eyes began to burn and swell. So this was how it began. She pushed down on the gas. The Civic sped across the road. The fence toppled over without much resistance. She aimed the car at the double glass doors in front. In the back seat Maya moaned. Sandra glimpsed at Michael, pale and clutching his stomach in the passenger seat. She braced the wheel. Upon impact the double glass doors simultaneously wrenched open and shattered. The car burst through the foyer and into the front office, at which point she engaged the brakes.

She tried her door; it would not open. She crawled onto the dash and shouldered herself through the already demolished windshield. She swept her arms across the hood to clear the way of debris and glass, then turned back for her children.

"Quick, hurry."

Sandra helped them out of the car. In the wreckage of the office, she found a set of keys. She grabbed the hands of her children, dragged them down a hall toward a stairwell, and descended it to the basement. Almost immediately her headache began to recede. She could even feel her children's grip on her hands tighten as they, too, experienced a respite of symptoms.

An overhead sign pointed Sandra in the direction of an armoury. She followed the path to a thick steel door with a bolt lock. She tried all the keys until one worked. The armoury was empty inside, save for a few ammo cases and belts.

Sandra ushered the children in ahead of her and, following, closed the door behind them.

IN THE FIRST TWO YEARS of mandatory migration, a section of unpaved jungle called the Darién Gap separated the Pan-American Highway at the shared border of Panama and Colombia. Back then families were expected to abandon one vehicle on the Panamanian side, cross the jungle in two nights, and resume the drive with another vehicle on the Colombian side. The first year, the UN installed markers to aid families in the crossing. They also built "Mid-Gap" to provide shelter at the halfway point. The second year, a tropical storm destroyed the markers. That same year thousands became lost in the Gap and were presumed dead, while thousands more were exposed to the sun and died shortly thereafter.

News of the markers' destruction had reached Sandra, Federico, and the children while they were stationed in the shelter at Panama City. Each shelter was equipped with a radio, and it was common practice for families to radio ahead about road conditions. When Federico and Sandra reached out to the shelter at Yaviza, the last stop before the Darién Gap, they were stunned to learn that they were approaching an impassable jungle, into which many families were already reported to have journeyed and disappeared.

"What do you think we should do?" Sandra asked.

"Let's get there first," said Federico. "Then we can decide."

In Yaviza, Federico attempted to radio Mid-Gap.

"Yaviza to Mid-Gap." He waited for a reply. "Yaviza to Mid-Gap."

"Maybe they're sleeping," Sandra said.

Federico and Sandra discussed possible solutions with the other families present. One family suggested they wait for news from Mid-Gap before leaving, while another suggested they turn back and attempt to survive six months in the highway shelters.

"Or I could go," Federico said. "Find Mid-Gap, come back, and lead the rest of us there."

"What if there is no Mid-Gap anymore?" Sandra asked.

"Either way, somebody needs to go. And it would be better if one of us goes than if all of us do."

The other families somberly agreed.

"Perhaps we should draw straws?" one mother suggested.

"There's no reason to," Federico said. "I've already volunteered."

Sandra preferred the straw option. "If one of us has to go," she said, "we should at least be fair about it."

"But it is fair," he said. "It's my idea."

Another father, David, offered to go along with him. Prior to the evacuations, David had worked as a surveyor in central Mexico and so had some experience navigating jungle territory. Like Sandra, his wife also protested, but he, like Federico, insisted on going. Everyone conceded that Federico and David together posed the best chance of surviving the unmarked route to Mid-Gap and back again.

When it came time for them to leave, Sandra said to Federico, "I have the worst feeling about this."

"Don't make me leave like that," Federico said.

"What do you want me to say?"

"Tell me to be careful. Tell me that you love me and that you'll see me when I get back."

"Please be careful," she said.

Federico kissed her cheek. "And?"

"And I love you and I'll see you when you get back."

WAKING IN THE DARKNESS of the armory, Sandra noticed first that the door was open and second that she couldn't feel Michael. "Michael?" Perhaps he had merely stepped out to use the washroom. She listened for the sound of urination or his step. But there was nothing.

She sat up. "Michael?" she called louder.

Maya stirred in her lap. She tightened her grip around Sandra's waist in defiance of the end of sleep. Sandra woke her anyway. Maya whined as she became slowly reacquainted with yesterday's injuries.

Sandra turned on the small flashlight she had set out on a nearby ammo box and shined it around them. For a second she wondered if Michael was still there sleeping, curled up alone in a corner of the room, ignoring her.

"Where's Michael?" Maya asked.

"He –" Sandra hesitated. "He must be in the washroom." No point in panicking just yet. She checked her watch. Eight-fifteen. They had slept through the alarm. Fortunately, they had only missed it by an hour. She helped Maya to her feet. "Let's go look for him."

After they checked the basement washrooms, Sandra and Maya climbed the stairwell to the ground floor. Sandra was relieved to see the Civic (not that it was even driveable) was where they had left it, because it meant that Michael couldn't have wandered very far. But where would he have gone? Probably he had walked into town to look for another vehicle. Any moment now she expected to hear a horn blaring outside, to see Michael pull up in a sleek, new automatic transmission, eager to prove himself capable to her.

Because the Civic was blocking the entrance, Sandra and Maya left the building by way of the back exit and walked around to the front.

"Wait here," Sandra said. "I need to get our things from the trunk."

"Did Michael run away again?" Maya asked.

That had been Sandra's first thought, too. "No," she answered, "I don't think so." She kneeled in front of Maya. "I need you to wait right here and keep a lookout for Michael. Can you do that for me?"

Maya nodded.

Using the flashlight, Sandra stepped carefully over the broken glass and fence pieces and crumpled drywall. When she was near the car, she shined the flashlight at the trunk. It wasn't closed like she'd thought, merely resting open on its latch. She opened the trunk and looked inside. One suitcase. Two backpacks, hers and Maya's. Michael's gone. Sandra wanted to scream. If she screamed loud enough, he might hear her, have pity on her, and come back. But she didn't want to startle Maya.

Sandra collected the suitcase and backpacks and made her way back to Maya, who met her at the edge of the rubble.

"I heard something," Maya said.

"Where?"

She pointed north, in the direction of town. "Over there."

Sandra hushed her daughter and listened. In this mostly lifeless world, even the slightest noise could be heard from miles away. She discerned a faint whirring. Definitely a vehicle. Yet it was so quiet that she might've mistook the sound for an artful breeze had she not been listening for it.

"That must be Michael," Sandra said. "Let's go find him."

She grabbed her daughter's hand and hurried toward Main Street. They would come back for their luggage later. Not long into their pursuit, Maya began to resist Sandra's pulling on her. "Slow down," she said. "You're hurting me." Sandra slowed for a moment to give Maya a break. She listened for the car again. She heard something like a car, but she couldn't be certain anymore. Sandra lifted Maya up and directed her arms around her neck. The extra weight of carrying Maya aggravated the injury to Sandra's ankle, the pain resuming with even more intensity than the night before. She knew it would give out eventually – and then what? Was Maya supposed to carry *her*?

With no other option, Sandra shifted her focus to finding a working vehicle. All down Main Street there were cars with their doors hanging open, already checked by Michael. Finally, she and Maya came upon a group of cars with their doors closed. Among them Sandra found a Pontiac Sunfire with keys left behind on the passenger seat and a gas tank two-thirds full.

Sandra sped back to the National Guard headquarters for their stuff and threw it in the back seat. Now she had a decision to make: either she could turn back and search for Michael along Main Street or she could continue east on Highway 174 to I-59 and try to cut him off there. She decided to take the interstate directly. Michael was at least half an hour ahead of them, as long as it had taken her to find the Sunfire. If she were to catch up with him on route to San Antonio, Sandra needed to be fast.

Four hours later Sandra and Maya arrived at the outskirts of Baton Rouge. Sometime earlier they had made a fortuitous stop for gas outside Hattiesburg, where they exchanged the Sunfire for a newer Dodge Charger. Sandra had hoped the increased speed would help narrow the distance between themselves and Michael. But so far nothing. She feared that she had overtaken him, somehow, perhaps while he was off on a gas detour of his own. At times during the drive, she had passed rest stops and thought, "At the next one I'll stop for an hour and wait." But then she would remember that they couldn't stop, that to stop for any other reason than gas might delay their arrival in San Antonio, which was the only way to catch Michael for certain. Otherwise, he would get a night's advantage on them and be gone all the way to Ushuaia.

The shelter at San Antonio stood at the city's southwest limit, in the small suburb of Von Ormy. Less than an hour before dawn, Sandra and Maya turned into the parking lot, empty except for a gold Dodge Caravan. Sandra recognized it as the Dominguez family vehicle and burst into tears.

The shelter was buried fifteen feet underground and accessible only by way of a bulkhead that extended out of the concrete as on the roof of a skyscraper. Sandra and Maya opened the door and descended the metal grate stairs to the bottom. Entering the shelter, they were greeted by the smell of beans and pancakes. Elena gasped upon seeing the dishevelled mother and daughter. Roger waved hello with his spatula. While he was distracted, Camilla, their daughter, dipped her finger into the pancake batter and tasted it.

Roger swatted her hand. "Déjalo."

From the bunk bed where she lay, Elena reached her arms out to Sandra imploringly, either too pregnant or too exhausted to rise.

"Come," she said.

Maya left Sandra and joined Camilla by her father's side. Sandra limped over to Elena's bed and knelt beside the pregnant woman.

Elena brushed her hand across Sandra's injured cheek. The tenderness of this touch was more than Sandra could bear. Elena held Sandra while she wept.

"He's gone," Sandra said. "I've lost him."

Elena ran her fingers through Sandra's hair. "It's okay."

"I've lost him, and I don't know what to do."

"It's okay."

NEXT NIGHTFALL Michael was still missing. Sandra had spent most of the day in fitful sleep, listening for the rumblings of vehicles, the creak of the shelter door above, waiting, hoping, drifting off, then startling to attention. Even Maya, who at five years old had never slept in a shelter bed by herself, crawled into the neighbouring bunk after one too many of Sandra's hypnic jerks.

As if he had never moved, Roger was once again at the hot plate. The uneaten beans from yesterday sizzled in the pan. On the burner beside them a pot of water boiled for coffee. He nodded kindly to Sandra as she rose. Elena, Camilla, and Maya remained asleep in their respective beds.

Roger scraped some beans off the pan and offered them in a bowl to Sandra. "Here. Eat."

She stepped across the cold concrete floor, took the bowl, and sat at a nearby table. She thanked Roger for the food.

"De nada," he said. He served himself and joined her.

They ate in silence. The beans were heavily spiced and better for it. Sandra had to be purposeful in her eating so as not to reveal how truly famished she was. She didn't want Roger to open another can for her out of solicitude.

While they were eating, Roger gestured at Maya. "Does she know?"

"About Michael?"

"Yes."

Sandra nodded. Roger continued eating.

A moment later she said, "I promised I would take him home. I thought he was coming here. But he must've gone home instead."

"Where is home?" Roger asked.

"Baltimore."

"And you are not . . . ?"

"Going after him?"

"Sí."

"I'm worried there isn't enough time."

"Will you wait here?"

"For a few nights."

And then she and Maya would continue the journey. Because she had done the same thing when Federico disappeared. Because all the other families had moved on, and there were two young children to think about. Four nights Sandra had waited at Yaviza. Even after the second party reached Mid-Gap and radioed back directions for safe passage, even then she had waited another night. She waited for as long as she could, until the possibility of missing the final ship to Antarctica became near certainty. Long enough that they were among the last families to cross.

"We will take her," Roger offered. "Maya, she will come with us."

"That's too much," Sandra said. "I can't ask that of you."

"Not asking. We will take her, and you will go." Roger scraped what was left on his plate back into the frying pan. He nudged Sandra toward Maya. "Say goodbye. Then you will go."

Sandra looked at her sleeping daughter. She trusted Roger and Elena to take care of her, and with a playmate in Camilla, Maya might even jump at the opportunity to ride along with them.

But then Sandra was not worried about her daughter's safety. She was worried about Michael's and her own. Assuming she was even able to find him, she knew what sort of life awaited them. Six months of highway shelters. Six months of boiling water and foraging for food. Six months without doctors or teachers or friends. Not to mention that Maya would spend those six months in Antarctica convinced her mother had abandoned her, a conviction that would become fact in the likely occasion of Sandra's death. Yet there was no other choice.

Sandra gently woke her daughter. Maya sniffled and wiped her nose. She had been crying in her sleep.

"Is Michael back yet?" Maya asked.

"Not yet."

"I'm hungry."

"Roger is making food." Sandra brushed Maya's hair out of her face. "Now I want you to listen to me. Camilla and her father and mother, you are going to ride with them for a while."

"Like a sleepover?" Maya asked.

"Yes, like a sleepover."

"What about you?"

"I am going to find Michael."

"I want to help!"

"I know you do," Sandra said. "But I want you to help by being a good friend to Camilla. Can you do that for me?"

Maya's lips trembled. "Are you going to die like Dad?"

"No, I'm not going to die. I'm going to find Michael and then we're going to drive as fast as we can to catch up with you. Faster than we've ever driven before." Sandra kissed her forehead. "I love you. I have to go now, or else I won't be able to catch up with you later, all right?"

Roger helped Sandra carry her suitcase up the stairs. He loaded it in the trunk, along with a second bag, full of canned food.

"I can't accept that," Sandra said.

"You will need it," Roger said. He closed the trunk before she could attempt to give it back. "You will need it for Michael."

She hugged him and thanked him again.

Then Sandra got into the car and drove.

Afterword: The Collection

I HAVE SEEN EVERYTHING, I have done everything, and I remember all of it. From the peak of Everest to the shores of Maldives, I have set titanium foot on every inch of Earth. I have swum every ocean, river, lake, and sea. I have explored their lightless depths and labyrinthine caves until my anatomy radiated from the pressure and the heat. Every language there was to learn, I have learned and spoken and written in and read. Every animal in my time I have touched, petted, coddled, bred. And when plants still grew, I made gardens of them all.

I am a Completionist. Completionism is what we have now instead of religion, though there are many of us who still believe in God and some of us who imagine themselves that way. There are two tenets of Completionism: knowledge and experience. The early Completionists fathomed them endless. But they did not consider novelty, and novelty does have an end. Beyond novelty there are only variations, differences made in combination.

No one predicted that we might approach immortality at the price of eternal boredom.

Regardless, we have long since moved underground. As such, there is no comparison between the boredom we knew then and the boredom we know now. Earth above, with its spectacular diversity, has for a thousand years been barren and uninhabitable due to the exacerbating combination of a heavy atmosphere and swollen Sun. Temperatures at the surface average three thousand degrees Celsius during the day and fifteen hundred at night. Though our bodies are built to withstand temperatures as high as two thousand degrees, the delicate circuits of our consciousness break down at a pitiful five hundred. And once lost, consciousness is impossible to recover; it is as if we have been lobotomized.

I knew the story of a man who, after three hundred years in the tunnels, decided his life was worth sacrificing for one last glimpse of the sky. He was a Completionist but a relatively new one. At ten kilometers from the surface, he finally capitulated to his autonomic nervous system and turned around. Even then it was too late: the man he was had been boiled to a soup within his skull.

This is the fate that awaits us all. In trying to escape the heat above, we have burrowed toward the heat below and trapped ourselves between them both. We have perhaps six months before the fatal equilibrium is reached. Our impending erasures (the MecEngs tell us only our minds will perish while our bodies persist as so many useless automatons) seem a cosmic reprimand for our vanity, our arrogance that we should become gods, and our once cherished Completionism, merely a cruel magnification of our loss. Had we died as human beings, with flesh and blood and disintegration, it might've been easier to accept. At least back then we acknowledged our foibles and fragilities. But for ten thousand years we have taken for granted our invincibility. We have collected our knowledge and experience like precious stones, only to have them poured out over us, so that we are crushed under their existential weight.

I WAS BORN IN 1985, when there were still borders, in the country of Canada. I lived a long and healthy life until the age of seventy-six, at which point I began to suffer cognitive decline. By the age of eighty-three I was completely senile. Five years later Google went public with the technology for transference, and my daughter, Nella, having been appointed my primary healthcare POA, volunteered me for the procedure. My shrunken brain was removed, scanned, and uploaded. My body was cremated, and the ashes, except for a small alloy stored like a cloudy diamond at the previous location of my suprasternal notch, disposed of as biological waste. I awoke inside my machine without the slightest idea who I was or how I got there. The story of my life I learned second-hand from Nella. She told me about her mother, Helen, my wife, who, regrettably, died while I was in a vegetative state. Nella told me that I was once a journalist, before settling into a career in copywriting. When I asked her why she decided I should, at the risk of sounding grandiose, become immortal, she told me that, while in hospital, and in a rare moment of clarity, I had expressed a profound regret at having never published a book. It was for the accomplishment of this unfulfilled dream that she presumed my consent.

Naturally, there were complications. No one expected the transition from man to machine to occur seamlessly, and in the end, the only thing lost was our imagination. We were born, as it were, creatively impotent. The MecEngs hypothesized the problem to be one of synthesis. Apparently, the human brain was immeasurably more capable of forging connections between unrelated or even disparate sensory information than was the quantum brain, though the MecEngs could not determine precisely why, or how they might fix it. Neither could any biologist or psychologist consulted provide a workable solution for us. Religious explanations were offered. Every major faith prescribed their own formula for the recovery of the faculty, but decades passed without a single recorded example of success.

Under these circumstances, Completionism was conceived. The founders of Completionism believed sensory input to be the means by which we would eventually transcend our hardwired limitations. Creation sprang out of an abundance of life, they argued; come enough knowledge and experience, we would evolve beyond our restrictive metallurgy. Of course, I had my doubts about it all. But since nothing else had worked, I converted anyway. Worst case scenario, I would spend a thousand years travelling the world and end up exactly where I started: with an infinite number of years left at my disposal.

Alternatively, I would find inspiration and finish my book for Nella.

WE PASS OUR DAYS DIGGING and shoring new tunnels. In so doing we defer our inevitable destruction – but at a loss. For every two days' work we add to our survival by approximately one half day. It might seem more reasonable to quit working altogether, to allow the end to come when it does, and to spend what time we have left in community and self-reflection. There are, however, many of us who still believe that at the last hour we will be saved, that this climate calamity, like the Ice Ages of old, will progress a certain distance, then pause and recede. What a shame it would be if we were to stop now and the reversal arrive a day too late.

And so we prolong our lives dubiously in expectation of this miracle.

I BECAME A COMPLETIONIST shortly after Nella's death. Like so many others during the early days of the technology, she had decided not to transfer, to die naturally. It was not uncommon then for spiritual machines, confronted with the death of a close family member, to request an erasure. (Erasure would only be legal for another hundred years or so, after which time immortality, like death before it, became a matter of course.) And because it had not been my choice to transfer, I was perfectly within my rights to choose to die.

But I simply could not do that while the book remained unfinished.

As for what form it would take, whether novel or collection, fiction or non-fiction, Nella, before she died, provided me with the starting point: a single, surviving journal from my thirties that included a rough outline for an article on "exit strategies." Vladimir, Marika, Granger, Tilikum – I referred constantly to their stories for inspiration. I had the pages memorized; their lives were never far from my thoughts. Nevertheless, the world had changed so much since the time of their living that they hardly seemed real people to me but ancient characters as enigmatic as Socrates. In that sense even attempting to expand their stories into something resembling a book would require from me an impossible ingenuity. In short, I needed more subjects. It was decided then: I would write a collection. The collection would comprise brief histories or sketches of real people I met while on my completion tours, or the stories told me by them, and include the already finished pieces on Vladimir and Marika, Granger, and Tilikum. For the sake of consistency, I would set the collection in their time, also Nella's. I wanted the book to be one she might've read and understood, if I had finished it thousands of years ago, when she was still alive.

I attended the Completionist seminary, installed their programs and algorithms, and set off for Paris. Beginning in those grey and grimy streets, I embarked on my completion tour of Europe. Being a relatively new phenomenon, transhumans were yet to be fully accepted by the general population, which is to say, we were treated as "other." Most people outright refused to speak with me, and the few who did, did so with an active suspicion; they met my inquiries into their lives with unwavering obstinance. I was not without hope that, in time, attitudes would change; after all, the collection depended on it. And until then there was always the tour to occupy me. My progress mapped itself internally on the built-in GPS. Every day I explored a new alleyway, entered a new building. I crisscrossed over roads and bridges and rooftops. I learned French *en même temps* and kept a journal for practice. Seven months was all it took to complete Paris. The next five years I spent wandering the Provence, living outdoors like a vagabond. Fortunately, shelter was no longer a necessity for me. I only needed the rare drop of oil in my joints and a charging station, which were everywhere and free.

Meanwhile, my mind filled with memories substantial and immutable. Completionism as a system of thought hinged on our capacity to remember every detail. Again, the belief was that a surfeit of memory would resurrect imagination within us, or perhaps form the base for a projected imagination, and, thereby, release us from the wages of immortal life: eternal boredom.

Know all, experience all, and all that is left for man to do is create or despair.

WE MOVE SLOWER NOW. The cooling fan in back of our heads whirls continuously: this noise is our tinnitus. Daily, the heat exposes faults in our construction – the later models are particularly susceptible to breakdown – and every fault is a fatal one. We expire one after another at arbitrary intervals. There is no telling who might be next. Many begin their workdays fully conscious and lose themselves entirely by the end of them. They are easily identifiable, these suddenly mindless machines, because they do not stop working when the bells are rung but continue forever at their task. We are forced by circumstance to work beside them. They were our friends, our family. We speak to them, but they do not answer us. We observe subtle differences in their movements, the peculiarities of self, departed, the perfection of automation, restored.

I watch a wife remove the alloy of her husband to wear as a pendant. She achieves this by violently hammering at the front base of his neck until the piece comes loose. Others follow suit. It is easy this way to identify those of us who are still alive inside. Some men and women carry four, five, six: the ashes of entire families. The Completionists are quick to co-opt this activity and devise rules for its practice. Only the most zealous followers comply. I am unpersuaded by their promise to separate me from my machine. I do not trust them to treat my ashes with due respect. Instead, I pry them free one night and bury them myself.

THIS WAS MY FINAL DRAFT.

A fortuitous discovery by the MecEngs of a submicroscopic cache invulnerable to heat afforded us, in our last days, the opportunity to leave something of ourselves behind. If you are reading this now, it is because you have found my cache.

I finished the collection for the first time four hundred years ago. I have finished it a thousand times since then, with each new draft, a different arrangement of stories, with each new story, a different measure of fiction and fact. And yet it could be argued that I never finished the collection, and never will, for it exists only as bytes on a computer chip and not bound as would behoove the pages of a physical book. It was not just experience stolen from us by heat, but also knowledge in the form of the written word.

Yes, I had evolved an imagination, as did we all, as I suppose was necessary for our continued sanity in this perma-climate of darkness and dirt. The Completionists heralded this occasion the Last Renaissance. They rejoiced in this proof of their authenticity as a faith. If they had bothered to consult unbelievers, whose imaginations returned simultaneous to ours, they might've realized it proved nothing about the efficacy of knowledge and experience but only the indomitableness of the human spirit; and that, in the end, Completionism was, like all religions from time immemorial, merely a lens through which to view death and make peace at its approach.

I suspect it is for this same reason Nella hoped for me to finish the book.

And I did. For her and for myself, I did.

Sources

BC Forest Discovery Centre. "Shawnigan Lake Lumber Co. No. 2." Accessed March 3, 2021. https://bcforestdiscoverycentre.com/our-train-collection-schedules/.

Sarah Boesveld. "'Lovely' elderly couple in double suicide were ill for a long time, shocked neighbours say." *National Post*, October 29, 2013. https://nationalpost.com/news/toronto/lovelyelderly-couple-in-double-suicide-were-ill-for-a-long-time-shocked-neighbours-say.

Gabriela Cowperthwaite, director. *Blackfish*. CNN Films & Manny O. Productions, 2013.

Mike Devlin. "What happened to Granger Taylor?" *Times Colonist*, February 8, 2019. https://www.timescolonist.com/islander/what-happened-to-granger-taylor-1.23621363.

Arin Greenwood. "What It Means To Say A Dolphin Committed Suicide." *Huffington Post Canada*, June 13, 2014. https://www.huffingtonpost.ca/entry/dolphin-commits-suicide_n_5491513?ri18n=true.

Hans von Hentig. *The Criminal and His Victim*. New Haven: Yale University Press, 1948.

Tyler Hooper. "The Man Who Went to Space and Disappeared." *VICE*, January 7, 2016. https://www.vice.com/en_ca/article/yvwjkv/the-man-who-went-to-space-anddisappeared-the-story-of-granger-taylor.

Jennifer Horvath, producer; Nicolina Lanni and John Choi, directors. *Spaceman*. Canada: CBC Docs POV, 2019.

Brian Clark Howard. "Why Tilikum, SeaWorld's Killer Orca, Was Infamous." *National Geographic*, May 4, 2021. https://www.nationalgeographic.com/animals/article/tilikum-seaworld-orca-killer-whale-dies.

David Neiwert. *Of Orcas and Men*. New York: The Overlook Press, Peter Mayer Publishers, Inc. Gerald Duckworth & Co Ltd., 2015.

Jewish Telegraphic Agency. "Elderly Holocaust survivor couple die in suicide pact." *The Canadian Jewish News*, November 30, 2013. https://www.cjnews.com/uncategorized/elderly-holocaust-survivor-couple-die-suicide-pact.

Jewish Virtual Library, "Osijek." Accessed May 16, 2022. https://www.jewishvirtuallibrary.org/osijek.

Marco Chown Oved. "Suicide pact capped lifelong love story." *The Star*, October 10, 2013. https://www.thestar.com/news/gta/2013/10/30/suicide_pact_capped_lifelong_love_story.html.

Real Life is Horror. "What really happened to Granger Taylor?" July 7, 2018. http://reallifeishorror.blogspot.com/2018/07/what-really-happened-to-granger-taylor.html

David Shultz. "Everything you always wanted to know about dolphin sex-but were afraid to ask." *Science*, December 8, 2017. https://www.sciencemag.org/news/2017/04/everything-you-always-wanted-know-about-dolphin-sex-were-afraid-ask.

Zvonko V. Springer. "Osijek - Essek - Mursa." Accessed May 16, 2022. http://www.cosy.sbg.ac.at/~zzspri/travels/osijek/OSIJEKAlt4.html.

Jennifer Welsh. "This Disgusting Scene Shows Why SeaWorld Allegedly Kept A Psychotic Killer Whale." *Journal Star*, November 5, 2013. https://www.pjstar.com/article/20131105/NEWS/311059966.

Wikimedia Foundation. "Kingdom of Yugoslavia." *Wikipedia*. Accessed May 16, 2022. https://en.wikipedia.org/wiki/Kingdom_of_Yugoslavia#CITEREFTroch2017.

Tim Zimmermann. "The Killer in the Pool." *Outside*, July 30, 2010. https://www.outsideonline.com/1924946/killer-pool.

Acknowledgements

An author's first acknowledgements are probably the most important. I can think of innumerable teachers, friends, acquaintances, co-workers, fellow artists who, over the years, provided me with either the encouragement or the inspiration that led to the creation of this work.

I want to start by thanking Freehand Books, specifically my editor Naomi Lewis, whose careful attention and thoughtful suggestions helped shape the final draft, as well as managing editor Kelsey Attard and designer Natalie Olsen for your hard work in eventually bringing this book to shelf. Also, a special mention to Deborah Willis for considering my unpublished novel *Spectral Lines*, which led tortuously to the present publication.

It has always been my dream to write and publish a book. When I was a young child, I used to handwrite "novels" and force them on my classmates and friends. I suppose they should be thanked first; their graciousness kept me from abandoning the craft outright. Next, I want to thank my public school English teachers. I would list them all if I could remember their names, if, say, I had a yearbook for every grade and could reference them. In place of a list, however, I have decided to share a few meaningful anecdotes. The aforementioned handwritten books were largely read and appreciated because a certain teacher counted them as literature during silent reading period. (Thank you to him and apologies to the classmates who chose to read "The Fight" or "Island of Species" when they might've read *Lord of the Rings* or *The Chronicles of Narnia* instead.) I also loved reading aloud to the class, especially when the assignment was an original story. My classmates loved that I loved reading aloud, too, 1) because it meant some of them didn't have to do it and 2) because I always pushed the boundaries of what we were allowed to write. One time I went too far, describing in gory detail the beheading of a horse by a scythe during the Crusades. To the teacher who allowed me to get that far before stopping me and forbidding me from ever reading to the class again: thank you. In high school I gave my unfinished novel "Haven" to a teacher to read. Sometimes I wonder if she really read it. If she had, she might have told me to forget English and focus on Math; it would have been the honest response. But she told me it was great and to keep writing. Thank you. Beginning classes at the University of Alberta, I wanted to get into the WRITE program so badly and was so convinced of my natural greatness that I boldly applied in my first year, though the course was restricted to second-year students only. Naturally, I was rejected. The next year, however, I was accepted. I've gone back and read the story, "The Venus Urn," for which Thomas Wharton accepted me into the program and have not a clue what he saw in me. But I am thankful that he saw something. I wouldn't be here if not for him. By the time I graduated, I had already decided not to use my degree in Education, but rather to pursue the writer's life and publication at all costs – except of course by actually writing. My friend Ian Amundrud invited me to come stay with him rent free in Victoria. Though it was not the reason he allowed it, I always promised to pay him back with money from my future book sales. (Fortunately rent was affordable back then, so the possibility still exists.) For all those months that I didn't pay rent, and all your additional encouragement through my early consistent failures, thank you. Years of procrastination followed my move to Victoria. I started a bildungsroman about my time in Edmonton as a singer-songwriter titled "The Album" (thank you Rhea March for giving me the opportunity to even write such a book). It took seven years and moving my girlfriends at the time, Megan O'Shaughnessy and Ashley Gawiuk, across the country with me to Edmonton for two distinct writing retreats to finish. Megan's early encouragement gave me the confidence to continue. Ashley's steadfast support led me through two other novels and eventually to beginning *Exit Strategies*. Then there are my beta readers for this book, Lea Silver and Charli Steketee. I also want to thank the Write as Rain group with special mention to Janna, Lisa, and Elan for reading previous works. Lastly, I want to thank the Royal BC Museum for the scheduling flexibility that allowed me to write every day.

And thank you again to Mom and Dad. Although I gave them a page at the beginning of this book, they should be mentioned twice for the sheer magnitude of their support.

Paul Cresey is a fiction writer based in Victoria, BC. He has been published in *Grain*, *Qwerty*, *The Dalhousie Review*, *The New Orphic Review*, *Burning Water*, and online at *prairiejournal.org*. He was the recipient of a Canadian Council for the Arts Grant for New/Emerging Writer in 2020 for his unpublished novel *Spectral Lines*. At one time a touring singer-songwriter, he was nominated for a Canadian Folk Music Award for Young Performer of the Year in 2008. His albums can be found on Spotify and Apple Music. A graduate in Education, Cresey currently works in Finance at the Royal BC Museum. *Exit Strategies* is his first book.